T0354121

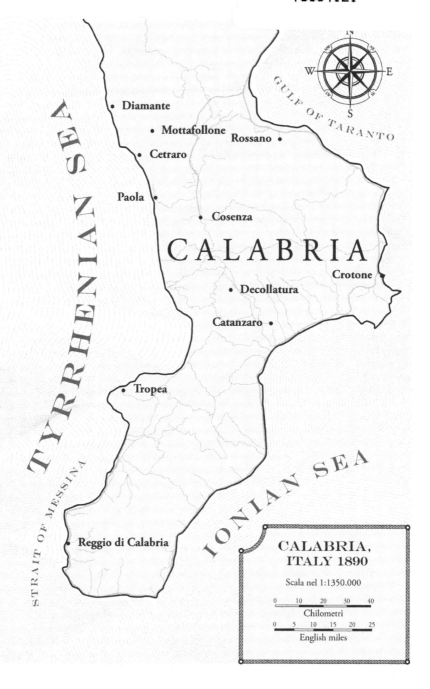

TYRRHENIAN SEA

STRAIT OF MESSINA

GULF OF TARANTO

• Diamante

• Mottafollone

Rossano •

• Cetraro

Paola •

• Cosenza

CALABRIA

Crotone

• Decollatura

Catanzaro •

• Tropea

IONIAN SEA

• Reggio di Calabria

CALABRIA,
ITALY 1890

Scala nel 1:1350.000

| 0 | 10 | 20 | 30 | 40 |
Chilometri
| 0 | 5 | 10 | 15 | 20 | 25 |
English miles

The INHERITANCE

by
Marianne Perry

The Inheritance

iUniverse books may be ordered through booksellers or by contacting:
iUniverse
1663 Liberty Drive
Bloomington, IN 47403
www.iuniverse.com
1-800-Authors (1-800-288-4677)

ISBN: 978-1-4759-5283-4 (sc)
ISBN: 978-1-4759-5285-8 (hc)
ISBN: 978-1-4759-5284-1 (e)

Library of Congress Control Number: 2012919525

Printed in the United States of America

iUniverse rev. date: 10/31/2012

Also by **Marianne Perry**

NONFICTION

Sault Ste. Marie Naturally Gifted: A Celebration of Our City, History, Natural Environment and People.

For my family.

ACKNOWLEDGEMENTS

Above all, I would like to thank my cherished parents; my mother, Dorothy Anne (Lima) Perry and my late father, Arnold Joseph Perry, for taking me to the public library when I was a child, introducing me to the world of books and bringing *The National Geographic Magazine* into our home.

I would like to acknowledge the kindness of three fellow Saulites: Morley Torgov, Canadian novelist, humorist and lawyer; the late Ken Danby, Canadian realist painter; and the late Brian Vallee, Canadian author, journalist and documentary producer. I will be forever grateful for their advice and encouragement.

I would like to thank Kim Moritsugu, the Canadian novelist who served as my mentor at The Humber School for Writers, for helping me craft the early drafts of this book.

I would like to acknowledge the late Professor Vincent Mancinelli, former Associate Professor, Department of Modern Languages, Algoma University College, for his assistance in translating old documents and providing valuable direction with respect to my genealogical research and traveling in Italy.

I'd like to express my thanks to the Fuzednotions Creative Studio Inc. team for their direction, guidance, patience and support. Without their dedication and expertise, *The Inheritance* would not have been published.

I would like to express my gratitude to my dear friends, Nancy and Peter Cresswell, for their genuine interest in my writing and for my iPad.

I would like to thank my beloved late godmother, Assunta (Sue) Perri Bonin, for sharing her stories about Nana and what she knew about life in Calabria in the early 1900's.

I would like to acknowledge my sister, Barbara Perry, for her support.

I would like to thank my precious children, Randi and Mitch Butcher, for giving me the wonderful book I have noted below as a Christmas present in 2009. They are the greatest blessings in my life.

Doeser, Linda. *Italian Cooking: The Food and the Lifestyle.* Parragon Books Ltd. 2004.

And finally, I would like to thank my husband, Bud Carruthers, for his insightful comments, our shared love of books, our mutual passion for travel and adventure, and, most of all, for believing in me and supporting my dream to be a writer.

PREFACE

I was born and raised in Sault Ste. Marie, Ontario, Canada as part of a large Canadian-Italian family. I have always felt connected to Italy and had a keen interest in learning about my Calabrian and Sicilian roots. I first traveled to Italy as a university student and have returned five times to date. I hope to visit Italy again and again and again. *The Inheritance* is a work of fiction set in Calabria in the early 1900's; there are, however, threads of truth woven throughout my story.

My paternal grandparents emigrated from Calabria in the early 1900's and eventually settled in Sault Ste. Marie. My maternal grandparents emigrated from Sicily around the same time and eventually settled in Toronto, Ontario, Canada. My father was born and raised in Sault Ste. Marie. He was one of nine children. My mother was born and raised in Toronto. She was one of four children. My parents met and married in Toronto after World War Two and, after a period of time, moved to Sault Ste. Marie where they raised their family. I am one of five children; two of whom died within the first year of their lives.

My father's mother, Maria Caterina Spagnuolo Andreoli, was born in Mottafollone; a mountain village near the town of Cetraro on the Tyrrhenian coast in the province of Cosenza in the region of Calabria. At twenty years of age, my grandmother and three others from her village went to Naples planning to board the steamship, *America*, which would take them to their new life in Canada. Life was hard in Calabria and poverty the norm; many had already left southern Italy and my grandmother and her companions had intended to join those they knew who had previously relocated to Sault Ste. Marie. Jobs were ample in this northern Ontario industrial town and, as a result, many had deemed it a good place to begin anew. Something happened while my grandmother and her companions were being processed to board the ship and, for reasons that have never been made clear to me, they became separated. My grandmother found herself alone on the ship and discovered, long after the *America* had set sail, that the authorities in Naples had prohibited one of her companions from boarding because of an eye infection. The three, they told her, had decided to return home and make the journey at a later date. My grandmother was by herself. She crossed the Atlantic Ocean as a steerage passenger. She knew no one else, had very little money and spoke only the dialect of her village. She arrived at Ellis Island on January 13, 1913 and, from there, took the train to Sault Ste. Marie. My grandfather, Pietro Perri, had emigrated earlier from Decollatura, Cosenza, Calabria and gone to Sault Ste. Marie to work as a labourer at Algoma Steel. My grandmother met him there and they were married in 1915. Her three traveling companions eventually arrived in Sault Ste. Marie. Neither my grandmother nor grandfather ever returned to Calabria.

The Perri grandchildren called our grandmother, Nana. Nana never learned to speak English and though my father mastered her dialect, I never did. My connection to her, nevertheless, was profound. She was equal parts gentle and strong and though she passed away when I was a teenager, I can still feel her presence.

We knew very little about my Nana's early life in Calabria. Other than a few family details and being poor like the majority who lived in Calabria back then, the information was sketchy. None of my Nana's nine children ever visited Calabria and, as I grew older and the questions remained unanswered, I became increasingly intrigued about what her life might have been like before she came to Canada.

Over the years in my quest to learn more about Italy and my Nana's life, I have researched the history, geography and culture of Calabria as well as conducted genealogical investigations. Nana had more than two dozen grandchildren and though a few of my cousins have also conducted family research, none had ever visited Calabria. As a result, I decided a few years ago to travel to Calabria, go to Mottafollone and see if I could learn anything more about my Nana's early years. I became the first of my Nana's blood to undertake this journey and for my father the trip became a family pilgrimage of sorts. While there, I maintained a daily journal and took photographs of Mottafollone, Cetraro and the surrounding area, which I later compiled into albums for my father and his siblings. Life is full of miracles and it just happened that I was in Cetraro on Father's Day. I called my father that Sunday in Sault Ste. Marie and the coincidence resonated with significance that we both believed was a blessing from Nana that said she was pleased with what I had done. I did learn new details about my Nana's life when I was in Mottafollone; most of her past, however, will remain shrouded in mystery. I have traveled to Italy since this particular trip and continued my research and genealogical investigation. My cumulative efforts have definitely given me a greater insight into the woman Maria Caterina Spagnuolo Andreoli was before she left Calabria and for this, I am thankful.

Please let me reiterate, however, that *The Inheritance* is a work of fiction. Did my interest in solving my family's mysteries inspire this story? Yes. Does this story reflect facts that I have learned about over the years? Yes. Have my travels throughout Italy influenced my book? Yes. Are any of the characters in *The Inheritance* real people? No. Does *The Inheritance* tell the story of my Nana's early life in Calabria before she boarded the ship in Naples and set sail for North America? No, it does not. I did, however, select the name Caterina for one of my characters in her honour.

For readers interested in viewing some of the photographs of Mottafollone, Cetraro and the surrounding area that I took on this particular trip, I refer you to my **website: www.marianneperry.ca.** I have also listed other websites and sources of information on the Resources page at the end of this book for those interested in genealogical research and traveling to Calabria. Thank you.

Marianne Perry,

Sault Ste. Marie, Ontario, Canada

The INHERITANCE

by
Marianne Perry

PART ONE: 1897-1909
Calabria, Italy

CHAPTER ONE

"*O glorious Saint Gerard Majella, preserve Nella from the excessive pains of childbirth,*" Padre Valentine prayed.

A feeble ray of morning light passed through the small window of the one room cottage. It was not the brilliant beam of gold that the priest had wanted but it was still a sign that there was hope for the young woman who lay quietly on the blood soaked straw mattress in front of him. Hers was not the first desperate situation he'd witnessed nor, he lamented, would it be the last. After four years, Padre Valentine still couldn't fully accept that his life would end in Cetraro; a desolate fishing village on Calabria's rocky Tyrrhenian coast.

The priest touched Nella's forehead. "*Release her dear God and shield the child she now carries.*" He made the sign of the cross and she started to scream again. He pulled his hand back. Nella's body twisted and turned and shaped itself into unnatural contortions. There was no reason for the priest to finish his prayer; no one would be able to hear his words. Padre Valentine wasn't even certain if God was listening anymore.

"She should have given up the baby two days ago," Mafalda said. She leaned her thick upper torso over Nella's flat chest. The *Gobbo* talisman attached to a piece of twine, which the old midwife always wore around her neck, began to swing side to side like a pendulum.

The rhythmical movement of the little gold statue of the hunchback mesmerized the priest and for an instant, he considered praying to the good luck charm.

"Padre, this can't go on for much longer."

Mafalda's voice broke the spell. He moved closer to Nella as Mafalda pressed her large hands down on Nella's narrow shoulders.

It was 1897 and Padre Valentine had worked with Mafalda since he came to Cetraro as the new priest at St. Ursula's Church. Padre Valentine knew that Mafalda would do everything she could to save Nella and her unborn child.

"Make her still."

The other midwife, Velia, yanked Nella's ankles, and pulled her spindly legs straight. She flattened the soles of Nella's bare feet against her heavy bosom. Padre Valentine did not know this midwife, and feared she might break Nella's bones.

"Padre, Nella knows her baby's not safe outside her womb." Mafalda glanced at Velia. "We'll have to take it."

Nella stopped kicking. Her round belly rose from her emaciated frame and a picture Padre Valentine had seen of Mount Vesuvius before it erupted and buried Pompei flashed through his mind. It was from a textbook that he had studied a decade ago when he had been a student in a theological seminary in Rome. The priest was ashamed that he had let such an image distract him. Nella needed his full attention now; that was why God had put him here. Padre Valentine tried to control his thoughts but sometimes he failed. He had never planned to be a priest in a poor Calabrian fishing village and sometimes, he still couldn't believe everything that had happened to him.

"I need clean rags," Velia shouted to Anna.

Anna spun around, she had been praying to the twig crucifix on the mantle of the open stone fireplace next to the olive jar filled with her summer roses. The front of her silk dress was stained with her servant's blood. Flowers that had been pink had turned red, as had the band of ribbons that circled her tiny waist. Several hours ago, Padre Valentine had urged her to return to the villa, he promised he'd let her know what happened to her servant. But she refused to do so. Attending the birth of a servant child violated

9

the code of decorum that her husband, Santo Marino, had set for his wife. Even though Santo was still away, the priest was worried that somehow he would find out. Padre Valentine still did not understand why, after ten years of marriage, Anna had not yet learned what he had long ago accepted, that Santo Marino was not a man to be challenged.

"Here." Anna snatched a rag from the pile on the floor and threw it to Velia. She took her place beside Mafalda.

"She'll live." Velia said. "I've never lost a sixteen year old mother."

This hadn't been true for Padre Valentine and Mafalda.

Velia shoved the rag into Nella.

"We'll have to take it now," Mafalda said.

Anna knew that her presence here would raise her husband's ire; nevertheless, when Padre Valentine had brought her to Nella's cottage yesterday, she could not abandon her.

"Take my place."

Mafalda shifted towards Velia.

"Hold her head."

It was difficult for Anna to believe that this was the same beautiful girl who had cared for her since her family moved to San Michelle four years ago. She placed a hand on each side of Nella's swollen face. Anna was relieved that Nella's husband, Edoardo, did not have to witness his wife's suffering. Nella had tried to give Edoardo a child before they had come to San Michelle, but she was a bleeder and her body had given up the infant before it was fully formed. Edoardo worked as a gardener for Anna's family; he was thirty-five and Anna knew that there was not much time left for him to be a father.

All of a sudden, blood spurted from Nella's body, and sprayed the front of Velia's dress. Padre Valentine needed to concentrate on something but the stone walls were bare.

The fetid air stirred the bile in his liver and he felt a bitter taste rise up in his throat. He rushed to the bucket of water by the door, grabbed the ladle off the floor and plunged it into the liquid;

10

it was a miasma of dark colors and dank odors. The priest wiped his mouth with the sleeve of his cassock; the dark material was sodden with a mixture of his sweat and Nella's blood, he was repulsed by his own smell. Padre Valentine needed to pray, but he couldn't think of anymore prayers to say and it seemed useless to repeat the other ones.

"There are no more rags." Mafalda stood up. Velia and Anna held their places.

Nella was still bleeding.

Mafalda raised her fleshy arms to the ceiling. "Oh, lavender," she cried. "Let your powers cast out the evil within our Nella." She reached into the pocket of her skirt, and scooped up a handful of dried purple petals. "Oh, lavender, bring her peace and give us her child." She sprinkled them over Nella's body.

Padre Valentine grasped the silver crucifix suspended on a leather cord that hung around his neck. The individual sculptures of the bull, winged lion, bird and virgin riveted on each point pressed into his palm. The crucifix had been a gift from his friend, Fiore, who was now a doctor in Naples and the priest had worn it in St. Peter's Square on the day of his ordination when Pope Leo X111 had blessed him. Padre Valentine released the crucifix. The imprints of the sculptures had marked his skin. Mafalda had stopped speaking. Why had his teachers not taught him how to deal with these superstitious people? They prayed with him in his church but whenever something frightened them, they resorted to the old ways. Padre Valentine hoped that he could reach their children, like this baby, if it lived.

The petals had absorbed Nella's blood and were no longer discernible. Mafalda closed her eyes and touched the *Gobbo*. The flow finally abated.

Anna pulled a white handkerchief edged with lace from the sleeve of her dress and patted Nella's forehead. Nella grew quiet.

"A flood," Mafalda shouted an instant later. Nella's body shaped itself once again into unnatural contortions.

"A river of blood," Velia screamed.

Mafalda grabbed a blanket and Velia forced her hands into Nella; Anna recoiled and her handkerchief dropped to the floor. Padre Valentine wanted to avert his eyes but he couldn't.

"*Bambina.*"

Velia pulled the baby out of Nella. "A girl."

The baby hadn't cried. Anna shifted forward. Velia placed it in the blanket Mafalda held. It did not move and Padre Valentine feared that it was dead and he had lost both a mother and her child. Surely God would not do this to him. He held his breath. Nella shuddered then lay still. Mafalda wrapped the blanket tightly around the baby and stepped away.

Anna kissed Nella on her cheek, and walked over to Mafalda. Anna's first birth had been difficult and it had taken her son a few minutes to cry but Caesare was now stronger and bigger than any other nine-year-old boy Santo had ever seen. Benito had been born less than a year later and Anna had worried about his small size but he was fast and smart. Nella's baby whimpered. If Anna hadn't been standing close to Mafalda, she wouldn't have heard it.

Padre Valentine approached Mafalda and Velia followed him. He stood next to Anna. Her youngest son, Lorenzo, born three years ago in Cetraro, was the first child that he had anointed with this holy water; Nella's would be the last. The vial would be empty; Lorenzo and this newly born infant would forever share a blessed bond. Padre Valentine trudged to the door, and slid the board up to unlock it. He used both hands to pull it open, and stepped outside.

The warmth of the noonday sun dispelled the chill within the priest and for an instant he forgot that Nella had just died. An early summer breeze ruffled the heavy folds of his cassock and softly shaped clouds sauntered across the blue sky. Edoardo was tilling his vegetable garden and the stalks were just beginning to peak through the soil with the promise of new life. The day was too beautiful for someone who worked in harmony with the earth to hold such horror. Padre Valentine had spoken the words he needed to say to Edoardo to other men before but this didn't make it any easier for him now; he hoped that God would help him.

Edoardo threw his hoe on the ground. "Padre. Is it over?" His legs covered the short distance between them in a few steps. He wore two different work boots; there were no laces in the eyelets and the leather was splattered with mud. "Can I see Nella now?"

"Come with me." He followed the priest into the cottage. Padre Valentine joined Mafalda and Velia in front of the fireplace; Edoardo staggered over to his wife.

"*Amare.*" He brushed matted strands of dull, dark hair off her wasted face with his rough and soiled hands. When he kissed her closed eyelids one at a time, his chapped and cracked lips barely touched their sunken surface.

"It's a girl," the priest said.

"*Bambina?*" Edoardo asked.

Anna stepped out from behind the two midwives. She held the infant; it was wrapped in a clean brown blanket. She went over to Edoardo and he touched the downy black hair that covered his daughter's crusted head. Her face was speckled with Nella's blood and when her hand moved, Anna noticed a patch of tiny red dots on her left wrist. She had never seen such a strange birthmark. Padre Valentine walked over to them and Mafalda and Velia followed. Anna placed the baby in her father's arms.

"*Bellisima,*" he said. "I'll name her Caterina."

Padre Valentine blessed them both.

It was late afternoon and Padre Valentine had already gone but Anna had wanted to make certain that there was someone to care for Caterina before she left. She was pleased when Mafalda told her that, Elda, a servant on the enclave who had been Nella's friend, would nurse the child. Oresto took her hand and she stepped up into the rear seat of her carriage then sat down.

"Would you like your shawl, *Signora* Marino?"

"*Si.*" He placed it around her shoulders and Anna welcomed the familiar warmth. Her mother had died when she was a young girl but her memories kept her company; Caterina would have none of her own. Edoardo would love his child but Anna knew that a father's love could never replace that of a mother's. Why did Caterina's life have to begin on such a note of sadness?

They passed brick and stone cottages and pens holding goats and sheep as they made the two-mile journey from the enclave back to the villa. Women and children were clustered around the well filling their buckets with water for their evening chores. They crossed onto the manicured grounds, gardens and flowerbeds of the 124-acre San Michelle Estate that Anna had come to love as much as her childhood home in Tuscany.

Five years ago when Anna was twenty-one, she had inherited a considerable amount of money when her father, a professor at the University of Pisa, had died; Santo had used a portion of it to purchase San Michelle.

Every morning Nella had helped her dress and every evening Nella had helped her prepare for bed. Anna's skin was delicate but Nella knew how to pour her bath so that the water was neither too hot nor too cold. She only had to tell her things once and Nella always remembered. Anna would miss her very, very much. The padding cradled her head and she closed her eyes.

"*Signora* Marino." Oresto's voice seemed to come from a distance. "We are here."

The pink colored limestone walls of the villa welcomed Anna home. Oresto helped her from the carriage, onto the crushed stones of the circular driveway. "*Grazie*. How is Fragola and your new *bambino*?"

"*Bene, Signora*." He grinned, making no attempt to hide his broken teeth.

"*Grazie* to you too, Grigio." She patted the old workhorse's grey muzzle. Oresto passed by her on the pathway, ran up the greenish-grey granite steps and opened one of the double symmetrical oak doors framed at the top with a Roman arch. Anna entered the villa.

"*Mamma*," Lorenzo yelled.

He raced down the staircase and it was as if Anna was looking at a portrait of herself at three years of age; Lorenzo was unequivocally her son. Tears came to her for the first time since Nella had died.

"Where were you? I looked everywhere."

She stood beside the demi-lune table.

"You're bleeding," he screamed. "Who hurt you, *Mamma*?"

"No one hurt me, Lorenzo." She pulled him towards her. "I'm fine."

"What's wrong, *Mamma*? Why are you crying?"

"Nella died. Her baby girl has no *mamma*."

"Who's going to take care of the baby?"

"We will Lorenzo. We will take care of Caterina."

"Take my son to his room."

Santo's voice startled Anna.

"Now, Rinaldo."

"No, I want to stay with *Mamma*."

"It's all right, Lorenzo. Go. I'll see you in a little while." Anna kissed his cheek. "I'll come and read you a story."

Lorenzo took Rinaldo's hand and they walked away.

"Did you just get back?" Anna asked. She brushed her hair off her forehead, and repined a loose tendril. "I wasn't expecting you for a few days." She adjusted her shawl to hide as much of the blood stained fabric of her dress as possible. "It's good to see you." She shaped a smile on her lips, and hoped that it made her face look welcoming.

Santo had left Cetraro a week ago to visit Arduino Buccella, a business associate who lived in Cosenza; a town located about 35 miles away. Over the past few years, Buccella had helped her husband expand his fishing operations along the Tyrrehenian Coast and Santo now owned everything from Cetraro to Cirella on the Calabria-Basilicata border.

"We finished our business and there was no need to stay."

"Were there problems?"

"Of course not. Why do you ask such a question?"

"Our sons will be pleased to see you." The severe features of his face softened for an instant just as she knew they would.

"I had lunch with Caesare and Benito. Bruno cooked the tuna they caught this morning."

It was only natural for her oldest sons to share their father's love of the sea for they were born in Diamante, a nearby village where Santo and his father had been fishermen and where Anna and Santo met. She and Mariangela, sixteen-year-old friends who attended the same convent school in Pisa, had been spending the summer with Anna's grandmother.

When Anna first saw Santo, he was walking along the beach. His sun-bleached shirt had no buttons and he wore canvas-colored trousers cut just below the knees; a corded rope was tied around his trim waist and he was barefoot. His earth brown hair was shoulder length; the only comb it had ever known was the wind. Santo called her "a child of the sun" because she was so fair; her eyes, he said, "were the color of the sea." His smile was dazzling; Santo was different than the other twenty-one year old men that Anna's father brought to their villa. Was it any wonder that she fell in love with him or that everything happened so quickly that summer?

Her father was infuriated when Anna's grandmother told him that she was going to have Santo's child. She arranged to have a priest marry them but he refused to attend the ceremony. They moved into a house that her grandmother owned and Santo continued to work as a fisherman. When Caesare was born, her father relented and he gave Santo his dowry. Within three years, Anna had given birth to Benito, her grandmother had died and Santo had used his dowry to buy the fishing operations in Diamante and Cetraro. Even though Anna's father was pleased that she was happy in her new life, they rarely saw each other for during this time period he remarried.

"Did Caesare and Benito go back out on the fishing boats?"

They had gone out on Santo's fishing boats in Diamante before they could even walk. Caesare and Benito would crawl around on the slippery decks and Anna was terrified that they'd fall into the ocean; they never did.

"*Non.* They've gone riding on the trails."

Her absence from the villa the past day had probably gone unnoticed. When Santo was away, Caesare and Benito weren't required to eat dinner with her, and often didn't. The only rule he gave them was that they had to stay together. This was unnecessary for right from the start; they had been inseparable, even insisting on sleeping in the same bed when they were young.

"Then, they're going for a swim."

Their villa was set on a cliff that overlooked a rocky beach on the Tyrrhenian Sea. Santo had taught Caesare and Benito to swim when they lived in Diamante but Anna still worried that the waves would pull them out.

"Lorenzo's been with his teacher but he's been asking for you."

Anna had told Lorenzo that Padre Valentine needed her to help him in the church but she had been gone longer than she'd anticipated.

Santo ran a finger along the line of his dark mustache and she noticed that he was wearing a signet ring. The gold initial "N" rose from a square, black stone on the finger that was intended for a wedding ring. Her husband lavished Anna with expensive gifts of jewelry but never wore any himself. "Where did you get that ring?" Her interest was not feigned.

"From Buccella."

"Why?"

"He wants me to run his fishing operations in Paola and Tropea. The ring was a token of his appreciation for me. I'm quite an asset to him, you know."

His head moved up a fraction and Anna knew that the ring signified a new and important connection between her husband and this man. How could she find out what it was, and what the "N" stood for? "Did you invite him to come to San Michelle for a visit?"

"No. Buccella's a very busy man."

The heels of his leather boots struck the terra cotta as he stepped towards her and Anna feared that he would shatter the tile. Santo was dressed as usual, in a crisp white shirt and creased black trousers. He shaved twice a day and had his dark, wavy hair trimmed regularly, his nails were clean and cut short. At thirty-one, Santo was still handsome but the fleshiness underneath his chin and around his waist were more pronounced than when Anna had married him. He crossed his arms on his chest.

When had he returned to San Michelle?

"Did you think that I wouldn't find out?"

"Nella died giving birth." She summoned tears to her eyes.

"I've always permitted you to visit the servants at *Natale* and to give them whatever gifts you want. It's proper to be generous at *Natale*. But not this."

"Her baby, Caterina, doesn't have a mother."

"No more, Anna."

The tears would not work this time; it was best not to say anything whenever this happened.

"You've gone to their graveyard when their babies died and I've tolerated this because I knew you wanted more children. Then last year I found out that you were giving Lorenzo's old clothes to families in the village. Do you know how embarrassing it was for me to see the children of my fisherman wearing my son's shoes?" Santo leaned over her. "I will no longer tolerate your foolishness."

His sweet cologne made her nauseous.

"You will not ruin Santo Marino's name."

She held her breath.

"You smell. Fragola will pour your bath. And get rid of that dress." He stepped back. "Bruno will have dinner ready at the usual time and we will all eat together tonight." He left the villa.

Anna walked towards the staircase; there was plenty of time for her to bathe and read Lorenzo a story before dinner. When would her husband leave San Michelle again? Soon, she hoped. Anna planted her foot on the first riser; she could hardly wait to take Lorenzo to see Caterina.

CHAPTER TWO

"We have a problem, Sisina," Anna said. She turned away from the large armoire in her dressing room and faced the sixteen-year old girl Santo had hired as Nella's replacement.

"Didn't I hang your dresses up properly, *Signora*?" She clasped her fingers.

They were so thin, Anna feared they'd snap. Why did Sisina insist on wearing such shapeless dresses? They made her body look like the trunk of a young tree.

"I took them out this morning and rearranged them just like you told me to do." Sisina cast her eyes down.

The carpet's twisting vine pattern would probably make her dizzy again. Anna could have it replaced but her five-year-old son, Lorenzo, loved to spend hours copying the intricate swirls.

"I put the colors with the colors and the prints with the prints," Sisina said.

Her ebony hair contrasted with her pale skin; she tied it behind her ears and it pulled at the temples on each side of her head, giving her face a permanent look of surprise.

"There's nothing wrong with what you've done." This wasn't entirely true but what did it matter? At least the girl was trying; Anna would separate her dresses later and perhaps she could find one for Sisina.

Sisina had worked for the Buccella family before San Michelle but her domestic skills were unsophisticated; it had taken her months to learn how to wash and press Anna's clothes and almost a year before she knew how to draw a proper bath. Sisina rubbed her lips; her cuticles were raw again. Anna would treat them with a chickweed infusion tonight.

"It's just that we've run out of space."

"Oh," Sisina said.

"Everything's full: the armoires, the chests of drawers. There's no more room."

The lid of the *cassone* on Anna's dressing table was open; her locket with the strands of her sons' hair lay beside the walnut jewelry chest that had once belonged to her mother. Her pink sapphire ring was next to an amethyst earring. Had Sisina lost the other one? Nella always took such good care of Anna's things.

"I have to see my husband now but tomorrow morning, we'll look around. I'm certain we'll find someplace."

"*Si, Signora.*"

Anna inspected her reflection in the mirror with the elaborately carved Florentine frame that Santo had recently purchased in Murano. Her eyes were an exotic blue-green shade; Lorenzo was the only one of her sons to have inherited them. Her nose was a tad long but the tendrils that cascaded down the side of her face and fell around the nape of her neck softened this feature. Sisina had done an excellent job of pinning her hair up this morning; Anna was making progress with her. She fluffed the delicate ruffle that lined the scooped neckline of her dress. Her husband liked the way its moss green color accentuated her fair skin and hair; her demure appearance was perfect for what she planned to ask him today.

It was time for Caterina and Edoardo to have a new cottage; the little girl was two years old now and she should have her own bedroom. No one would ever take as good care of her as Nella had and this was the least that Anna could do for her child. She took one last look at herself then continued down the corridor. She needed Santo's permission for this as he'd never let her take such action by herself but Anna knew how to get what she wanted. She passed by the door to his bedroom and descended the stairs.

Bruno watched Anna enter his kitchen. The skirt of her dress hid her tiny feet; it was as if she was floating towards him. Anna was an angel; Calabrian women were short and heavy. Dark hair sprouted from their chins and they had mustaches. He had been her family's cook from the first day they had moved into the villa. Lorenzo popped up from his chair.

"*Mamma*, look what I've drawn," he said. He picked his sketch off the table and held it up for her.

"That's wonderful, Lorenzo."

Her words sounded so big; Bruno knew that Anna was the best mother in the world.

"The cedro trees look exactly like the ones outside. Your teacher will be so pleased."

Cedro jam was Anna's favorite; he'd make some for her this afternoon. Bruno spooned the last bit of tomato sauce over the eggplant. He had prepared *melanzana al funghetto* for Santo's lunch, just as Anna had asked him. Edoardo had brought him the firmest eggplant from his garden; its skin was a deep, vibrant purple. He could hardly wait to have some.

"The *melanzana* smells delicious," Anna said.

Her roses had a sweet scent and Anna made her own perfume; Bruno liked it more than the smell of his own cooking. He wanted to make her *buccellato* but he was afraid that he wouldn't put in the right amount of raisins and anise; Bruno wanted his cake to be as good as the one Anna's cook baked for her when she was a child.

"You're the best cook in all of Calabria," Anna said.

He smoothed his apron. It was tight over his paunch; maybe he should go for a walk with Padre Valentine once and awhile; the priest kept telling him he needed some exercise. Tomato sauce was splattered on the white bib; Bruno wished he'd remembered to put a clean one on. Anna sat on the chair and pulled Lorenzo onto her lap. He wiped his face. There was flour on his hand. Why didn't he have a mirror in his kitchen?

"And some day, I will be the best artist in all of Calabria," Lorenzo said.

"You will." She kissed his cheek.

The curls made Lorenzo look like a little Anna. The door behind Bruno opened and the summer wind brought the salty scent of the sea into the room. Edoardo held Caterina in his arms.

"Renzo," Caterina said. She thrust her arm forward; there was a dirt-covered ball of something Bruno could not identify in her hand. "I grew this." She squirmed and Edoardo placed her on the floor.

Her bare feet skimmed the stone surface as she raced across the room; Bruno was afraid she'd slip and hurt herself. Why didn't she have on the shoes Anna gave her?

"*Mamma* Anna, look, too." She climbed over Lorenzo's knees and shoved the bulb against his nose. "I made garlic. Smell it."

"It stinks." He jerked his head back.

"Don't hurt her feelings," Anna said.

Tears welled up in Caterina's eyes and she slid off him.

"Let me see it," Anna said.

She moved away.

"But it's garlic," Lorenzo said.

Caterina jumped up and down and reminded Bruno of a puppet in a box that Santo had bought Lorenzo one *Natale*.

"Can you draw it, Renzo?"

"*Sì*," he said.

"Now?" she asked.

"Soon," Anna said.

She hopped towards her.

"Where are your shoes?"

"They're too small."

"Then I'll have to get you another pair." Anna embraced both Caterina and Lorenzo.

The red in her hair was the same as Nella's; Bruno wondered if Lorenzo would ever be able to paint colors. Caterina wriggled out of Anna's arms and ran over to him.

"Cook it," she said. She waved her hand back and forth.

"You're going to be as good a gardener as your father." Bruno wanted to take the garlic bulb but bending over was hard for him to do.

Edoardo scooped up his daughter.

"We'll come by later," Anna said. Lorenzo leaned against her.

"When?" Caterina asked.

"After Lorenzo's lesson is over."

"Renzo draw my garlic?"

"*Sì*," Lorenzo said.

"We're going for a walk on the trails so Lorenzo can do some sketching but we can stop by for a few minutes," Anna said.

Caterina nestled her head in the crook of her father's neck.

"I made lots of *melanzana*," Bruno said. "There's some for you and Caterina to have for supper." He had made extra but Caesar and Benito ate so much, he was a little worried that he hadn't prepared enough. He better hide a dish for himself if he wanted to have any. Life was much simpler when Caesar and Benito were away; Bruno always knew how much food to cook.

"I'll bring you more vegetables later," Edoardo said.

"I have to take my husband his lunch now," Anna said. "And you better get back to your teacher."

"See you later, Caterina," Lorenzo said.

"*Ciao*, Renzo."

He left the kitchen.

Edoardo patted Caterina's cheek. Anna kissed her and she closed her eyes. He nodded at Anna, then Bruno and left.

Bruno walked over to the counter. He spooned the food onto a china plate then covered it with a silver dome; cold *melanzana* was something the *Signore* would not eat.

"You are very good to my family," Anna said.

Why was he warm? Bruno wasn't cooking anymore. He placed

the plate on a tray. "Is there anything else that I can get for the *Signore?*"

"*Non, grazie.*"

He handed Anna the tray and watched her walk out of the kitchen.

The priest had cost Santo more than he'd anticipated and the doctor's medical expenses were higher than he had planned; still, Santo was certain that someday his investment in Padre Valentine and Fiore would prove valuable. He had been in his office all morning recording and analyzing figures in his ledger and was getting hungry. Where was his lunch?

There were piles of paper and stacks of books everywhere on the desk. Buccella was having problems with the men in Paola; they weren't catching enough tuna but Santo had figured out what to do. Santo was a clever man. He didn't have much time for Anna today.

"You've been working so hard lately," Anna said. "You must make certain you eat."

Santo placed his silver fountain pen in its stand, closed the ledger and put it in his desk drawer.

"I had Bruno prepare *melanzana al funghetto* for you."

The men Buccella had introduced him to were fit; he'd been trying to eat less lately. He shifted some papers to make room for the tray. He was looking forward to his afternoon ride with Caesare and Benito; they had already mastered the stallions he had bought them. Santo wasn't leaving for Paola for a few days, and he had time to lose a few more pounds.

Anna set the tray down carefully; she did not want to scratch the walnut wood like a former servant once had done. It had taken another servant a long time to sand the entire surface, and refinish the wood so that the desk looked new again.

How had she resisted Bruno's cooking all these years? Santo

watched her walk around his desk; she still had the slim figure of her youth.

"Rinaldo is packing your suitcase." She sat down in the chair facing him. "You seem to be taking a lot of suits."

She glanced at the signet ring Buccella had given him. Santo had told her that the "N" stood for Buccella's father, Nino, who had started the family's business that he was now a partner in; this was the truth, just not all of it. What he had told Anna was exactly what Buccella had told his wife and it had worked for him. There was no need for her to know that the "N" also stood for "*Ndrangheta.*"

A group of Sicilians who had been banished from the island for insurrection by the Italian government in the 1860's moved to Calabria, and formed a secret organization called the "*Ndrangheta*" with the intention of controlling the region. Nino Buccella had been a pivotal figure.

Buccella had been impressed with the way Santo improved productivity in his fishing operations and from the moment they met, they worked well together. Over the years, Buccella had established himself as one of the most powerful men in Calabria; Santo was becoming increasingly recognized as one of his key players.

"I thought you were just going to Paola for a few days."

"I'm not sure how long we'll be gone. We're going to see Eugenio afterwards and we'll be in Taranto for a while."

"You're taking Caesare and Benito with you again? But they just got back from Sibari. You said they'd learned enough for now about your olive business."

"Buccella wants to see them again."

"What for? It wasn't that long ago since they were in Cosenza. Why can't he ever come here like the other businessmen?"

"They're not boys anymore, Caesare's eleven and Benito's ten. When I was Lorenzo's age, I was already fishing with my father."

"He's only five. You can't take him away from me yet."

"He should come riding with us this afternoon; his brothers were never scared of horses."

"Lorenzo has a lesson with his teacher; you know he loves his books."

Why hadn't Anna had a daughter for herself? Santo took his fountain pen out of its stand and dipped the tapered point into the marble ink well.

When Anna had given the ink well to Santo last *Natale*, he'd made her glue a piece of felt cloth on its base so that it wouldn't mark the wood. The rows in the shelves, which filled the wall next to her, contained his collection of leather, bound books on ancient Rome. He could barely read and write when they first met. Had he forgotten that she was the one who taught him? There was no point in arguing today, not if she was going to get what she wanted.

"You remember Mariangela, don't you?"

"Of course, Anna." Eugenio was his cousin; their fathers had been brothers, and they had all fished together in Diamante. Diamante was a long time ago and Santo was no longer a simple fisherman; the past no longer interested him. Why was Anna talking about Mariangela?

"She took care of Caesare after Benito was born."

"You know I would never forget that." Santo had asked Buccella to help Eugenio establish a fishing operation in Taranto and Buccella had agreed for he wanted a presence on the Ionian Sea. Anna moved closer to the desk; Santo would permit her to stay for only a few more minutes.

"Do you remember when she almost died from the chills?"

It had been a terrible malaria epidemic that had broken out in the area around Diamante.

"We were lucky, Santo."

"You're right." He had Anna's dowry and so many people had died in the epidemic that he was able to buy the fishing operation in Diamante for little money; it still felt good to own the business where Santo had first worked with his father.

"Soon it'll be the second anniversary of Mariangela's death." This wasn't true but Anna knew that Santo never remembered such things so it didn't matter.

Mariangela had died shortly after her daughter, Francesca, had been born. The smell of the garlic was making Santo hungry; he was going riding so he could have a little bit of the eggplant. Anna would be leaving any minute now and his food would still be warm.

"I would like to go to Taranto. I've only seen Francesca once and I've never visited Mariangela's grave."

Santo had never met another woman who had the eyes of the Tyrrehenian Sea, not yet, anyway. Her face was unlined and it was hard for him to believe that she was almost thirty. Still, Buccella was right, old women were tedious. Francesca would be a good diversion for her, and Anna was her godmother. "I'll take you to Taranto soon."

"*Grazie.*"

"You must go."

"Make sure you eat." She walked around the desk. She'd ask him now. "Bruno needs more vegetables. You're bringing so many businessmen now to San Michelle that Edoardo needs more gardens. He knows a perfect spot but there's an old cottage on it and a servant family is living in it."

"Tell Oresto to tear it down."

"What about the servants?"

"Have Oresto build them a new one."

"Whatever you say." She kissed him on the cheek, left his office and headed towards her sitting room.

What was Santo up to? Anna had seen him put the ledger in the desk drawer; she'd look at it after he'd left for Paola. She walked down the hall, entered her sitting room, crossed the floor and stood in front of a small panel on the wall depicting four angels playing musical instruments. She named the first one, the one with the lute, Avanina, after her mother. The one with the harp was Mariangela and the one with the flute was Nella. When Anna died, she would be the angel playing the trumpet. She picked her needlework off the table and inspected the design of the young boy holding a puppy; she'd have to rework some of the sections. She put it down and went over to the window by her chair. Would she ever be as good an artist as her mother? Probably not, but Lorenzo would definitely be a better one.

It was a perfect view of her favorite rose bed and over the past few days, the red petals had begun to turn pink. She was going to have Edoardo's old cottage torn down and several of these rosebushes planted in memory of Nella; the new cottage would be built next to Elda's, Caterina's godmother. Anna sat down and rested her feet on the stool. The red spots on the child's left wrist had shaped themselves into the mark of a rose. Was this a sign that they were destined to have a special relationship? Perhaps. She'd have a nap then get Lorenzo and together, they'd tell Edoardo and Caterina the wonderful news; Santo would be off riding with Caesare and Benito so he'd have plenty of time to sketch the garlic bulb for Caterina.

CHAPTER THREE

Grigio pulled the wagon along the uneven ground and Bruno placed the reins at his feet. The sun had not yet risen on this mid-August morning but there was no need to guide the old workhorse; the animal had traveled the road between the enclave and the villa enough to know its way by rote. The large wheels creaked and the dried wood groaned as if the wagon was complaining that the load of vegetables it carried was too heavy.

"What do you know about the men who are arriving tomorrow?" Edoardo asked.

"They work for Buccella and most of them have never been here before." He took a fig out of his sack and gave it to Edoardo. "I heard Anna tell Benito though that Buccella's not coming." Grigio whinnied. "Even he's happy that the *Signora's* back."

"I have more of Caterina's carrots for Grigio," Edoardo said.

Did she think that Bruno would let Grigio starve? He grabbed a handful of grapes and shoved them into his mouth; the juicy pulp was refreshing.

"She was so worried that he wouldn't get enough to eat when Anna was in Taranto."

Just because everyone else paid more attention to the new Arabians didn't mean that Bruno would. Caesare would never win the Palio anyway; he was too big for a horse race. He looked at the figs and wished that the pear-shaped fruits were covered with chocolate; he'd eat one anyway.

"Every day that Lorenzo was gone; Caterina looked at Grigio's sketch. I think he'll have to make her a new one."

"Where's Oresto?"

"He wanted more time with Giuseppe so we loaded the vegetables last night. He'll meet us in a little while. The little boy's not much better."

"But he told me that he drank my chicken broth." No matter how busy Santo kept him today, he'd make more; he'd add a few chickpeas too and Fragola could mash them for her son.

"I'll unload the cart," Edoardo said. "Oresto will help you put them away and I'll go pick some tomatoes and come back later."

The fig had been firmer than Bruno thought. He didn't want to break another tooth so he shoved the fruit to one side of his mouth to let them rest. It wasn't his fault that he didn't have strong teeth; life in the Sila Mountains had been difficult after his father died. His family had cows but his mother was forced to sell their milk and the cheese she made to the people in nearby Cerisi. Santo had ordered so many different kinds of cheeses for these men that Bruno knew he would not miss the chunk of *caciocavallo* he had tucked behind the bags of flour.

"There's so much to do before tomorrow," he said. The fig was softer in his mouth. "Rinaldo has to wash all their shirts, and press all their suits."

"I know," Edoardo said. "He told me. Not just Santo's but Caesare's, Benito's and Lorenzo's too."

Bruno chewed his fig.

"The only time Santo makes us work like this is when he has the big *Natale* parties." Edoardo sipped water from his canteen. "You're cooking swordfish and eels too?"

"And Caesare's favorite, that smelly tuna. It stinks up my kitchen."

"But Anna will give you some of her roses."

"*Si.*"

Their scent lasted a long time and it was like having Anna in the kitchen with him; cooking with his mother was one of Bruno's favorite memories and he made sure that he thought of

30

it often so he would never forget it. He reached into the sack for some almonds, popped them into his mouth and listened to the crunching sound. At least he had all his front teeth; he didn't look as ridiculous as Oresto. Why did that man always smile with his mouth open? The villa came into view; their day had begun.

Caterina stood on the chair, and peered through the window of her cottage. The sun was sinking and soon it would drop behind the other cottages and sheds and she wouldn't be able to see it anymore. *Pappa* had told her last night that he would be home before the sun went to bed so she knew he'd be back soon.

The sour smell of vinegar made her nose crinkle. She glanced down at the bucket of water from the well that Elda had helped her fill a short time ago; next time she would use more water and less vinegar. She always kept this window clean, sometimes when the wind blew dirt onto it; she'd wash it several times in one day. She always wanted to be able to see her *Pappa* coming home right from the start so she didn't mind; she never considered washing this window as one of her chores.

"*Mio Pappa*!" Caterina jumped down from the chair and her bare feet slapped against the hard dirt floor. She'd left the door open so that she could get to him as fast as possible. She ran past the lavender bushes and leapt into his arms.

"*Tesora mia*," Edoardo said, "My treasure." He swung her body around in circles. She laughed when his straw hat flew off his head. After a few minutes, he put her down. "You're getting too old for me to do this."

"I'm only five." Caterina thrust her arm up, opened the palm of her hand and stretched out her fingers.

"Padre Valentine's teaching you to count now?" He sat on the ground.

"*Si, Papa*. I told him I wanted to show Lorenzo that I'm as smart as he is when he got back from Taranto." Caterina straightened her arms by her side. "Listen to me." She closed her eyes. "*Uno, due, tre, quattro, cinque, sei, sette, otto, nove, dieci, undici, dodici, tredici, quattrodici, tredici, quindici, sedici, diciasette, diciotto, diciannove, venti.*"

"You can count to twenty."

"I'm as smart as Lorenzo."

Edoardo pulled her close and Caterina took the rag from his pocket and wiped his forehead.

"I picked more tomatoes today than you have numbers to count." He sat her on his lap. "Did you help Nicoletta do her chores for *Zia* Elda?"

"*Si, Pappa.* I peeled the potatoes and Nicoletta cut the onions for the stew but *Zio* Ermengildo wouldn't let us watch him kill the goat. Nicoletta wanted to but he said that it wasn't right for his daughter to see all the blood."

"*Zio's* right."

"I didn't want to see blood." She put the rag back into his pocket. "Why are so many men coming to Anna's villa?"

"Who told you that?"

"I heard *Zio* tell *Zia* Elda."

"You know you're not to go to the villa when Anna's away."

For an instant, her dark eyes no longer suited the face of a child. "I know that *Pappa*."

"What other chores did you do?"

"We washed clothes in the stream." She swung her arm behind his neck. "Then we had to find dried corn cobs for the fire."

"No time to play?"

"Guess what, *Pappa*?" She jumped off his lap.

"What *mia bella*?"

"*Zia* taught us the tarella dance!" She began stomping on the ground. "Get out spider," she yelled. She spun around in circles and her long hair came untied and covered her face but Caterina didn't care that she couldn't see. "Get out of my body."

"It's the tarantella, Caterina, not the tarella." He grabbed her at the waist.

"Padre. Renzo." She wriggled out of Edoardo's arms as she saw them approaching. "Renzo. I can count to twenty."

Padre Valentine waved at Edoardo and Caterina.

"You taught her how to count to twenty when I was in Taranto," Lorenzo said. "Francesca can't even count to ten and she's the same age as Caterina; she's *stupida*."

"You shouldn't say such things about your mother's goddaughter."

"She chatters all the time and gives me headaches."

"Do you want to hurt your *Mamma*?"

"Never, Padre." He kicked the dirt with the toe of his boot."

Caterina zigzagged towards them. The priest had spent the last few hours with Fragola and Giuseppe was getting weaker every day. Why couldn't Caterina give him some of her energy?

"Renzo, did you see me dancing?" Caterina hit his knee with her fist.

"I'm eight years old now. Can't you remember to call me Lorenzo?"

"I can remember how to count to twenty. I'm as smart as you and I'm only five." She tugged at the priest's cassock. "Right Padre?"

"*Si*." He squatted. Caterina's face and dress was smudged with dirt. The tip of the lavender stalk that Edoardo always made her wear peaked out from the neckline of her dress.

"I was dancing the tarella, Padre. Did you see me?"

The priest nodded as he wiped her face with his sleeve. He glanced at Edoardo who was still sitting on the ground a short distance in front of them.

"Renzo. Can you draw me dancing the tarella?"

"It's called the tarantella. Not the tarella."

Padre Valentine retied her hair in a ponytail with the red ribbon that Anna gave all the girls every *Natale*.

"You should see all the carrots in my garden, Renzo." She slapped her hands against her dress and puffs of dust flew up.

33

"Grigio ate twenty of them when you were in Taranto but there's still twenty more. Come and see. You too, Padre." She scampered off.

"I'll be there shortly."

Lorenzo followed Caterina.

Edoardo offered the priest his hand. "Were you with Fragola and Giuseppe?" He helped him to his feet.

"*Si*." He smoothed the folds of his cassock.

"How was he today?" He picked his straw hat off the ground and they began walking.

"The cough is still in his chest but your hyssop infusion helped him sleep better last night."

Caterina and Lorenzo rounded the cottage and disappeared from sight.

"*Bene.* God can't take another son from Oresto. Not after Luigi last winter."

Nothing could be done to save Giuseppe; Padre had seen enough sickness in his ten years at San Michelle to know this.

"I'll make another infusion and bring Fragola some fresh lavender too. Soon he will be better."

There was no need to tell Edoardo the truth; Padre Valentine had come to accept the fact that lies, which helped protect the innocent from further pain were justified. Caterina was on her hands and knees at the edge of the small garden plot Edoardo had prepared for her. Lorenzo stood behind her. "Anna showed me the dresses she brought back for Caterina. They're very sweet."

"Nella must be smiling all the time in heaven. I'm glad Santo took her to see her goddaughter; the train ride gave her time with her sons too."

"The trip made Anna very happy."

"Look, Renzo." Caterina pointed at the tips of the shoots breaking through the soil. He knelt down beside her. A leaf blew in front of them and as it floated away, Caterina sprung up. "Let's try and catch it."

Lorenzo jumped up and the two of them ran haphazardly in all directions, following the leaf as the wind constantly altered its path.

"Such beautiful children," Edoardo said.

Padre Valentine watched Caterina and Lorenzo in silence.

CHAPTER FOUR

Lorenzo adjusted the notebook on his knees. His satchel was on his right, and he'd arranged his charcoal sticks, white chalk and putty eraser in a straight row on his left. A cool easy afternoon sea breeze passed by the side of his family's villa where he had spent the last hour sketching; it carried the scent of the nearby cedro and lime trees to him. Lorenzo wished he knew how to draw smells. He picked up a thin charcoal stick; the arched windows on the third floor in his drawing were still too big. *Pappa* would be home tomorrow and he had hoped to have it ready to show him.

Before he was three years old, *Pappa* had brought Lorenzo's first teacher to San Michelle, by the time he was six, Lorenzo could read and write. He was now ten, and had been studying Latin for the past year. *Pappa* was impressed with the words Lorenzo had learned to describe his family.

Pappa was the *patrician*, the wealthy nobleman. Caesare was the Roman *centurion* and *Pappa* said that someday he could be the boss of all the *plebeians* who worked for them. Benito was the Roman *quaestor* because he was good with numbers so *Pappa* said he'd put him in charge of all their money. Lorenzo didn't know what the Latin word for him was yet because *Pappa* hadn't decided what he was going to be. His teacher had told *Pappa* that Lorenzo was bright and could be the lawyer that *Pappa* said he needed to keep them out of trouble.

A large shadow engulfed Lorenzo and a massive hand seized his notebook. "What pretty pictures are you drawing now?"

Caesare's muddy boot almost stepped on his satchel.

"Give that back to me." Lorenzo jumped up.

"Flowers and trees." Caesare flipped through the pages. "This doesn't even look like our villa."

He couldn't reach the notebook.

"And stupid pictures of old workhorses and servant girls." Caesare waved it above his head. "If you're going to draw birds, why don't you draw a man's bird like the quail I killed today?"

"Give that back to me."

"You're a *bimbo*." He tossed the notebook to one side; it landed in front of the fuschia bougainvillea hedges. "You're too scared to swim in the sea and the only horse you can ride is Grigio."

That wasn't exactly true. Lorenzo swam in the streams that crossed San Michelle, and he knew how to ride a horse; his legs just weren't long enough to handle the stallions. Lorenzo tried to scramble past Caesare to get his notebook.

Caesare snatched him by the collar and forced him onto the ground, the hard earth pressed against Lorenzo's bony shoulder blades. "Here." He reached behind him, grabbed the dead quail and shoved it into Lorenzo's face. "Draw this for me."

The wide nostrils of Caesare's flat nose flapped open and close as his heavy breaths hit Lorenzo's face. The large pores on his coarse skin were filled with specks of dirt. His bristly hair was soaked with sweat. You look like a pig, and you smell like one too, Lorenzo thought. He kicked Caesare with his shoes and even though he knew that Caesare wouldn't feel his blows, he kept kicking.

"Get off him, Caesare."

Benito grabbed Caesare's hand and Caesare tightened his grip on Lorenzo's neck. For a moment, Lorenzo couldn't breathe. Then Caesare released him and Lorenzo's head struck the earth; Caesare lumbered off.

"What did you say to him?" Benito tossed the bird away, and helped him to his feet. He tucked Lorenzo's shirt into his waistband then took a handkerchief from the side pocket of his trousers.

"Nothing."

"Were you speaking Latin again?" Benito wiped Lorenzo's chin. "You know he can't understand that."

Why did Caesare always make fun of him? He'd read more books and he was six years younger; even Caterina knew more words than his brother did.

"Don't do it anymore."

"Come on, Benito. The fishermen are waiting for us." Caesare snorted and rocked from side to side.

"In a minute." Benito did not turn away from Lorenzo. "*Capisco?*"

Lorenzo knew that Benito was right.

Benito brushed the dirt from his hair. Lorenzo was glad that they both had curls, even though his were fair like *Mamma's* and Benito's were dark like *Pappa's*; they were still the same curls.

"Get Bruno to clean you." He stood up and patted the top of his head.

"Tell Bruno to cook this for me."

Caesare threw the quail and the bird landed at Lorenzo's feet.

"Do as he says, Lorenzo."

Benito walked away.

Herb gardens that Edoardo had planted broke the stretch of ground behind the villa and the sea. Bruno sat on the cement stoop at the back entrance to his kitchen. The sections with basil, parsley, oregano and rosemary were full. Soon it would be time to hang them from the ceiling of the storage cellar below his kitchen to dry. The cedro trees were heavy with their yellow fruit and the lime trees were full of white blossoms. Gulls circled noisily above the ocean, then disappeared from site as they dove down to the rocky beach to eat the fish that had washed up along the shore. All you birds do all day is eat, Bruno thought. He put a handful of chickpeas in his mouth. The bushy plants beside him were full of *cecci*. He was glad that Santo wouldn't eat "this peasant food," it meant that there was more of it for himself. Caesare and Benito charged past the fruit trees and Bruno watched them until they headed down the cliff. He was relieved that Caesare did not run through any of his herb gardens this time.

Lorenzo rounded the corner of the villa.

"What happened to you?"

There were tears on his face and his shirt was stained with blood.

He pushed himself off the stoop. Why were his legs so short? He needed to get to Lorenzo as fast as possible.

"Are you alright?" Why wouldn't Lorenzo answer him?

"Come into my *cucina*." He took the quail from his hand. "I made minestrone soup, the one with the vermicelli that you like."

"You're hungry?" Food always made everything better.

Lorenzo nodded.

"*Bene*. I'll have a bowl with you."

"That was good *zuppa*." Lorenzo opened his notebook on the kitchen table as Bruno placed a glazed ceramic green bowl full of oranges in front of him. "*Grazie*."

"What are you drawing now?"

There was food stuck between his teeth again but Lorenzo didn't tell him.

"That's exactly the way Caterina looks when she feeds Grigio her carrots."

He turned the page.

"Who's that? That can't be me; I'm not that fat." He went back to the counter.

How old would Lorenzo have to be before his arms were long enough to wrap around Bruno's stomach?

Square white tiles with a blue fish motif in the center filled the space between the counter and the dark oak cupboards attached to the wall. Bruno had placed the quail on a plain platter so its blood wouldn't stain the wood. One of the thin head plumes was missing and the bird's blood had dried on its mottled, brown feathers; Lorenzo decided that he would never eat quail for as long as he lived.

"I'm getting sick of this bird," Bruno said. "Everyday Caesare kills one. He can't get enough of its eggs. I bet you and Caterina don't have enough numbers in your heads to count all the eggs I fried for Caesare's breakfast. Benito even gave him his two but he still wanted more. Then Benito ate almost all of my *prosciutto*." He brought a pitcher full of a lemon and sugar drink that Lorenzo liked to the table. The pitcher matched the ceramic fruit bowl and Lorenzo decided to ask his teacher to show him how to paint with colors.

"Are you feeling better now?"

He placed his hand on Lorenzo's shoulder; his fingers looked like the sausages he made from the hogs raised on their estate.

"I'm not a *bimbo*, Bruno. I'm ten years old."

"If you're so big, why did you leave everything outside?" Padre Valentine walked into the kitchen, and placed Lorenzo's satchel on the table in front of him. Lorenzo prayed that he would not start to cry.

"Padre, sit down." Bruno tapped the rim of the pitcher. "Let's all have a drink and we'll have a talk."

"Have you filled another notebook?" Padre Valentine said a little while later. He sat beside Lorenzo at the kitchen table; Bruno was cleaning the quail.

"Just about. *Mamma* wanted me to do some sketches of Caterina for her *Pappa*."

"I'll have my friend from Naples send you some new ones."

"Fiore, Padre? The doctor?"

"*Si*. You remember everything, don't you?"

Sometimes Lorenzo wished that this weren't true.

"Your teacher says that you're getting smarter everyday."

40

"I learned another word in Latin today. *Ma...gi...ster.*" He enunciated every syllable.

"Teacher. *Bene.*"

"What did you call Grigio's cart?" Bruno asked.

"*Biga.*"

"*Non.* That's a small chariot pulled by two horses, Lorenzo."

Bruno turned around. "You're not always right." He pointed a finger at him.

"And don't you dare show him that picture of me until you fix it." He resumed picking the rest of the feathers off the bird.

Lorenzo winked at the priest, and silently mouthed the word "later."

"What are you staring at?"

"You have a Roman nose," Lorenzo said.

"What's wrong with Padre's nose." Bruno glanced over his shoulder.

"The upper part's bony and high; it's a Roman nose. My teacher told me."

"He needs a new teacher, Padre."

"Isn't it almost time for your *Mamma* to read to you?"

"She should be back soon, Padre. Oresto took her for a carriage ride."

"There's a fourteen-year-old girl from the village whose *Nona* died; they prayed together in church. She's alone now and must find work. Your *Mamma* wants to hire someone to take care of her dresses; with all the parties your *Pappa* has now, Sisina needs help. I'd like to bring her to San Michelle so she could meet her."

"Why don't you wait for your *Mamma* in her sitting room? You could work on that picture of the roses for her."

"*Si.*" Lorenzo stood up.

"Tell your *Mamma* I need to talk to her later about the girl." He handed him his satchel.

Lorenzo hugged the priest, and smiled at Bruno. He left the kitchen.

Padre Valentine carried the empty pitcher to the counter. He stared at the decapitated quail. Bruno offered him some soft nougat.

"I added more almonds and extra honey to the *cumpittu*. The last batch wasn't sweet enough." He popped a piece into his mouth.

"*Non, grazie.* I suppose I should tell Anna about Caesare's bullying. Lorenzo won't; he doesn't want to worry her." He walked over to the stone fireplace, and straightened the wooden cross in the middle of the mantle.

Bruno crossed the room and stood close to the priest. "The last while when the men have brought their fish to my kitchen, they've said that Caesare and Benito have been spending a lot of time drinking in the village. A few days ago, Caesare was arm wrestling with a man, and he wouldn't stop, even after the man admitted Caesare had won. He broke his arm. There are a lot of girls too who have no father to give them a dowry and Benito's very handsome." Bruno cleared his throat. "And very charming, Padre."

"Why didn't Santo take them this time, Bruno?" Padre Valentine wanted to be close to Caesare but it was difficult; he couldn't talk to him about books. Even though Benito was as intelligent as Lorenzo, he was only interested in learning about things that he could do and he, too, was not keen on discussion. The priest had spent time on the fishing boats with them over the years, which seemed enjoyable. Caesare, in particular, liked to show him how far he could swim. Strange though, Padre Valentine thought. If Benito did not yell at Caesare to come back, the priest had the feeling that Caesare would keep swimming out to sea.

"You have to talk to Santo. Caesare and Benito are reckless in the village and Caesare, well today; he could have hurt Lorenzo. Here, have a piece of nougat."

"I'm cold, Bruno." He rolled the candy around with his fingers. "I'll build us a fire."

"You're a priest. You can get through to him."

Nobody could get through to Santo, least of all Padre Valentine. He placed the nougat on the mantle, and picked up some kindling wood from the stack beside the fireplace.

"I'll talk to Santo when he gets back." What else could he say to Bruno?

Bruno took the nougat and put it in his mouth.

Lorenzo stopped in front of the mirror on the wall. He stood on his toes and stretched his neck; his reflection showed more of the curls on the top of his head than it had a few weeks ago. Soon his legs would be long enough to ride a stallion and he'd win the Palio. Caesare was *stupido*, if Benito didn't go with him, Caeare would probably take the wrong train and never get to Siena. Benito should ride in the Palio instead; the horse always went faster for him and he never had to use a whip. Lorenzo walked a little further down the corridor and entered his mother's sitting room.

The needlepoint picture of a young boy petting a dog hung above a narrow table. *Mamma* had spent a long time pulling different colored threads through the cloth with a needle; there was no pattern on it when she began and Lorenzo thought it was magic when the shapes started to appear. "Avanina, Mariangela and Nella," he said aloud as he looked at the angel panel. Lorenzo wondered if his *Mamma* had picked out a name for the one with the trumpet. Her chair and stool were covered in the same floral fabric and the rose and green designs reminded him of the gardens of San Michelle. His mother walked into the room.

"There you are," she said.

"You have to see Padre right away."

She sat down and took his hands in hers.

"He found a girl in the village who can help you with your dresses."

"That's marvelous, Lorenzo. Now, tell me. What have you been sketching?"

"I'm still working on the windows in the villa but the arches don't look right."

"The sketches that you showed me yesterday were very good."

"They're not ready to show *Pappa*."

Why wasn't her approval enough? Would it be the same if she had a daughter? She picked a book from the stack on the table. "Remember when all you could draw were stick figures?" She flipped through the pages. "Just keep practicing and someday I know you will be the greatest artist that Italy has ever known."

"Better than Leonardo and Michelangelo?"

"Of course, Lorenzo. Leonardo never knew his *Mamma* and Michelangelo's died when he was a little boy. You have their gifts and a *Mamma*."

"I'm so much luckier than they were."

"And so am I."

"Do you think you can trick me with a fable today?"

The first time Anna had heard Leonardo da Vinci's fables was as a young girl attending school in Pisa; she had been reading them to Lorenzo for years. First, she would select a story and when she was finished, he would try and guess Leonardo's message. They both knew the stories and the messages by heart; nevertheless, they loved playing this game.

"Let's begin."

Lorenzo sat on the stool; he rested his elbows on his knees and cupped his chin in his hands. *Mamma* wore gold earrings that *Pappa* had brought her back from one of his business trips that resembled the sun in Cetraro on a hot July day. She had a white handkerchief tucked in the sleeve of her blouse; the lace edging reminded Lorenzo of the spider webs in the corners of Grigio's stall. *Aqua marina*, he said to himself, the Latin words his teacher had taught him that meant "sea water" and described the blue-green shade of the eyes that he and his *Mamma* shared.

After she finished reading, Anna asked, "What is Leonardo's message?"

"A lion roars, and makes her cubs open their eyes just like a *Mamma* who praises her children for reading makes them wants to read more."

"You're a clever boy. But now we must go. They're some things I must do." She put the book on the table. "Benito's having dinner with us and he wants to look at your sketches. Caesare's staying on the fishing boat but Benito's going to spend the whole night in the villa and have breakfast with us in the morning." Anna touched Lorenzo's cheek. "Isn't that lovely?"

"*Mamma?*"

"*Si*, Lorenzo."

"Can I show Benito all my notebooks?"

"What a brilliant idea. I know Benito will be very impressed. Let's get them right now."

CHAPTER FIVE

Padre Valentine quickened his steps; a cluster of barns, stables, sheds, corrals, and pens loomed in front of him. He did not want to be late for his afternoon lesson with Caterina. He tucked the text under his arm; it was one of Lorenzo's. Caterina was determined to learn how to talk Latin to him. What a waste, the priest thought. Caterina's life would be like that of her mother's. She'd work for the Marino family, marry another servant, and bear his children, then die. But she was more fortunate than most Calabrians for because of Anna; Caterina would never have to worry about food and shelter. Such an intellect would serve no purpose for a girl of her blood; nevertheless, Caterina's mind was a gift from God and the priest felt compelled to honor it.

The stable that had been built for the Arabians was a few feet away. At exactly the same time that Padre Valentine passed by the open door, Benito tore through it. He crashed into the priest and they both collapsed onto the ground.

"Caesare was supposed to have spent last night on the fishing boat," Benito said. He rolled onto his hands and knees and sprung to his feet.

"Benito, what's the matter?" Padre Valentine pushed himself halfway up; his legs were caught in the material of his cassock. Benito panted and paced like an agitated horse that senses a storm is coming. The priest untangled himself.

"There's been an accident, Padre." Benito lunged towards the priest and pulled him forward. They crossed into the stable.

Toppled bales of hay cluttered the space. A muckrake and a pitchfork lay on the ground, their tines pointed menacingly upward. An empty barrel was on its side; the muddied water in front of it looked like a rivulet. Buckets were inverted and smashed; the apples and oats they once held were scattered about.

Padre Valentine edged forward; Benito, at his side. Caesare was sprawled on his stomach; his body filled almost the entire area of one of the four stalls. The sour smell of old alcohol hung in the air. A hoarse rattle sounded; Caesare had begun to snore. The priest may not have noticed the girl in the next stall had Benito not been staring at it; the light from the small window barely reached the dark corner where it lay. The priest inched ahead.

"I found them like this. She hasn't moved."

Her shoulders pointed in one direction and her hips in another; it was as if her upper and lower torso belonged to two different bodies. There was no need for the priest to put his hand on her torn blouse or ripped skirt. The unblinking eyes that stared upwards, the dried blood that pooled in her nostrils, the red streaks that ran down from the corner of lips and the violet-red markings that bruised her twisted neck told him what he did not want to know. It was the girl from the village that Padre Valentine had been hoping Anna would hire.

"Is she..." Benito lurched forward, and vomited. Yellowish-blue liquid spewed out of his mouth, poured onto his black leather boots and discolored the gold buckle.

How had she ended up here? Why hadn't she waited for him in the village as they had planned? Padre Valentine stepped into the pool of vomit; it soiled the hem of his cassock. He put his arm around Benito, wanting to comfort the fifteen-year-old boy, but Benito pulled away from him. "Your father's back. Go and get him. I'll stay here." Benito did not move and the priest feared that he had been rendered insensible by the realization that Caesare had raped and murdered this girl. "Go!" Benito fled from the stable.

Santo walked across the hardwood floor of his sitting room, and stood in front of the white marble fireplace. He rubbed his hands; the fire that Rinaldo had made was perfect. He had not seen Caesare and Benito for three weeks and he looked forward to having dinner with them. Buccella had sent him to Naples again. Things were now settled enough that they could accompany him on his next trip. He sat in one of the matching chairs, a short rest would restore him; it had been a long train ride.

A bronze statue of "*Gattamelata*" was set in the middle of the mantle. The soldier of fortune poised on a dark horse outfitted in equestrian armor was a replica of the original in the Doge's Palace he had toured when he was in Venice. Some of Santo's business associates were convinced it was the original piece, so exact was the artistry. The statue had been a lucky purchase but Santo wasn't really surprised, he was a lucky man.

Sisina entered the room and set a tray with a cup of tea on the table next to him. Her parents were from Sicily. Both had been killed when she was a baby and she was sent to live with Buccella. Sisina's mother had been Buccella's cousin but Sisina did not know this; she thought she'd been orphaned as a child, and was a servant like the others. Buccella planned to tell Sisina the truth about her blood when it became useful for him to know this; in the interim, she would be safe at San Michelle.

"Would you like anything else, *Signore*?"

"Tell Rinaldo to bring me a glass of brandy. *Per favore*." He sipped the sweet, warm drink. Buccella always added *millefiori* honey to his tea and now everyone in his family drank it this way.

Buccella hadn't seen Sisina in seven years but regularly asked about her. Santo would be leaving in two days with Caesare and Benito to go to Cosenza; Buccella was expecting a report on the business that he had transacted in Naples. While there, Santo would tell him, once again, how hard Sisina worked to please him. Rinaldo entered the room, placed a snifter of brandy on the tray and left. The liquid in the pear shaped glass was a rich shade of brown with golden hues and reminded Santo of the time he met Padre Valentine. The year was 1892 and Buccella had sent him to Naples to meet with representatives of one of the clans of the "*camorra*", a Neopolitan secret organization equivalent to the "*Ndrangheta.*" Buccella's sister had attended the same convent school in Rome with one of the daughters and he wanted to investigate the possibility of their families developing a partnership. Buccella had warned Santo that the "*camorra*" weren't as noble as the "*Ndrangheta*"; the founding men had been members of a prison gang, they would have to be careful.

Santo had taken a horse-cab to Central Station situated on a street lined with taverns. He was sitting in a booth when he noticed a man at the corner of the bar swirling his brandy around in a glass, as if he were contemplating a serious issue. His face was a wind whipped red with chapped lips. There were strips of blood stained cloth wrapped around his fingers and Santo surmised that he was one of the countless who worked in the harbor loading the steamships that sailed regularly for North and South America. Five thousand people would board the "Georgia" that Santo had seen that afternoon and spend three weeks in steerage crossing the Atlantic Ocean before they arrived at Ellis Island, New York. Thousands of Calabrians, unable to make enough money to care for their families, had already left. Buccella had bought much of their land for little money, some for the 40 *lira* per person that the voyage over cost. Santo sipped his drink and the man turned in his direction. If Santo hadn't been watching him at that precise instance, their eyes would not have met and all that ensued would never have occurred. It was such a lucky moment.

The man's unbuttoned shirt revealed a white amice. Why would a man drinking at a bar have on the linen cloth that only a priest wore underneath his alb? Unless of course, he was a priest. And if this were true, what was a priest doing in a bar? Santo offered to buy him a drink, then another and another, and within a short time, he learned his story.

His name was Serro Valentine; he was twenty-one years old,

49

and from Terni, an industrial town in northern Umbria. Serro had toiled alongside his father in the steelworks but as he was bright, their parish priest taught him to read and write and eventually, sponsored him as a seminary student in Rome. Serro had just been ordained when he visited his friend, Fiore, a medical student at the University in Naples. That was one year ago and Serro had never returned to Rome. He wasn't sure how everything had happened or how he'd lost control of his desires. The woman was Fiore's sister and when Serro found out that she was going to have his child, he knew that he couldn't abandon her. Serro had left the church, married the woman and the child had recently been born; they all shared an apartment and the men worked loading ships in the seaport. Serro supported his family and Fiore covered the costs of medical school. Serro and his wife shared no love, only a sense of duty to their child.

"It was the church I wanted to marry," Serro had said to Santo.

"A man could honor two wives," Santo had replied. This was what Buccella believed. "It was just a matter of making the proper arrangements."

A pact was agreed upon. Santo would provide Serro's wife with a monthly stipend to cover living expenses for herself and the child and, in return, Serro would become the new priest at St. Ursula's Church in Cetraro. Santo would permit him to continue his studies in Cetraro and visit his wife and daughter in Naples when Santo deemed appropriate. In addition, Serro would fulfill whatever obligations Santo required of him. Before Santo left to return to San Michelle, he also struck a deal with Fiore. In exchange for covering the cost of his studies, he would set up his practice in Naples to watch over Serro's wife and child. Serro's wife was content with the arrangement; she had no need or interest in remarrying. She would tell their child that her father had died and Serro was simply a family friend. In Cetraro, Serro would be introduced as the priest from the theological seminary in Rome whom Santo had met on his travels. If either Serro or Fiore violated this pact, Santo would expose the truth.

The tea and brandy and fire had warmed Santo. He stretched his legs, and folded his hands on his lap. Buccella had been impressed when Santo told him he owned both a priest and a doctor. Santo closed his eyes. Naples was a lucky city for him. He drifted away.

"*Pappa*. Wake up."

Santo thought he heard words.

"*Pappa*."

Someone pulled his arm. He opened his eyes and Benito's face gradually took shape.

"There's been an accident."

One hour later, Santo watched as Padre Valentine and Benito heaved Caesare's unconscious body onto the open back of the cart. They covered it with empty burlap sacks. Benito and Caesare were to take the train to Cosenza where Buccella would keep them safe. Santo would let them know when they could return to San Michelle. Benito stepped up into the cart, and left; the words between them had been few, only those which were needed to explain what had happened. He had surmised that Caesare had gotten into a fight and decided not to spend the night on the fishing boat. He probably went to the stable to see if the Arabians had arrived yet and the girl must have been asleep in the stall. Santo turned to Padre Valentine. "Wait here until I bring another cart around."

The girl was not much older than Padre's own daughter. He returned to the stable and covered her with a blanket. Santo was relieved when he had told him that she was an orphan from the village and not one of his servants. No one would miss her, he had said and things weren't as complicated as they could have been. The priest knelt down and prayed but he wasn't sure whom his prayers were for, the dead girl or the man he had become.

"Dump her in the back," Santo yelled.

The priest walked outside. Santo held Grigio by the halter; it was Bruno's cart and partially loaded with vegetables and sacks of flour and sugar. "Put her here," he said. "We're lucky. It's almost dark."

Padre lifted the girl off the dirt floor; the bones in her body did not feel as if they were where they properly belonged. He set her down in the back of the cart and Santo covered her with turnips, eggplants, onions, and potatoes.

"Let's go." Santo jumped up onto the seat. Padre Valentine sat beside him and tapped Grigio's hindquarters with the reins. "It'll look like you're bringing food to Bruno's kitchen and I just got back and they'll think we're talking. We'll throw her off the cliff. Her body will never wash up." He glanced behind him. "Where's the whip? Can't this old horse go any faster?"

They were soon behind the villa. The priest pulled on the reins and Grigio stopped in front of a ridge of rocks. Santo leapt from the cart.

"Climb halfway down, and throw her off. Straight out."

Santo demonstrated his order as if Padre Valentine was too stupid to understand what he was supposed to do. The priest approached the edge. The waves were high and choppy and their crests were full of foam. The wind carried the salty sea upwards and the spray slapped the priest's face. It hit Santo with such force that he fell backwards.

"Hurry up." Santo scrambled to his feet. "It's starting to rain."

Padre Valentine picked the vegetables off the girl's body one at a time. Santo stood next to him, his clothes clung to his body. He had lost weight since the priest had last seen him. What a ridiculous thing to think of at this time. He was insane. He must have always been. The priest tucked the blanket tightly around the girl as if it was a shroud.

"Take off that cassock. You'll trip."

No one ever saw the undershirt and trousers he always wore underneath. The priest disrobed; he felt naked in front of Santo. How could he ever hide what he was going to do from Anna? He did not know how he had already hidden so much. Padre Valentine lifted the girl off the cart and walked past Grigio; the horse turned his head away, even the animal was ashamed of what the priest had become.

"Fling her over your shoulder. The way the men carry the big tuna."

A twisting path led down to the beach. The priest grabbed onto the outcrops but there was barely any light and he nearly lost his hold.

"That's far enough. Toss it now."

Her body bounced off the rocks and disappeared into the water. Santo had not even asked what her name was and Padre Valentine had forgotten to tell him. "I am so sorry, Clorinda."

Night had fallen and there would be no stars or moonlight. They were stopped in front of the villa.

"Meet me in my office tomorrow morning. Be early." Santo jumped off the cart.

The priest would go to church, and pray but he wouldn't blame God for not listening.

"Where have you been?" Anna asked. She stood in the doorway. "Lorenzo and I waited in the dining room for hours. No one knew where you'd gone. Not even Rinaldo."

That damn priest had taken too long and Santo hadn't had time to make up a story; the truth was certainly something he'd never share with his wife.

"Why are you wet and dirty?"

"Something terrible has happened." He ran up the stairs.

"Caesare and Benito? Are they hurt?"

"*Non*, Anna. They're fine." Santo ushered her into the villa.

CHAPTER SIX

Anna inserted a clove of garlic into the soil around the rosebush. Insects had invaded the flowerbeds the past few days, and sucked the sap from the plants.

"Is there anything else you'd like, *Signora*?"

Oresto's reflection appeared in the large salon window in front of her. He placed her watering can beside her gardening implements. "*Non, grazie*." She turned around. "Are you going to church now?"

"*Si, Signora*. Padre is going to pray with us. Then we are going out on *Signore's* fishing boats to throw flowers in the sea where Clorinda drowned."

"I wish I had more roses to give you." The villagers had been searching all week for Clorinda's body. If she wasn't given a proper burial, they believed that her soul would wander the earth forever, never finding peace. "But these insects have damaged so many of them."

"You have given us many beautiful flowers, *Signora*. You and the *Signore* have been very kind." Oresto nodded and left.

The wide brimmed straw hat gave Anna little respite from the late morning summer sun. She wiped her brow. Santo had been so distraught the night of the accident that it wasn't until the next morning when Padre Valentine came to the villa, that she fully understood what had happened.

After Benito finished having breakfast with Anna and Lorenzo, he had returned to the fishing boat where Caesare had spent the night. Padre Valentine had been in the village in the

morning and had talked to Clorinda about going to San Michelle
with him the next day to meet Anna. When he was finished, the
priest wandered down to the dock and decided to join Caesare and
Benito for an afternoon of fishing; Caesare was eager to catch fish
for Bruno to cook for dinner as Santo was returning that day from
Naples. Padre saw a girl struggling in the water below their villa on
their way back; it was Clorinda. Caesare jumped in, and swam over
to her. She was frantic but Caesare managed to grab onto her and
almost made it back to the boat when the wind suddenly arose and
a wave engulfed them, pulling her out of his arms. Benito ordered
Caesare into the boat. They continued to search for Clorinda but
her body never resurfaced. They returned to the dock and Padre
went to find Santo. Caesare and Benito planned to rest for awhile
before resuming their search. Anna had not seen her sons since the
accident as Santo had sent them to Cosenza the next morning. An
urgent business matter had arisen from his meetings in Naples that
Buccella needed to be made aware of and Santo did not feel he
could leave because of the accident. What could be so urgent that
her sons could not find the time to say goodbye to their mother?
Anna picked up her last glove of garlic.

"Are you having any luck?" Edoardo knelt down. There were
lavender stalks in his hand.

"*Non*. I've never seen insects like this before. How's Caterina?"

"Still upset at Padre for forgetting her lesson. And for not even
going to see her to explain why."

"I told Caterina that Padre has barely spoken to me since the
night of the accident."

"He should have said something to her."

"He's not himself, Edoardo." Anna broke up the garlic. "Bruno
says he's hardly eaten anything this past week." She inserted a clove
into the ground. "Padre thinks he may have told Clorinda to come
to San Michelle that day, he didn't mean to but he's quite certain
that's what must have happened."

"I'm going with Oresto on one of *Signore's* boats."

"The lavender's for Clorinda?"

"The sea may never give up her body and her soul may never be at rest but at least, while she's wandering, the lavender will protect her." Edoardo walked away.

Hot red pepper had always deterred stubborn insects in the past; Anna opened up the pouch and spread it on the soil. Why did Santo care about Clorinda? Why was he being kind to the villagers? There was nothing in it for him. There was something about the story of Clorinda's drowning that Santo and Padre Valentine had told her that didn't make sense. Anna wished she knew what it was.

The pepper she had applied yesterday had no effect on the insects.

"*Mamma*," Lorenzo called. He was carrying his notebook and his teacher waited on the stone platform behind him.

"What a lovely morning for sketching," Anna said.

"*Pappa* says I have to get some fresh air before I have lunch with him."

Anna ran her fingers through his hair; he jerked his head back.

"Why won't anybody tell me what happened? *Pappa* pretends he doesn't hear my questions and Padre walks by me as if he doesn't see me."

"Nobody really knows for certain."

"Why was Clorinda on the beach? You always told Caterina and me never to go down there. Don't village girls know this?"

"Padre thinks he told Clorinda to come to the villa to meet me and she went down to the beach."

"If that's true, why doesn't Padre know that's what happened?"

"Sometimes when something terrible happens, it takes awhile for people to remember."

"And why didn't Benito come and tell me that *Pappa* was making him go to Cosenza? He promised to look at my sketches again at dinner."

"Benito was exhausted after all that happened. He never told me either, Lorenzo." She put her arm around his shoulder. He tried to pull away but she held on to him. "Caesare jumped into the water and Benito brought the boat as close to them as he could but the waves were rough and Clorinda's body slipped away. Your brothers were very brave."

"I'm going on the trails."

Anna knew that Lorenzo didn't want to hear anymore. She let him go and he walked away; her last son had not said goodbye to her either.

"*Signora?*"

"What is it, Sisina?" Anna rubbed her hand against the front of her gardening apron. After a number of years, her skin condition had reappeared. She hoped that Sisina's burdock poultice would soothe the irritation. At least Anna didn't have to worry anymore about Santo seeing it.

"*Signore's* almost finished his lunch and he wants to see you; he's taking the train to Cosenza later today."

Her servant knew more about Santo's schedule than his wife; this should bother Anna but, in reality, it didn't and it hadn't for longer than she cared to remember.

"What dress would you like to wear?"

Black, Anna thought. Even though she had never met Clorinda, her sense of loss was genuine. "The patterned one that you just pressed."

"And you'll be wearing your grandmother's pearl necklace with it?"

"*Sì.*" Sisina had improved tremendously over the years. She left. Padre Valentine and Rinaldo were in front of the villa. The priest was holding a brown package. When would he be able to talk to her? She brushed the dirt off her apron and when she looked up, Padre Valentine was leaving and Rinaldo was walking towards her. She approached him.

"*Buon Giorno, Signora.* How are your flowers doing?"

"Not well. I'll check them again tomorrow. Hopefully the garlic and pepper will have helped by then."

"*Signore* will wait for you in his office."

"*Grazie.*"

Rinaldo went back into the villa. Anna stood at the base of

the steps. The geraniums in the pedestal pots on each side were the same cerulean blue as the sky. She took off her straw hat, it had flattened her curls; she didn't even care that Sisina did not have time to wash her hair before she saw Santo. A number of her servants were walking down their driveway, they were going to church again to pray for Clorinda. What had really happened to make Santo act as if he cared for her? Anna entered her villa and suddenly everything made sense to her. Santo would do anything to protect his sons and Lorenzo had been with Anna all night. Somehow, Caesare and Benito had been involved in Clorinda's drowning. And Padre Valentine knew everything. What had her Caesare and Benito done that was so heinous that Santo needed a priest to help him cover up the truth? Anna wanted to know.

Santo covered Lorenzo's notebook on his desk; he didn't want Anna to see it yet. She touched her pearl necklace; it had been her grandmother's and she had worn it on their wedding day. Her grandmother believed that it would guarantee their marital bliss. How wrong she had been. Anna was becoming increasingly difficult; life was so much easier when he didn't have to bother with her.

"I want to know what really happened," Anna said. "I've been your wife for seventeen years and I've given you the sons you've wanted."

"I've already told you."

A man like Santo Marino had no use for a wife after she'd given him sons. He was not going to go over everything again. Anna needed to rub more cream on her hands; they were starting to look rough from all her ridiculous gardening. Santo was glad he didn't have to hold them anymore.

"Will you be inviting Buccella to your *Natale* parties this year?"

"He's too busy to come to San Michelle." He touched his

signet ring. "That's why I'm going to Cosenza." Santo didn't want to hear any more of her questions.

He waved the notebook in the air.

"What are you doing with that?"

"Pictures of flowers and birds. Lorenzo's ten; this must stop."

He flung it across the desk; it whizzed by Anna's head and landed on the floor behind her.

"I've sent Padre to Naples for a new teacher. The one he has now will stay until he arrives." Santo pointed his finger at Anna. "And your afternoon fairy tale reading sessions with him, they're over too." He leaned back in his chair. "It's not my fault that I haven't had as much time with Lorenzo as I did with his brothers. I've been working hard at building my business for my family."

"Lorenzo's not like Caesare or Benito. You can't take his art away from him."

"He'll be a lawyer. Buccella says every family business needs one. I've decided."

"When will Caesare and Benito be returning to San Michelle?"

"When I tell them to." Santo stood up. "You must go. I have work to do."

Anna closed the door to Santo's office; she had work as well. Over the years, Santo had filled a number of ledgers and when the desk drawer could no longer store them all; he'd moved some elsewhere. It had taken Anna a while but she'd found his hiding place behind the volumes that lined the third row of his bookshelf. She still hadn't been able to make much sense out of the numbers but she'd keep trying. She strolled down the corridor to Bruno's kitchen; she felt like eating something sweet.

Edoardo pulled out the weeds that had sprouted at the base of the wooden cross that marked the place where Nella had been buried seven years ago. Anna watched him from the edge of the graveyard. When had his hair become silver and his shirt too big for his frame? He was forty-two; would Anna look this old in nine years? It didn't really matter; Santo had stopped noticing her a long time ago. When she had gone to the dining room last night for dinner, he had already left for Cosenza. And of course, he, too, hadn't said goodbye. When had their love for each other changed? Anna didn't remember the precise moment or the exact day when it had happened for her. When did change become permanent, she wondered, and when did people crossover and become different from who they were the day before? She walked over to Edoardo.

"It seems to take longer every time." He rubbed the protruding knuckles of his hand. "There must be more weeds."

Regardless of how many weeds there were, Edoardo wouldn't stop until he'd removed every one of them. She picked up the basket full of her favorite crimson roses and went from one grave to another. So many of the servants had lost children the past few years. Fragola and Oresto had two sons buried here, Luigi and Giuseppe. When would she see Caesare and Benito again? And when she did, would she notice something different about them? If it took her the rest of her life, she'd find out what had really happened. Anna placed a rose on Luigi's and Giuseppe's graves then returned to Edoardo. He was sitting on the back of his legs and resting his hands in his lap. She placed the remaining roses on Nella's grave. Why did life separate people who love each other? Anna wondered what was better, to lose someone you loved or to live with someone you no longer had any feelings for.

"I'm going for a walk," Edoardo said. He pushed himself off the ground.

"I'll watch our children. Put your straw hat on. The sun..."

"You sound like Nella." He headed for the woods that framed the graveyard and disappeared from sight. Almost immediately, the quiet was broken by raucous voices.

Caterina pumped her arms when she saw Anna through the trees. Grigio was faster than Lorenzo so she could slow down but she didn't; she liked the way the air rushed through her hair.

Anna saw Caterina first; Lorenzo was behind her, as usual. Their three-year age difference was not readily apparent for at ten, her son was short and slight; she knelt down and braced herself for what she knew was coming.

"*Mia Mamma*!" Caterina leapt into Anna's arms. Lorenzo was panting and gasping behind her; she found it hard to believe but it seemed as if he was getting slower every time they raced.

"*Mia Mamma*!" Lorenzo said.

His damp curls wet Anna's face. She embraced both children.

"*Non*! *Mia Mamma*!" Caterina tried to push Lorenzo away.

They spilled onto the ground and their laughter melted together; no one would ever take Caterina or Lorenzo away from Anna.

CHAPTER SEVEN

"I'm glad you're back," Anna said to Sisina.

They stood outside Santo's office. Buccella had requested her presence at his home for the servant who had raised her was dying; she and Santo had returned yesterday after an absence of six weeks.

"I missed San Michelle very much."

"Is my husband finished his lunch?"

"*Si, Signora,*" Sisina said. She walked away.

Anna entered the room.

"Lorenzo's new teacher is excellent." Santo began to talk before she'd sat down. "I've approved the course of study he recommended for the next year." He folded a piece of paper in half. "He will be arriving soon."

"Where's Padre Valentine? I thought he was supposed to bring Lorenzo's new teacher here."

"He went on to Rome after Naples to study in the seminary."

"When is he coming back?"

"Not for some time." Santo inserted the paper into an envelope.

"I still don't understand why you and our sons must live at Buccella's."

"The next two years are going to be busy. Buccella and I will be spending a lot of time in Naples. Caesare must concentrate on honing his skills for the Palio..."

"What about the Arabians that are coming to San Michelle?"

"They're going to Cosenza. Buccella has a marvelous stable

for them. And Benito needs to learn as much as he can about the business. The logistics are easier if we are all in Cosenza."

"When will I see my sons?"

Santo shrugged his shoulders.

The question as to when she would see her husband again was not one that Anna cared to ask.

The first year Santo came home for only a few days but Caesare and Benito did not accompany him; during his absence, Anna sat at his desk and reviewed the ledgers.

In 1892, the year she received her inheritance, Buccella sent Santo to Naples for the first time and began negotiations for him to buy San Michelle. Anna grabbed a pencil, and copied numbers onto a piece of paper. The same amount of money had been paid every month from 1892 to 1904. Other sums had been paid intermittently. Who was he sending money too? And for what reason? Why weren't there any names recorded? She didn't even know how much money they had anymore and it was her inheritance. Anna threw the pencil across the desk; it rolled onto the floor. Books and flowers and needlepoint. Was she good at nothing else? She crumpled up the piece of paper. How was she going to find out what her husband was doing and what he'd gotten her sons involved with?

"*Signora.*" Sisina poked her head into the room.

"Come in." Anna moved some papers and Sisina set the tray next to the ledger. "The *biscottini* looks good." She took a bite of the golden brown cookie. "Bruno bakes wonderful buttery sweets."

"How are your letters coming?" Sisina picked the paper and pencil off the floor and placed them on the desk.

The servants thought that Anna was writing to friends in Pisa whom she hadn't seen during her eighteen years of marriage. "They're taking a long time. So much has happened that I want to share with them." She held up a sheet of her personal stationery, a cynanine blue vellum with the initials "A" and "M" embossed at the top in the center. "I'll need more paper soon."

"I'll order it for you, *Signora*. Would you like anything else?"

"*Non, grazie.*" She sipped her *cappuccino*.

Sisina stepped away.

"Sisina."

"*Si, Signora.*"

"Your poultices have worked miracles, my skin is perfectly clear again."

"*Bene.*" She left the room.

The numbers in the ledger gained Anna's attention once more. She did not hear Bruno enter Santo's office until he was beside her.

"What's the matter?" His face was as white as the flour that usually dusted it.

"He's dead."

"What are you talking about?"

"Edoardo found him. He didn't wake up from his sleep."

Anna had never seen Bruno cry before.

"Grigio, *Signora*. Our old horse is dead."

Bruno approached Grigio's grave. He was so upset that he'd barely been able to eat dinner last night or breakfast or lunch today. He held a bunch of carrots that Caterina had given him from her garden. Anna had selected the site at the edge of San Michelle; Montea, the highest mountain in the area, was visible. Anna, Edoardo, Caterina and Lorenzo were already there. They were going to say prayers for Grigio. Bruno had not gone to the stall to look at Grigio; he wanted to remember him pulling his wagon. Edoardo had marked the grave with a white cross and Lorenzo had printed Grigio's name. Bruno was pleased that an oak tree provided shade, the workhorse hadn't liked the heat the last few years. He stood between Caterina and Lorenzo.

"How old was Grigio?" Lorenzo asked.

"I don't know. He was here when I came and he was old then."

"Who will pull the wagon you and *Pappa* ride in every morning?"

"So sad, Caterina. So sad."

Anna gave Caterina and Lorenzo a rose from the bouquet in her basket. They knelt down and placed them on the freshly turned soil.

"Do you think Grigio will let *Mamma* ride him in heaven?" Caterina asked Lorenzo.

"I'll bet he'll pull her around in a cart."

"Why not a wagon? And how do you know heaven has roads? Did you read it in one of the new books your teacher gave you?"

"Everyone knows heaven has everything so why wouldn't there be roads?"

"Padre left me a year ago and I don't learn things anymore. I don't have a teacher."

"I will be your teacher, Caterina," Anna said.

"Can you teach me to talk Latin?" She stood up.

"No, but..."

"Let's pray now," Edoardo said. He took Caterina's hand.

"*Pappa.* Is it Padre's fault if Grigio doesn't get into Heaven?"

"What do you mean Grigio won't get into Heaven?" Bruno asked.

"You can't get into Heaven if there's no priest to pray for you," Lorenzo said.

"Everything will be fine," Anna said. "Grigio will get into Heaven."

Bruno believed Anna, she was too good a woman to ever tell a lie.

"God will listen to our prayers," Edoardo said. "And Grigio was such a hard worker that God can hardly wait to have him in Heaven."

Before long, Bruno knew that Grigio would be God's favorite workhorse. Anna led them in prayers. A short time later, he said, "I want to stay here for awhile. By myself." The others left. He placed the carrots on Grigio's grave. "Don't forget to eat in Heaven," he said aloud. Bruno wondered who cooked for God.

"Would you like anything, *Signora*, before I start dinner?" Bruno and Anna stood outside the door to Santo's office. "I'm cooking *Pollo All'Agro*."

"Lemon chicken," Anna said. "I can hardly wait." Even though she wasn't very hungry, she would eat as much as possible tonight.

"I'm starving too."

"Please have Sisina bring me tea." Bruno left and Anna walked over to the bookshelf. She hoped to notice something in the numbers this time that she had missed before. She slid her hand behind the volumes lined up in the third row. The ledgers were gone. She hurried over to the desk and pulled open the drawer. There were no ledgers there either. Who had found out what she'd being doing?

"Let's start our lesson this morning by reviewing what we read about Galen last week," Anna said. She had enjoyed teaching Caterina and Lorenzo the past year and a half and was pleased that Lorenzo's teacher shared his books so willingly.

Caterina placed the sack holding their lunch on the ground. She jumped up and tried to touch the purple gladioli; in a few hours the thick canopy would be a welcomed shade for the heat of the June day.

"Galen was the Greek physician who lived from A.D. 130-200," Lorenzo said. "His medical theories formed the basis of European medicine until the Renaissance."

"Excellent, Lorenzo." Anna had told his teacher that he would spend the entire day with her.

"Your words don't say anything, Lorenzo. Galen was the man who said that there were four parts in our body: happy, bad, sad and sick."

"*Si* but Lorenzo is right too. You need both parts for the complete answer."

The front of the villa receded behind them. They passed by tracts of land planted with rows and rows of grapevines; the small green fruit was plentiful, there would be much winemaking this year.

"You're favorite, *Mamma Anna.*" Caterina snapped a stalk from an evergreen shrub covered with tiny light-blue flowers.

"*Rosmarinus Officinalis,*" Lorenzo said.

"If Padre wouldn't have left us, I'd know how to say rosemary in Latin, too." She ran ahead to the pen full of sheep and lamb.

Padre Valentine had left Cetraro without explaining to Caterina why he missed their lesson; he had not, in fact, said one word to her after Clorinda's drowning. Caterina rarely mentioned the priest's name.

"Why hasn't he written us even once in a year and a half?" Lorenzo asked. "*Pappa's* busy but he finds time to write me. And Benito sends me notebooks and you pretty gifts."

There had to be something terrible about Clorinda's drowning to have made Padre Valentine disappear from their lives; Anna refused to believe that the priest would have intentionally hurt Caterina and Lorenzo. "Sometimes, there are no explanations for the things people do," she said. "We have to trust that in time, Padre will return to us." A row of pillar cedars formed a line to their right. "I'll meet you and Caterina underneath those trees and we'll start our lesson." She took the blanket from Lorenzo and he walked away. The priests from the nearby villages of Malvito and Mottafollone had come down from the mountains to say mass in St. Ursula's Church but it wasn't the same; everyone missed Padre Valentine. She spread the blanket on the ground.

"I wonder what Bruno made us for our morning treat?" Caterina said. She sat next to Anna and opened the sack. "*Biscottini di mandorle.*" She gave Anna a macaroon cookie covered with slivered almonds in the air.

"Today I am going to teach you more about making tinctures and decoctions."

"What flowers do you want me to gather?"

"Wild roses and bring back the leaves so we can make an infusion tonight for Sisina. She told me this morning she's not feeling well."

"And we're going to continue with our study of sonnets." Lorenzo took a slim book out of his satchel and passed it to his mother.

"*Sì*. But go with Caterina now and work on your sketches." Anna gave Caterina her cookie. "Take some treats with you."

The sweet smell of the cedar trees that enveloped Anna was a perfect scent for Francesco Petrarca's poems. Santo's love for her had once matched that of Petrarca's for Laura. Caterina had picked some roses and Lorenzo was trying to draw her but as soon as he'd start sketching, she'd run off. Lorenzo would chase her, she'd stop and they'd do it all over again. Anna opened the book. She had never solved the mystery of the missing ledgers but for awhile, she would forget about the man she was married to and remember the man she had fallen in love with.

Santo stepped outside his villa; it was his first morning back and he looked forward to spending August at San Michelle. His new 1906 Itala automobile was parked in the driveway; he'd make sure that water was poured over the stones to keep the red paint shiny. Santo had driven back to Cetraro from Siena with Caesare and Benito in it after Caesare had won the Palio; they'd had a wonderful time celebrating his victory. Everything had gone well the past two years; he and Buccella had proved that the *Camorra* and *Ndraghetta* could work together. Santo went back into the villa. There was always work to do. A few minutes later, Sisina walked into his office with the tea he had asked for earlier.

"Would you like anything else, *Signore*?"

"Sit down." He sipped his tea. "My wife acts so foolish."

"*Si, Signore.* She spends a lot of time with the servants. And teaching Caterina."

"Lorenzo's teacher told me this morning that he can no longer tolerate her interference."

"Is there anything else you'd like me to do?"

"Just the same. Sending me those ledgers was smart. Buccella is proud of you. And so am I."

Sisina blushed.

"You will be rewarded when the time is right." Santo took another sip of tea. "Always the right amount of *millefiori* honey. You may go Sisina. *Grazie.*"

"*Mamma.*" Lorenzo bounded towards Anna. Santo had his hair cropped last week when he returned and Anna wondered if she'd ever see his curls again.

"You've had lunch with *Pappa?*"

"*Si* and *Pappa's* so pleased with my studies that he's letting me go sketching for awhile."

Benito hurried down the pathway. His light shirt was soaked in a sweat that revealed his sinewy upper torso and the tan trousers covering his long legs were smudged in dirt.

"*Buon Giorno, Mamma.*" A sheen coated his sun-colored skin and his dark hair had separated into short fine ringlets.

Anna reached into the sleeve of her dress and gave Benito one of her delicate, white handkerchiefs.

"*Grazie.*" Benito patted the finely chiseled features of his handsome face.

When had those tiny flecks of honey appeared in his brown eyes? It was almost impossible to believe that this eighteen-year old man was her son. Anna hadn't seen Benito since Clorinda had drowned two years ago and she'd completely missed his passing into adulthood. Every time she had planned to visit him in Cosenza,

Santo had told her not to come because there were important business matters that required Benito's attention.

"Did you win your game, Benito?" Lorenzo asked.

"Of course."

"I've almost filled up the notebook you brought me back from Naples."

"Do you have it with you?"

"*Si.*"

"Show me your sketches."

"Here," Lorenzo said. He took the notebook out of his satchel.

"That's a good drawing of our villa. The middle floor is a little squished but the arched windows on the top are perfect."

Benito could never have hurt Clorinda. How could she have entertained such a thought?

"We'll show those to *Pappa* tonight at dinner." He gave Lorenzo back his notebook.

Did Benito stilll have space in his life for a mother? Anna prayed that this was the case.

"*Stupido,*" blurted a gruff voice. Caesare barreled towards them. He stood between her and Benito.

Manure stained his cream jodhpurs and chunks of dung stuck out from under the soles of his custom made leather riding-boots; Anna was repelled by the smell of her own son.

"Alberto fed the stallion the wrong food. I wanted to race him along the coastline but his stomach is cramped."

Caesare smacked the riding crop in his gloved hand. Anna had overheard him tell Lorenzo that he used the whip at the end of the Palio to win the race.

"I threw him out of San Michelle."

It wasn't clear to Anna if she even regretted not seeing Caesare the past two years. What kind of mother was she?

"I'm the boss of the horses."

How could she have born a child with black eyes? "Alberto's wife helps Sisina with my dresses."

"*Pappa* always said you were too soft with the servants."

70

A flush of heat warmed her face.

"He wants you to be more like the wives in Naples."

"When are you going to draw a picture of your brother who won the Palio?" Caesare snapped the strap of Lorenzo's satchel against his chest.

"Let's go for a swim and clean up," Benito said. "And I'll tell *Pappa* that Sisina needs a new girl for your dresses." He and Caesare walked away.

"Go sketching now." Anna adjusted the strap of Lorenzo's satchel and he left. Benito had not said goodbye to him.

Lorenzo ran past the villa, crossed in front of the barns, stables, sheds, pens and corals, skirted the edge of the servant's enclave and dashed into the open fields. Caterina was waiting for him outside the wooded area at the entrance of one of the trails that criss-crossed San Michelle.

"Here, Lorenzo." Caterina waved her skinny arms in the air. Her dress was stretched tight across her flat chest.

"That dress is too small for you."

"*Mamma* Anna gave it to me last *Natale*. Don't you remember?"

"Why don't you wear trousers?"

"Hurry up. The rabbits aren't going to wait all afternoon." She led Lorenzo down the trail and after awhile, stepped into the woods and pointed to a mound of leaves at the base of an old oak tree about fifteen feet in front of them. "There. See?"

"Be quiet."

They sat on the ground and Caterina watched him sketch the rabbits. As soon as he was finished, she said, "Now what?" She sprung up. "*Pappa* showed me this beautiful plant the other day. Its flowers were purple and there were a lot of butterflies around it. The spot's nearby. I could take you there. *Pappa* showed me how to mark the way."

"I better go back."

"How much longer before your *Pappa* and brothers go away?"

"Soon, Caterina. I have to check my schoolwork before *Pappa* looks at it tonight. He says now that I'm twelve, there's nothing more important than my studies." Lorenzo picked up his satchel and they made their way side by side down the trail. When they reached the enclave and parted, they spoke their usual words.

"*Mio amico,*" Caterina said.

"*Mia amica,*" Lorenzo replied.

"*Sempre,*" they said in unison.

CHAPTER EIGHT

The train arrived in Cetraro late that morning. It was early September and before Santo left last week; he'd sent word to Padre Valentine that it was time for him to return. Santo had rewarded the priest for helping him protect Caesare from facing the consequences of raping and murdering Clorinda by allowing him to study in Rome. Over the past two years, Padre Valentine had seen Santo infrequently and Caesare and Benito not at all; the priest wasn't even certain where the three of them were now.

Padre Valentine was on his way to visit Edoardo and Caterina. If he hadn't given in to his desires sixteen years ago, he wouldn't have had his daughter, Ortenza, and if he hadn't been a man of principle, he wouldn't have married the woman. If he hadn't done these things, he wouldn't have been in a bar in Naples at the end of the day, dwelling as usual on how abysmal his life had become, and met Santo Marino. Padre Valentine never understood why at that particular moment, he had been so vulnerable that he agreed to the pact Santo offered him; had the identical scenario presented itself on another day, would he have made the same decision? Padre Valentine tried not to think of what might have been; that if he hadn't gone to Naples in the first place to visit Fiore, none of this would have happened. He would have become a priest who devoted his life to studying theology, the reason he entered the seminary in the first place. And in the end, perhaps, Clorinda would still be alive.

The woman who was legally his wife had remarried and borne other children; her second husband and Ortenza believed that her first husband had drowned in the harbor when Ortenza was an infant and that Padre Valentine was an old friend of *Zio* Fiore's. They understood as well that their anonymous benefactor was a wealthy businessman who wanted to help the priest in exchange for the charitable work he did in Calabria. Fiore had never married and over the years, established a successful medical practice. Ortenza, now fifteen, was his assistant. What a bizarre set of circumstances; Padre Valentine's life would make a compelling work of fiction.

Ortenza had a tumultuous mass of shocking auburn hair, mossy green eyes, a milky complexion and a robust build; she bore no resemblance to either Padre Valentine or her mother. He and his daughter enjoyed light conversation but neither had any yearning to spend time together; greetings were friendly but not joyous and good-byes were courteous but not difficult. How could a daughter not know that she was in the presence of her father and how could a father have a daughter who was a stranger to him?

Edoardo's cottage came into view. Ortenza was healthy and content and her mother had a husband and children who loved her. If Padre Valentine ever challenged Santo, all of this would be lost. And after all, he wasn't the man who had raped and murdered Clorinda. The priest admired the lavender bushes in bloom.

Soon the sun would be going to sleep and *Pappa* would be home; Caterina was nine and got supper ready for them almost every night. She sat on the orange crate at the kitchen table. Gathering kindling wood with Nicoletta for their fireplaces had been fun today; it was the first time that their *Pappa's* had let them go on the trails alone since Lorenzo's brothers left. She picked up a fava bean and pressed down on the long, pale green pod with her finger. Everyone wondered how Lorenzo could have a brother with a pig nose. It was just like after Clorinda drowned; Caterina's *Pappa* wouldn't let her garden unless she was with Elda. The pod's seam opened and Caterina removed the seeds and placed them in the bowl.

In the past thirty days, she'd barely spent any time with *Mamma* Anna and Lorenzo. Whenever Lorenzo's *Pappa* came back, he wanted them both to himself. Caterina understood this. If she had a wife beautiful and kind like *Mamma* Anna and a son smart like Lorenzo, she'd miss them so much when she was away that she wouldn't want to share them either. Caterina had cleaned two hundred and five fava beans, that was enough. She slid off the orange crate and walked over to the window. An instant later, she ran outside.

"You're two years late for our lesson Padre."

"I had to go away for awhile."

"*Pappa* said you were so worried about Clorinda because the sea took her body that you've being living in a church where the Pope lives and saying special prayers for her soul."

He knelt down and touched her cheek.

"Why didn't you say goodbye to me?" She brushed his hand off her face. "Your prayers didn't work. The sea didn't give her body back." Caterina moved back. "And you better write the Pope a letter and ask him if Grigio got into Heaven."

"What happened?"

"Grigio died and if you wouldn't have left us, there would have been a priest to say the prayers for the dead and we'd know for sure that he got into Heaven."

"I'm sorry, Caterina."

"*Mamma* Anna's my teacher. But she doesn't know Latin so I can't talk to Lorenzo in it."

"How is your *Pappa*?"

"Are you going to have supper with us? Is that why you're here?"

"*Sì.*"

"Do you promise never to go away again?"

"I promise."

Caterina grabbed Padre Valentine's hand, pulled him into the cottage and locked the door behind her.

Grigio's halter and blanket were still in his empty stall; Padre Valentine shut the door of the stable. The afternoon was as lovely today as it had been yesterday when he saw Caterina and Edoardo. The priest had spent last evening alone in his church, he'd missed praying there. He walked towards the villa. Edoardo had cooked *pancetta* and fava beans flavored with garlic and olive oil; Padre Valentine couldn't remember the last time he had enjoyed a meal so much. The priest lost track of how many times Caterina told him that she had cleaned two hundred and five fava beans.

"Why didn't you ever say anything to *Pappa* about Caesare and Benito when they were here?" Lorenzo stood behind his mother as she worked the soil in her rose bed. "No matter how much food Bruno cooked, Caesare said it was never enough. And no matter how many shirts and trousers Rinaldo pressed, they were never the ones that Benito wanted to wear."

Anna took off her gardening gloves.

"And *Pappa* always found something wrong with my schoolwork, even when my teacher said it was excellent."

"I tried to talk to your *Pappa* but nothing I said mattered." She stood up and faced him.

"I was in the village yesterday with my teacher and I overheard some people say that Caesare and Benito ran away in the night after Clorinda drowned because they had something to do with it. And that's why *Pappa's* kept them away from San Michelle these past two years."

"They're wrong, Lorenzo. It was a horrible accident."

"Do you know what my teacher taught me this morning?"

"*Non.*"

"In ancient Rome, if a father sold any of his sons three times, he no longer owned them."

"What are you talking about? *Pappa* loves his sons more than anything else in the world."

He knew his father loved Caesare and Benito more than his mother did; he never left them alone. "If *Pappa* had to sell any of his sons, it would be me."

Anna grabbed his arm.

Lorenzo was shocked at how tightly she squeezed it.

"Your *Pappa* would never sell you. You're a brilliant son and he's very proud of you. Stop thinking such nonsense." She released her hold. "Let's get Caterina and we'll go for a walk." She kissed his cheek. "I'll change my dress and I need my hat. I won't be long." She left.

When would his mother realize that he was twelve years old and no longer a little boy? Lorenzo didn't want to be angry with her; he just didn't always understand his family and wished that she could explain things to him.

"Did you finish your Latin studies?"

Why was he hearing Padre Valentine's voice now? Probably because the priest's leaving was something else that his mother had never been able to explain.

"Perhaps we could read together again."

Lorenzo turned around. Had his imagination conjured up this picture of Padre Valentine standing in front of him?

"I brought you some books from the Vatican."

He touched the silver crucifix. It was not an apparition.

"Lorenzo."

He had so many questions for Padre Valentine but there was really only one that he wanted answered.

"Are you staying?"

"*Si.* What happened to your curls?"

"Your Roman nose looks bigger."

77

He let the priest embrace him. "You're skinny." He moved back.

"I'm sure Bruno will take care of that."

"You promise you'll never go away again."

"I promise."

Lorenzo let the priest embrace him again.

The crimson red rosebushes were in full bloom; Padre Valentine wondered if Anna still brought bouquets to his church. Lorenzo had gone to get some notebooks to show him his sketches. Anna descended the stairs, stepped onto the wide platform and strolled down the pathway; she held her straw hat in her hand and swung it back and forth in an easy rhythm. Even though he could not hear it, the priest knew she was humming. There was no hurry in her movements, her motions were full of grace; Anna was still the ethereal beauty that he remembered. The priest approached her and her hat slipped from her hand.

"When did you return, Padre?" Anna asked.

"Yesterday."

"Why didn't you even write us one letter?"

"I don't know."

"We've missed you terribly."

"I'm sorry, Anna."

"I didn't know what to tell Lorenzo."

"He's grown up so much."

"You've seen him?"

"A few minutes ago. He went to get his notebooks to show me his sketches."

"He's a gifted artist."

"And you taught Caterina how to count to two hundred and five?"

"You've seen her?"

"At supper last night. With Edoardo."

"She's barely mentioned your name since you've been gone."

"I didn't mean to hurt the children."

"I know, Padre. Did Caterina forgive you for missing her lesson?"

"*Si.* But I don't think she'll ever forget."

For the past two years, Padre Valentine had intentionally immersed himself in theological studies. He had not known how to deal with all that had happened and so, he forced himself to pretend that it hadn't. But now that he was back at San Michelle, the priest did not know how he had been able to stay away for so long?

"How's Bruno?"

"I can hardly wait till he sees you."

Padre Valentine picked up her hat and Anna took his arm. They walked down the pathway and rounded the corner of the villa.

Bruno stood at the counter in his kitchen and squeezed the tomato. "Nice and firm." He'd slice a few of them, then the mozzarella thin the way *Signora* liked it. He'd layer the tomatoes and the mozzarella, tear the basil leaves into tiny bits and sprinkle them over everything. Finally, he'd drizzle olive oil on top. "I make the best caprese salad in all of Calabria," he said out loud.

"You do."

"Padre."

"And I haven't tasted it for two years."

"You've come back to us." Bruno waddled over to the priest. He wished his paunch were smaller so that he could have held him closer.

"You haven't been going for walks."

"You're skinny." He pulled a chair out from the table. "Sit down. I'll give you something to eat. You're staying, aren't you?"

"*Si.*"

Anna sat next to Padre Valentine.

"*Bene.* You have to go with me to Grigio's grave and say prayers.

79

Caterina said God might not let him into Heaven."

"I've heard."

"You've seen her?"

"And Edoardo."

"Lorenzo knows he's back too," Anna said.

"*Perfetto*. Tonight, I cook a special dinner for all of us to celebrate."

Sisina entered the kitchen. "Padre."

"Make tea for all of us." Bruno pointed his finger at her. "And be sure you put lots of *millefiori* honey in Padre's."

During the next year, Padre Valentine reestablished his routine of saying mass, visiting the villagers and servants, assisting the midwives delivering babies and spending time with the children. Everyone sensed that Padre Valentine still blamed himself for Clorinda's drowning and so they asked him no further questions as to why he had left without any explanation and stayed away so long. Anna never broached the subject as to what involvement Santo and her sons might have had in Clorinda's drowning; the truth could not change what had happened, so it no longer mattered to her. And like everyone else, it was enough for Anna that Padre Valentine had returned to them.

Another year passed and it was now November; Santo, Caesare and Benito would celebrate *Natale* at San Michelle. Lorenzo had plenty of time to fill a notebook with sketches for Caterina and Edoardo as a special gift. He stood inside their two-room cottage and contemplated the scene in front of him.

The dirt floor contrasted with the smooth white marble in the main salon of his villa and there were no wool and silk tapestries depicting barbaric hunting scenes on the walls. He breathed in, and inhaled the sweet and bitter scent of herbs. Was he skilled enough yet to convey their aroma in a sketch? The faded green stalks of basil, parsley, and rosemary were suspended from wooden beams that crossed the space above him. Crystal chandeliers imported from Murano hung from his ceilings. His mother and Edoardo sat on rustic chairs at the kitchen table. It was a thick plank to which four vertical pieces of twisted wood were nailed. They were drinking from mismatched clay cups. Images of his mother's colorful *Majolica* pottery popped into his mind. A cross, constructed of twigs and twisted rope, was set in the middle of the mantle of the stone fireplace. He liked it better than his father's statue of Gattamelata and decided that he would sketch its simple design.

"Come here," Caterina yelled. "I'm in my bedroom. Look at what Padre gave me for my tenth birthday."

Her bed was made of straw piled on top of a board set on large stones. There were several woolen blankets and a stuffed burlap sack was her pillow. Dresses and shawls that his mother had given her hung from nails on the otherwise bare walls. A cedar box that Edoardo had made her a previous *Natale* sat on the orange crate next to her bed.

"Do you know what his birth name was?" Caterina held up a holy card.

"St. Francis of Assisi. Who in Italy doesn't know that?" Now that she had both his mother and Padre as teachers, Caterina was always trying to prove to Lorenzo how smart she was.

"*Non.* 'Giovanni.'"

"I bet you don't know the name of the mountain where the angels visited him."

Lorenzo didn't.

"La Verna." She put the holy card in the cedar box and took out another one. "Lorenzo."

When had she stopped calling him 'Renzo'? He couldn't remember. And her face didn't seem as round and full as it had been the last time that he sketched her.

"Do you know who the saint was that argued with Pope

Gregory X1 so much that he moved the church back to Rome?"

Soon Caterina wouldn't be a little girl anymore; Lorenzo would include a lot of sketches of her in the notebook; Edoardo would treasure them.

"St. Catherine of Siena. Padre told me."

He'd make sure to draw one for Padre Valentine.

She shoved the holy card in his face. "St. Catherine of Siena was the youngest in her family and had twenty-two brothers and sisters and even though St. Catherine never went to school, she knew how to write letters and everybody listened to her."

How could she say so many words without taking a breath?

"Who's going to wake you up when you die, Lorenzo?"

"What kind of question is that?" he asked.

"St. Catherine will be the one waiting for me in Heaven because I'm named after her. She'll be wearing the same white gown she has on in this picture and there will be a golden halo around her head."

Lorenzo di Medici had been a ruler in Florence and one of the first to recognize Michelangelo's talent. Lorenzo would ask Padre Valentine about his saint.

"Did you know it takes you awhile to wake up after you die?" Caterina put the holy card in the cedar box. "When you first wake up, you're sleepy. Padre told me that St. Catherine will wave at me so I can pick her out from all the other saints. That's how I'll know I'm dead and I'm in Heaven. I'll see St. Catherine first then I'll see *Mamma* and Grigio."

"Caterina," Edoardo called. "Come and see what Bruno made us."

She skipped out of the doorway. Caterina was still a little girl. Lorenzo followed her.

A little while later, Lorenzo and Caterina sat at the table with his mother and Edoardo. They were eating *passulate* cookies; Lorenzo preferred the walnuts rather than the raisins because the

Romans believed they made the brain smarter. His mother took a piece of apple from Edoardo.

"Next month will be *Natale* already," Edoardo said. He ate a bit of cheese.

Lorenzo's father insisted that his family spend every *Natale* at San Michelle for this was when he held lavish parties for his business associates. He took another cookie. Lorenzo wished that he could sketch this scene in the notebook.

CHAPTER NINE

"You've fastened the clasp perfectly," Anna said.

Sisina's reflection was in the mirror. The cuticles around her fingers were smooth; Anna's chickweed infusion had worked well. With her weight gain, her features had less severity and her body more shape. At twenty-five she had matured into an attractive woman.

"You have beautiful jewelry," Sisina said. "I'll get your dress."

The diamond pendant and matching drop earrings were garish but they were from Benito and she wanted to wear them. It was December 5th, St. Nicholas's feastday and tonight was the first of her husband's *Natale* parties.

"Here, *Signora.*"

The green velour dress that Santo had brought her from Naples cinched her waist and she could barely eat. There was so much material that she was terrified she'd trip and embarrass her husband. Sisina helped her put it on.

"You look lovely, *Signora.*"

Anna thought she looked like a ridiculous ornament; nevertheless, what other choice did she have but to do as her husband wished.

"We better go," she said to Sisina. "I don't want to keep my husband waiting."

A stream of guests poured through the main door of the villa into the entranceway.

"*Buonsera*," Santo bellowed.

They passed the staircase and walked down the long corridor.

"*Benvenuto* to San Michelle." He swept his right arm upward in a dramatic flourish then angled his body sideways. "My wife, Anna."

Santo was glad Sisina made certain his wife was dressed properly for these festivities. If he'd left it up to Anna, she might wear her straw gardening hat that made her look like a peasant. Anna smiled and nodded just as he had reminded her to do earlier that evening. He extended his arm across her body and announced, "My first son, Caesare. My second son, Benito. My third son, Lorenzo."

"*Buon Natale*," they said one after another.

Rinaldo took their coats and Santo's guests entered the large salon.

What is your name and how do you know my husband? Has he invited you to his most lavish party, the one on Christmas Eve? Are you coming to the party on *Capodanno*, New Year's Day? Anna had been smiling and nodding for the last hour. One more month until January 6th when *La Befana* gives everyone presents, then this will all be over. She glanced at Caesare, now twenty, and Benito, nineteen. Did they remember decorating their house with holly on St. Lucy's feastday when lived in Diamante? On their first *Natale*, Santo had given her honey to represent their sweet future and Anna had presented him with a bowl of nuts, a symbol of her promise to bear him sons. She had kept her promise and given Santo his sons; she'd just never expected that he would take Caesare and Benito away from her.

Caesare guffawed. Benito put his arm around Lorenzo's shoulder and the two of them laughed at the same time. Anna still had no evidence to confirm her belief that her sons were implicated in Clorinda's drowning. She didn't really need anything though to substantiate her fears; a mother innately knew her children. It would be easier if Anna no longer loved Caesare and Benito but she did; a wife could stop loving her husband but a mother could never stop loving her children, even if she wanted to. Some things were impossible to change.

"Has the train brought you that Fiat yet?" a man asked Santo. "We all want to see it."

"You just want a ride."

"Of course. There aren't too many fancy cars in Calabria."

"I've changed my mind. In the new year, Caesare, Benito and I are going to take the train to Naples and after we've finished our business, we'll go to Milan and drive the Fiat back to Cetraro ourselves."

"*Bravo*." The men clapped.

"And next summer, I'll have a party so you can see it and maybe I'll take all of you for a ride."

The men cheered.

"What a smart husband you have, *Signora*."

The loud music of an accordion sounded and Santo excused them.

The tables were laden with food especially prepared for the evening; Bruno had been cooking for days. There were trays of *Novellame*, an anchovy caviar like spread, *mozzarella* from the region of Campania and *pesca spada alla bagnarese*, a swordfish dish that was one of Bruno's specialties. Lorenzo took his place by his father's side; he was to help him distribute gifts to the guests. This was the first official function he had been given at a party and he did not want to make any mistakes. Lorenzo was glad that Benito had picked out a proper suit for him.

"Another fine son," a man said to his father. "And so handsome," the woman beside him added.

"He's going to be the lawyer in my business."

There were handcrafted marionettes of warriors from Acireale,

Sicily for the men and glass ornaments created by Venetian artists for the women. When the presentation was over, Santo dismissed Lorenzo. He wandered throughout the room and saw his mother retreat to a corner. He knew it was hard for her to walk in that dress. Lorenzo made his way over to her.

Sometimes, Anna wished that she could just disappear. She pushed herself as far back into the corner as possible and scanned the faces in the room. Why had Santo never invited Buccella to San Michelle? Why didn't he want her to meet him? Lorenzo was crossing the room. This was the first party that Santo had given him an official function and he seemed to have liked the attention. He was happy that Benito had picked out a suit for him to wear; Anna couldn't believe how much older it made him look. He was fourteen now and she expected that Santo would soon introduce him to Buccella and their world. How much time did she really have left with him? Anna could not even imagine her life without Lorenzo. A male guest passed by and she checked his hand; she had yet to see another "N" signet ring. Was this a good sign or an omen of bad things to come?

Caesare and Benito were standing side by side. Caesare was no longer wearing his suit jacket and most of the buttons on his white shirt were undone. Benito's silk suit had been cut to flatter his lean frame. He turned his face in Anna's direction and smiled at a young woman in a red dress; for an instant, Anna thought she was staring at the Santo she had fallen in love with twenty-one years ago. How could one son look so much like his father and another bear no resemblance to either parent?

Benito waved at Lorenzo. His physique was perfect. Lorenzo's legs were too long for his body and he had to wear a jacket and pants that were different sizes. Benito had said "nobody would notice" and he had been right. He wished he still had Benito's curls. Caesare bumped into a servant and the tray of glasses fell to the floor. Lorenzo refused to believe that he and Caesare shared the same blood.

Lorenzo followed his mother's line of vision. Benito was smiling at a young woman in a red dress. His mother turned away. He knew what she was thinking; Benito was becoming like *Pappa*. Was it natural for a son to favor his mother as much as Lorenzo did? It was time for them to leave this party.

"It's Christmas Day already," Anna said. She sat at the table in Edoardo's cottage.

"How long can you and Lorenzo stay?" Caterina circled her arms around Anna's neck.

"*Pappa* doesn't have time for us so we can stay all afternoon," Lorenzo said. "He's busy with his business associates and Caesare and Benito, of course, are with him."

"There are men who need to meet with your *Pappa*. And you know that this is the one-day he approves of you and I coming here." Why wasn't Lorenzo used to things by now? There had never been brotherhood between he and Caesare and it was always unclear when exactly Benito had time for him. Sometimes, everything seemed too much.

"Will you hold the basket, Lorenzo, so I can give out the oranges and figs?" Caterina asked.

"Of course," Lorenzo said.

"And you've brought blankets for each family," Edoardo said.

"Padre's friend, Fiore, got them for us. They're the same ones the hospitals in Naples use to keep patients warm."

"What about the red and green ribbons, *Mamma* Anna?"

"You can give all the little girls one of each."

"The chocolate?" Caterina licked her lips.

"That's for the young boys," Lorenzo said. "You can't have any."

"Why are you so grumpy, Lorenzo? It's *Natale* and you get more presents in one day than all of us get in all of our lives."

Anna pretended to scratch her nose.

"Your carriage is ready outside," Edoardo said.

"Do you want us to get started now, *Mamma*?" Lorenzo asked.

"Please." He bent down and Anna kissed his cheek.

"I'm sorry," she whispered.

"Me, too," Lorenzo whispered back.

A few hours later, Caterina walked into her cottage and Lorenzo followed behind.

Edoardo was looking at the notebook of sketches that he had given him last *Natale*.

"You get bigger everyday, Caterina," Edoardo said. "You don't even look like this little girl anymore."

They took their places at the kitchen table and Anna gave them a cup of warm milk mixed with coffee and broken cookie pieces.

"My favorite *dolce* to drink," Caterina said.

A comfortable heat circulated throughout Lorenzo's body as he sipped the warm liquid.

"This is the best *Natale* in the whole world of Calabria," Caterina said.

Lorenzo decided he would sketch this scene of his mother, Edoardo, Caterina and him celebrating *Natale*. Why couldn't he have two families?

Early the next morning, Edoardo approached The Church of St. Ursula at the edge of the village. There wasn't much time, he and Oresto had to unload supplies for Bruno as Santo was having another party this evening. He knew that Padre Valentine would be here; perhaps, if Edoardo asked him one more time, the priest would help him.

The letter from his cousin in Reggio di Calabria arrived a few weeks ago, Padre Valentine had read it to him. Edoardo's cousin and family would be leaving Calabria in the new year. They would go to Palermo, Sicily, board the S. S. Italia, sail across the Atlantic Ocean and land in Ellis Island, New York in the United States of America. Then, they would take a train to Pittsburgh, Pennsylvania and live with one of Edoardo's brothers who had settled there earlier.

Edoardo was fifty years old, his parents had died before he and Nella came to San Michelle and everyone else in his family had left Italy. After his cousin was gone, he would only have Caterina. His cousin wanted to see him before he departed so that they could say a proper good-bye. Edoardo could make the journey in three days. Why wouldn't the priest ask Santo for permission to let him go?

The church was nestled within towering oak trees. Its rough stone exterior was solid and unmarked despite the passage of time. Edoardo pulled open one of the heavy double wooden doors and walked inside. He dipped his fingertips into the clear holy water in the stone font where the priest had baptized Caterina. How had Nella known beforehand that their child would be a girl? When Edoardo had asked her what name she'd like if it were a boy, she had said, "It'll be a girl, Edoardo." Did mothers possess knowledge about their children that was beyond that of fathers?

The picture of St.Ursula hung above the font. "*Pappa*," Caterina had said to Edoardo. "Padre Valentine said the bad men killed her because she wouldn't give up her God. She was brave, *Pappa*." Why had their church been named in honor of this martyred woman? Even Padre Valentine didn't know the answer to this question.

The narrow table lined one of the grey stone walls in the small chapel at the transept of his church. Padre Valentine lit a candle in the back row. He walked over to the railing that divided the room into two sections; the thick woolen socks Anna had given him for *Natale* could not insulate his feet from the cold that radiated up from the floor. The statue of St. Lucy was on the ledge positioned in the middle of the wall. Edoardo didn't like the dish with two eyes in it that she was holding. She's the patron saint of blindness, the priest had explained to him. Still, Edoardo refused to kneel at the railing and pray to her.

"Padre."

Why was Edoardo standing in the arch-shaped entrance across from him? He should have been helping Oresto and Bruno.

"You must ask Santo. I have to go to Reggio di Calabria."

"I've already told you. This is his busiest time. I will not ask him."

"These people are my cousins."

"*Natale* was only yesterday. There are still so many more parties."

"There must be something you can do, Padre."

"Santo will be leaving San Michelle in a few weeks, you can go then."

"That will be too late." Edoardo knelt down in front of the priest. "Why can't you understand, Padre? Isn't there anyone you'd want to see one last time?"

Would it matter if he and Ortenza ever saw each other again? "I will not ask Santo. And you cannot leave without his permission." The priest stepped back.

"I am going," Edoardo said. He stood up. "Will you pray for me, Padre?"

Even if the priest did, would God listen to him? If it had been Edoardo who Santo had approached in the bar in Naples, Padre Valentine knew that he would have rejected the pact. Padre Valentine was not worthy to pray for Edoardo. "I will ask St. Christopher to take care of you on your travels." He turned around and walked away from Edoardo.

The old workhorse stopped again and Bruno tapped the reins on the animal's rear; it began to pull the cart. "He's not Grigio but at least he'll get us home tonight. Eventually." Bruno placed a chocolate covered fig in his mouth. He'd only been able to take a small one because he'd lost another tooth last week.

"Even you must be tired of cooking," Edoardo said.

Bruno smacked his lips and put the reins between his knees; he pulled his toque over his ears. " We're running out of fish."

"Oresto's brothers said the wind has been so strong lately that it scared all the fish away." Edoardo rubbed his hands up and down the sleeves of his woolen jacket. "One day I need to wear this, the next day I don't."

"Girolamo went out yesterday but the fog was thick and he had to turn the boat back."

"Giulio caught so few fish last month that Santo wouldn't pay him any *lira*. Elda gave him her new blanket so his *bambina* wouldn't get cold."

"I tried to give this horse some carrots yesterday but he wouldn't take them." Bruno grabbed a handful of nuts from his pocket.

"The animals are all a little skittish, Bruno. Did you see the way the stallions were running around the corral this morning? Even Caesare had a hard time getting them into their stables. Perhaps there's a bad storm coming. I hope it's not one with the *maesatrale* wind."

"Maybe we should pray to St. Christopher. Padre says he's very powerful." He tilted his head backwards and poured the nuts into his mouth.

"There's something I must tell you, Bruno," Edoardo said.

"You have a problem?"

"*Si*."

"You didn't eat much today. Are you sick?" Bruno asked.

"*Non*."

"Caterina?"

"She's fine."

"What is it *mio amico*?"

"I need you to help Elda watch Caterina."

"Why?"

"I'm going away for a few days," Edoardo said.

"What are you talking about? It's *Natale*. You can't go anywhere," Bruno replied.

"I'll tell you when we get to my cottage."

It was still dark when Bruno left Edoardo's cottage several hours later. He climbed into the cart, picked up the reins and tapped the rear of the old workhorse gently. The animal plodded forward and they headed back to the villa. Why had he failed to change his friend's mind? What was wrong with his words? Bruno wished he could talk as good as he cooked.

Morning had yet to come when Bruno led the mule out of the stable and tied him to the fence post as Edoardo had asked. He would be here shortly but Bruno couldn't wait any longer; Santo was hosting another party tonight and there was much work he had to do. He'd saddled the animal and packed a small sack of provisions for the journey that Edoardo would make along the coastal rode to Reggio di Calabria; he'd included a little bag of candied citron and licorice for his cousin's children. Bruno understood that Edoardo wanted to say goodbye to his cousins but he agreed with the priest. Why did Edoardo have to be so stubborn? Why had he refused to believe his best friend and a man of God?

There were black swirls in the sky and he could hear the stallions neighing in their stables. Even nature didn't want Edoardo to leave. Bruno pulled his toque down as far as it would go. Why wouldn't Edoardo listen to Padre? The words of a priest were holy; his soul, pure. Had Padre not showed his goodness to all of them? Would Edoardo's rejection of Padre's holy words make God angry? No; he told himself. Edoardo was a good man and God would be disappointed but not angry with him. Still, Bruno felt so sick that he doubted if he'd ever be able to eat again. He rolled the blanket, put it in front of the horn of the saddle and checked to make sure the strap of the canteen was securely attached.

Bruno had promised Edoardo that he'd tell Caterina and Elda that Edoardo would be busy helping him with the parties for the next few days and wouldn't have time to see them. Edoardo had already celebrated *Natale* with Anna and Lorenzo and they had to attend these parties too so they wouldn't expect to see him either. There would be so many people in the villa Edoardo was certain that no one would miss him. Bruno hoped that this was true. If Santo found out that Edoardo had left without his permission, his anger would probably be even worst than God's. He pulled an apple from the pocket in his trousers and gave it to the mule. Only he and Padre Valentine knew the truth and they had to make sure it stayed this way.

"Edoardo would be gone for only three days," Bruno muttered as he tried to comfort himself. He patted the mule's muzzle. The animal was sure-footed and sturdy and he'd take good care of his friend.

"Watch where you go and make sure he chews those fennel seeds," he said aloud.

The coastal rode was close to the sea in parts and Edoardo's eyesight wasn't that good at night; Bruno hoped that Edoardo would bring enough lavender.

Edoardo knelt down beside Caterina's bed. It was almost morning and it was time for him to go. Bruno would have the mule ready and he wanted to start his journey before the sun rose. Even though his friend disagreed with his decision, Edoardo knew that he would honor his word and keep his daughter safe. He wished he could be as certain about Padre Valentine's prayers; the priest had spoken with hesitation but he had to see his family one more time.

Edoardo pulled the blanket snug around his daughter's neck. "She is *bellissimo*, Nella," he whispered so as not to awaken her. She'd want to come with him, he knew, and it was too long a journey for a little girl. He slipped a fresh stalk of lavender under her pillow and kissed her goodbye. Until he returned, he would hold this picture of Caterina in his heart.

CHAPTER TEN

The cold had awakened Caterina from her sleep; she didn't understand why her *Pappa* hadn't put enough wood on the fire before he left for the day. She stoked the flames. This had never happened before. Something crashed outside and she hurried over to the window. A bolt of lightning lit up the space in front of her cottage. *Zia* Elda was chasing Nicoletta's little sister. She opened the door. Fortunata was in Elda's arms. Caterina fought the wind until she reached them.

"Take her inside," *Zia* shouted. "There's a storm coming. I'll get the others."

"*Mamma*," Fortunata screamed. Caterina dragged her into the cottage. Children streamed in and they crouched down in a corner. Where was Nicoletta? The wind rushed Elda into the room.

"*Mamma*," Fortunata wailed.

The child needed her mother so Caterina released her.

They heard the cries of a wounded animal.

"*Pappa*. Is that you?" Caterina shrieked.

"It's the wind, Caterina." Elda grabbed Fortunata and they clung to each other.

"*Non*. It's *Pappa*." Caterina pushed a child out of her way.

"You can't go outside," Elda screamed. "Cat..."

The door slammed shut behind Caterina and severed her name. She inched forward. "Where are you *Pappa*?" Flying branches razed her limbs and hailstones pummeled her body. Uprooted trees blocked her path, the ground rumbled beneath her feet and the rain poured down in thick sheets. She fell. "*Pappa, find me.*"

The bowed walnut footboard of Santo's bed reminded him of a sea wave. Plates of half-eaten food rested on top of the fruit veneer bombe dresser and empty wineglasses sat on the night table next to him, there were stains on its inlaid ivory surface. Rinaldo had just changed him into a clean nightshirt and Santo hoped that he wasn't going to throw up again. The window was still filled with night; Santo closed his eyes and welcomed the sleep that came.

"*Pappa.*" Benito flung the sheets off him. "Wake-up." He grabbed his arms. "There's a storm." He yanked his father to the side of the bed.

Something crashed outside and a bolt of lightning sliced the darkness.

"Caesare needs our help."

Santo ripped off his nightshirt.

"Here are your clothes."

He shoved his arms through the sleeves, pulled on his trousers and forced his feet into his boots without putting on any socks. Benito tossed him a jacket. They tore out of his bedroom, raced down the corridor and charged down the stairs.

Oresto was in the entranceway; his sodden clothes clung to his barrel-shaped body. His muddy boots had left a trail of prints behind them.

"Why are you here?" Benito stood beside Santo.

"The sheep and cows broke out of their pens."

"There's rain coming in through my window, Santo. What's happening?" Anna held onto the railing and made her way towards him; Sisina followed her.

He took her hand.

"Benito. You're wet. Why isn't Caesare with you?"

Lorenzo dashed down the stairs. "They're stallions in the driveway."

Padre Valentine hastened down the corridor. "The waves are rising over the cliffs. I've sent Bruno into his cellar. Rinaldo too."

"The maestrale wind's very angry," Oresto said.

"Stop it. You sound like a *bimba*." Santo slapped Oresto's shoulder. He faced the priest. "Take Anna and Lorenzo to the large cellar. Wait there until I return."

"You'll bring back Caesare and Benito?"

"Of course, Anna. Stay with her, Sisina."

"*Pappa*. I'm going with you and Benito."

"*Non*." Santo pushed him away. He turned to Benito and Oresto. "Let's go."

"Help your mother down the stairs," Padre Valentine said. Lorenzo guided Anna; Sisina was behind them. The priest shut the door and followed them into the cellar. Padre Valentine pushed a bin of potatoes out of the way and they huddled together on the earthen floor. Anna sat next to him.

"What's going on, Padre?"

"It's a bad storm, Anna. It'll pass."

Sisina leaned against a wall lined with shelves full of fruit preserves.

"I wanted to go with *Pappa* and Benito."

"He didn't want to worry about you, Lorenzo," Anna said. "What about the servants?"

The priest patted her hand.

"Their cottages don't have cellars. Will Edoardo and Caterina be safe?"

"They will be fine, Anna," Padre Valentine answered. Elda would watch after Caterina but what about Edoardo? Where was he now? Why hadn't he listened to him and Bruno? The sour smell of onions in the bushels began to burn the priest's eyes and the biting scent of curing meats and sausages hanging down were making him nauseous. Padre Valentine touched his silver crucifix. "It's time to pray."

The stallion stormed past Santo. Had he been standing in its path, he would have been trampled. Santo ran into the stable; Benito and Oresto were behind him. Caesare was leading a stallion out of the paddock; he had wrapped the reins around one hand and held a whip in the other. A rumble of thunder boomed. The horse erupted. Its tangled mane flicked across the white blaze on its black face and its hooves kicked the air above Caesare's head.

"Hit that damn animal," Santo yelled. He threw a pitchfork to Benito and a rake to Oresto. He picked up a spade.

The horse's hooves struck the ground close to Caesare's feet. They were near the edge of the stall. He lashed the animal with his whip. The stallion snorted and strained and tensed every one of the muscles in its 1,200-pound body as it pulled backwards.

"Let go of him," Santo yelled. "We've got to get to the villa."

Caesare glanced back at Santo and the horse leapt forward. It rammed his head into Caesare's chest and drove him into the stall, pinning him against the wall. Santo struck the horse with the spade; the edge of the iron blade cut into the animal's shorthaired coat and blood flowed through the jagged gashes.

Benito plunged the pitchfork into the animal's ribcage. It shrieked and spun around. The reins slipped from Caesare's hand and he slid to the ground. The horse charged towards Santo and Benito; they jumped out of its way. Oresto tripped over his rake and the horse trampled him. Oresto's screaming did not last long. Santo and Benito darted into the stall and helped Caesare to his feet.

"I'm...fine," Caesare said. He swayed from side to side.

The horse paced up and down, its eyes bulged and froth surged from its mouth.

"How are we going to get out of here?" Benito asked. Caesare stood steady beside him and watched the animal.

Why didn't Santo know what to do? Afterall, he was the father.

"I'll get his attention and you can run past him," Caesare said.

"*Non*," Benito said. "That's dangerous."

"Now," Caesare yelled. He grabbed Benito's arm and flung him forward moving towards the horse at the same time. The animal lunged towards him. "*Pappa*. Go."

He ran out of the stall and tripped over Oresto's body. He pushed himself halfway up and looked over his shoulder. The horse reared and Caesare threw his body on top of him. Santo couldn't breathe and he couldn't see but he could hear the hooves strike his son. Santo knew that he'd never be able to forget the sound of Caesare's cries. The horse shrieked and retreated; Benito pulled Caesare's body off his. The horse collapsed, Benito had pierced its forehead with a pitchfork. They dragged Caesare's unconscious body into a stall.

"Find some blankets." Santo took off his shirt and tied it as a tourniquet above the knee of one of Caesare's legs. Within a minute, Benito returned. He ripped his shirt into strips and bandaged his brother's wounds; Santo hoped there was enough material to absorb all the blood.

"We'll stay here until the storm settles then I'll go to the villa for help." He covered Caesare with a blanket and folded his jacket for a pillow. He leaned against the wall; Caesare's head rested on his lap.

"You're a brave and noble son, Benito. Caesare and I would have been killed if it weren't for you." Benito started to cry. Santo wrapped a blanket around them; he wasn't sure which son had been injured the most. Santo wished he remembered how to pray. Where was his priest when he needed him?

There was only one day for Edoardo to get to Reggio di Calabria. The wind was stronger than he'd expected and it had started to rain. Edoardo wasn't sure where he was or how long he had been traveling along the narrow coastal road that followed the sea. There had been no morning sun to tell him how much of the day had passed and the sky was too dark for him to read. He had chewed all of the fennel seeds Bruno had given him and his eyes were getting tired. Edoardo wished he could rest. He thought of his sleeping daughter, Caterina. Knowing that she was safe gave him peace. Soon, he told himself, he'd see her again. A bolt of lightning flashed across the sky and lit up a high ridge of land that jutted into the sea. Edoardo was disappointed for this marked the outer edge of San Lucido; he had only passed Paola, the mule was going slower than he anticipated.

The rocks on the seabed had started to shift a few hours ago. The movement was not strong enough to open any chasms on the mainland but it was sufficient to make swells beyond their natural size. At the same moment that Edoardo and the mule were at the mid point of the ridge, the crest of the waves rose to thirty feet and in one fluid motion, swept down and dragged them into the sea. Everything happened so quickly that Edoardo did not have time to ask God to forgive his sins. Edoardo, though, did not have to worry about whether or not God would let him into heaven for at the exact moment that he passed from this life into the next, Padre Valentine was praying for him.

"I want to go with you," Lorenzo said.

"Stay with your mother," Padre Valentine ordered. He stood at the top of the stairs. "As soon as I know it's safe, I'll come back." He stepped into the corridor and shut the cellar door.

Bruno approached the priest with a quickness that he had rarely witnessed before. He must have been in his kitchen.

"*Signora?*" He was panting.

"She's in the cellar with Lorenzo and Sisina. Are you all right, Bruno?" As soon as everything was back to normal, the priest vowed he'd make Bruno go for regular walks with him.

"*Si.*"

"Where's Rinaldo?"

"Upstairs," Bruno replied.

"You should sit down. I'll take you back to your kitchen."

A voice behind him said, "Padre."

Rinaldo stepped beside the priest.

"How are the other servants?"

"Fine," Rinaldo answered. "They got to the cellars."

The priest said a silent prayer of thanks.

"Where's *Signora*?" Rinaldo asked.

"In the cellar with Lorenzo and Sisina."

"The upstairs is damaged," Rinaldo said. "Most of the windows have been shattered; there are shards everywhere. The carpets are ruined, vases are in pieces, pedestals are broken and dressers have toppled over. Downstairs is bad, too. There's a tree trunk in the large salon and *Signore's* library is ruined."

"Those things don't matter, Rinaldo."

"Have you seen *Signore* and his sons?"

"*Non*," Padre answered.

They walked into the kitchen and Padre Valentine slipped on the wet floor. He grabbed onto the edge of the counter and regained his balance. Fragments of dishes were mixed in with squished fruits and spoiled food. Rinaldo flipped a chair upright and Bruno sat down. The priest opened the door; the rain had stopped but a grey mist prevented him from seeing anything. "I'm going to get *Signora*."

When he opened the cellar door; Lorenzo was waiting for him. Within minutes, Lorenzo, Anna, and Sisina stood beside Padre Valentine.

"Where's Santo and Caesare and Benito?" Anna gasped.

"I'll look for them now."

"What about Bruno, Padre?"

"He's in the kitchen with Rinaldo."

"Caterina and Edoardo?" Anna panted.

"I'll find them, Anna."

"I'm going with you, Padre," Lorenzo said.

"I'm coming too," Anna said. "You're not leaving me here."

Padre Valentine would take Lorenzo with him but what could he get Anna to do? "Gather some blankets," he said to her. "And find some food."

Anna nodded.

"If any of the children are hurt, we'll bring them here."

"*Sì*, Padre."

"Help her, Sisina."

"I will take care of this," Anna said. "Be careful, Lorenzo."

Padre Valentine and Lorenzo made their way to the servant's enclave. The mist had dissipated; the sallow sun gave scant light and meager warmth and by its position, the priest speculated that it was be mid-day. The rain began again, it pelted their bodies and within a short time, his cassock was soaked. The waterlogged material forced him to slow his pace, Lorenzo altered his accordingly and together they witnessed the wreckage of the storm.

The grounds of San Michelle were dotted with gaping holes where tree trunks had been uprooted. Shrubs had been flattened and saplings snapped in half. Fences had been blown away, a stable had collapsed, sheds were missing, and doors were lying in the middle of fields. There were broken sheep, cows, pigs and dogs everywhere. A group of servants approached them as they neared the enclave.

"Padre Valentine." Fragola grabbed his hand. "Have you seen Oresto?"

The priest remembered he had left with Santo.

"We can't find Nicoletta." Elda collapsed in front of him.

Ermengildo sank to the ground beside his wife. "Where's Edoardo?"

"Who's with Caterina?" Lorenzo asked.

"I tried to stop her." Elda sobbed.

"Who?" Lorenzo asked.

"Caterina."

"Where is she?" Lorenzo repeated.

"I had to hold Fortunata," Elda cried. "She's so little."

"There was nothing else you could have done," Ermengildo said. He put his arm around her.

"Where's Caterina?" Padre Valentine asked.

"She ran out of the cottage. She wanted her *Pappa*," Ermengildo said. "Help us, Padre."

"I'll stay with them, Lorenzo. Find Caterina and take her to your mother."

Lorenzo ran helter skelter around San Michelle. Where was Caterina? Why couldn't he find her? "Caterina," he shouted. "Where are you?" He tripped and hit his head, momentarily stunning himself. He lay still for a few minutes and the answer came to him. He struggled to his feet and stumbled off. Lorenzo knew exactly where Caterina was. Why hadn't he thought of this before?

Caterina was curled up on the ground in a fetal position still wearing the white dress his *Mamma* had given her two days ago for *Natale*. It was torn and stained with brownish red blood. Her bare arms and legs were slashed with razor thin cuts, her face was streaked with dirt and her lips were colored a terrifying purple. "Caterina," he whispered. Lorenzo bent down and lifted her from the wet earth of her mother's grave.

Padre Valentine stepped into the main entrance of the villa. Stones from the driveway mixed in with bits of wood and leaves covered the terra cotta. Footprints, smeared into each other, led to the base of the staircase; the carpet on the steps was soiled. They had not been able to find Oresto or Nicoletta. The priest hoped that his prayers had worked and that Edoardo had come back and Lorenzo had found Caterina.

"Where have you been?" Anna scurried down the corridor towards him. "I've been waiting for so long. Have you found Santo and Caesare and Benito?"

"*Non.*"

"Is Lorenzo with you?" she asked.

"He's not here?"

"Where are my sons?" Anna struck his shoulder with her fist. The priest flinched.

"Caterina? Edoardo? Where's everybody?"

The front of her dress was splattered with blood like the day Caterina was born; the priest did not want to know to whom it belonged.

"I'm going to find them." She shoved him out of her way and flung open the door. "Lorenzo."

He stepped across the threshold and his knees buckled.

"Move Anna." The priest dashed past her.

Lorenzo swooned and Caterina's body slid into his arms.

Anna caught her son as he fell; she guided his head onto her lap.

Padre Valentine held Caterina and wished that he had more warmth to give her.

"Ca...ter...in...a." Lorenzo's irregular breaths broke up her name.

Grazia, Dio. Padre Valentine prayed silently. Anna kissed Lorenzo then reached across the short space; her trembling hand stroked Caterina's matted hair. The silence between them asked the question that neither had the courage to express.

"*Signora.*" Sisina appeared in front of them.

"The children need blankets," Anna said.

When Sisina returned, Rinaldo was with her. They covered Caterina and Lorenzo.

"*Signore,*" Rinaldo said.

Santo's flaccid chest was laced with mud and his trousers were bloodstained. He staggered towards Anna, knelt down on one knee and touched Lorenzo's cheek. Lorenzo stirred and shifted his body in his mother's arms.

"Where's Caesare and Benito?"

"In the stable."

"What happened?" Padre Valentine asked.

"Something terrible."

"My sons?"

"They're alive, Anna," Santo said.

"Bring them to me," Anna pleaded. "Bring them to me."

"Here, *Signore*." Rinaldo was holding a jacket. The priest had no idea where he'd found it.

"Padre." Santo stood up. "We'll go to the stable now."

"*Pappa*?" There was scant life in Caterina's voice.

"Give her to Sisina," Santo said to the priest. He put on the jacket.

Sisina sat on the floor and the Padre Valentine placed Caterina in her arms.

Santo leaned over and touched Lorenzo's cheek again. "I'll be back for him." He and Padre Valentine hurried out of the villa. "Telegraph Fiore. I want him here as soon as possible." They raced down the steps. "And Padre, pray for Caesare."

The priest had already started.

PART TWO: SUMMER 1913

Calabria, Italy

CHAPTER ELEVEN

The morning train for Naples would be leaving Florence in a little while. Lorenzo hurried down the streets in the Medici-San Lorenzo complex; he didn't want to miss it; after four years he was going to see his mother. "Can't you two move any faster?"

"You gave me too much wine last night," Matteo said. "Look at how my hands are shaking." He massaged his slender fingers. "I wouldn't even be able to work on my cameo brooch. You do this to me every time I go out with you."

"I told you to eat something," Lodovico said. "You were drinking too much for that skinny body of yours but of course, you never listen."

"I had some *prosciutto* and bread. I just didn't get any sleep."

"You snored so loudly that I got up and went to my studio and chiseled until one hour ago. I don't care that our fathers were brothers. When we get back, you're going to find another place to live." Lodovico waved his hand at Lorenzo. "What are you racing for? Did you forget that we're catching the train with you?"

"Probably," Matteo said. "He drank more than me."

"I'm not the Arabian that Caesare rode in the Palio." Lodovico snorted and stomped his foot on the cobblestone.

Lorenzo walked towards Lodovico.

"And you're only carrying your own satchel, do you have any idea how heavy Matteo's is? I'm not a mule."

"If you were an animal, you'd be a Percheron," Matteo said.

"Why did you bring so many books? Did you forget that the

University of Pisa has a library?"

"Verrocchio's assignment is due next week and I have more research to do." Matteo took a handkerchief from his shirt pocket. "I need to rest for a minute."

"You take forever to do one little thing. What's the matter? Is a wisp of hair out of place?"

"Lodovico, it's more difficult to be an artisan than a sculptor." Matteo removed his eyeglasses, wiped the oval lenses and gold rimmed frame, patted his face and put them back on. He folded the handkerchief and returned it to his pocket.

"That's it." Lodovico lifted the strap of Matteo's satchel over his head and threw it down. "Who was the one who got a commission and a beautiful piece of marble to carve an angel for the Giuliano Family Tomb?"

"Be careful," Matteo warned. "I never had a satchel with such supple leather until Lorenzo gave me that one."

"I'm like Michelangelo," Lodovico said. "I can already see the angel's shape in the marble; she's going to be the most divine creature to ever stand on a sarcophagus. Give me your flask. I need some water."

"We can stop for awhile," Lorenzo said. They were approaching Piazza San Lorenzo. He rubbed his forehead; despite the cool air, it was damp with perspiration.

Flecks of stone peppered Lodovico's hair and a layer of dust coated his shirt. "Would you like a drink?"

"*Non, grazie,*" Lorenzo said.

"You're still worried about Verrocchio, aren't you?" Lodovico asked.

"I should have asked him for permission to leave," Lorenzo said.

"You know he wouldn't have given it to you. Your *Pappa* told him nothing was to interfere with your studies."

"He'll believe us when we tell him you're not at class because you're sick," Matteo said. "And besides, you're his favorite student."

"If I have to hear one more time about Lorenzo, the gifted

artist and brilliant scholar and champion fencer, I'm going to be ill," Lodovico said.

"And don't forget, he's a lady's man too. Oh, Lorenzo, you have the most incredible eyes." Matteo fluttered his eyelashes.

Lorenzo knocked Matteo's cap off his head.

"Are you going to miss the *bellisima* Loredana?" Lodovico asked.

"Non." Lorenzo said. "She's just like the others. Too agreeable."

"That doesn't seem to bother Benito," Matteo said.

"I wish he'd come to Florence more often," Lodovico said.

"I'm glad he doesn't. I'd never get any sleep if he did and my art would suffer," Matteo said.

"I still think that he could bring Caesare with him; I'd make sure that he didn't get into trouble. Maybe your brothers will be at San Michelle."

Benito and Caesare had not seen their mother either in four years. Caesare had spent considerable time recuperating in Naples after Fiore had amputated part of his leg and they now lived with their father in Cosenza with Buccella. Despite Padre Valentine's insistence that Lorenzo was wrong, he still felt that Caesare was connected to Clorinda's drowning and was indifferent as to whether or not he ever saw him again.

"Make sure you send us a telegram to let us know when you're coming back to Florence," Lodovico said. He picked up Matteo's cap. "We'll meet you at the train station."

"I'm sure things will work out with your father," Matteo said.

"I don't think I've ever seen him smile," Lodovico said. He handed Matteo his cap.

"He only smiles when he makes money," Lorenzo said.

"Then he should be smiling all the time." Lodovico slapped his back.

"Let's go, I'll carry Matteo's satchel," Lorenzo said.

The stands in the Piazza San Lorenzo market were still covered; the merchants had yet to arrive. In a few hours the public square would be bustling with people. The statue of Giovanni delle Bande Nere was in the open area.

"Someday my work will be better than Baccio Bandinelli's," Lodovico said.

"You could have been the model for his Hercules," Lorenzo said.

"Someday, I will sell my jewelry in a shop on the Ponte Vecchio," Matteo said. "Right next to the Bulgari's."

"Definetly," Lorenzo said. "The cameo brooch that you made for my mother is exquisite."

"I know Padre told us that she wears it all the time but I want you to draw me a sketch and show me exactly how it looks on her, the first time you see her wearing it."

"Of course, Matteo."

"When are you going to show Benito the jeweled cross we made?" Matteo asked. "You know how excited he is about introducing a line of jewelry into your family's business."

"I want to show *Mamma* first. When I get back I'll send it to him in Naples."

"*Bene.*" Matteo stroked his goatee. "Your idea to use the aquamarine stone was brilliant."

"We'll have to think of a project for us," Lodovico said.

"My angel sketches are almost ready. I'd like us to make a statue for *Mamma's* rose garden."

"I'll start looking for the perfect block of marble right away," Lodovico said.

"We better get going," Lorenzo said.

They passed the Church of Santa Maria Novella and a short time later entered the central railway station where the train was already at the platform. They boarded immediately. Lorenzo sat across from Lodovico and Matteo. The train followed the course of the Arno River as it made its way to Pisa.

"Do you think he's going to start about how the Arno valley's the background in the Mona Lisa, how his mother read him Leonardo fables when he was a boy and how he's like Leonardo da

Vinci?" Matteo leaned his head on Lodovico's shoulder.

"*Si*. We're probably going to have to listen about how he's left-handed and golden-haired and sketches in notebooks too."

"Let's give him his presents now."

Lodovico retrieved Matteo's satchel from underneath the seat; Matteo opened it and handed Lorenzo three parcels.

"These are from me."

The first contained an assortment of charcoal sticks, a piece of white chalk and a putty eraser.

"For your flower sketches."

There was a bundle of soft and hard pencils in the second.

"For studies of fruits and vegetables."

"Wine red, gold ochre, raw sienna, sepia," Lorenzo said. "It looks like a rainbow."

"Open the last one," Matteo said.

It was a notebook; the light grey paper had a slight tooth that was ideal for charcoal sketches.

"I want you to draw me pictures of San Michelle."

It had not been an aberrant winter storm that had struck Cetraro but the aftershocks of an earthquake with its epicenter around Reggio di Calabria and Messina. Vito Mabruco, one of Buccella's men that his father had hired to supervise the repairs, had done a remarkable job of restoring the villa and grounds.

"Here are my parcels," Lodovico said. Matteo put his gifts on the seat.

The first one was a pad of handmade cottonrag paper with ragged edges and the manufacturer's watermark in the corner.

"It's not that cheap woodpulp stuff Verrocchio makes you practice on," Lodovico said.

The off-white paper was semi-rough and irregular, just the right texture for painting. He lifted the first sheet; it was heavy enough and didn't require stretching before use. "It's perfect."

"*Bene*. Open the next one," Lodovico said.

"Are you that happy to see me go away?" This would be the first time the three of them had ever been separated

"Hurry up," Matteo said. "The train's going to be arriving in Pisa soon."

The second gift was a white ceramic palette with rounded recesses to mix paint and water.

"You've got so many sable brushes, I only bought you one," Lodovico said.

"But I picked it out," Matteo said. "It's time you threw the old rigger away."

He held up a small sponge. "And I thought of that too."

The last parcel contained two dozen small blocks of semi-moist colors.

"The viridian's a close match to the aquamarine stone in our jeweled cross," Matteo said. "And if you paint a picture of your mother, it would be perfect for her eyes."

Santo had sent his mother and Sisina to Taranto to live with Eugenio Mella while San Michelle was being restored. She'd had a stroke shortly afterwards but Lorenzo's father had said she'd fully recovered.

"Everything you've given me is beautiful." Lorenzo wished he knew words, which could express how thankful he was and how much he loved his friends but he didn't so all he said was, "*Grazie.*"

The sound of screeching brakes announced the train's arrival in Pisa, Matteo stood up and Lorenzo put Matteo's cap on his head.

"It's so light now, even you can carry it." Lodovico handed him his satchel and helped him adjust the strap on his shoulder. "I'll meet you at 12noon at the train station in Pisa in five days." He patted Matteo's shoulder. "Be careful."

"I'm not going to say goodbye," Matteo said. "Instead, I'll say a *presto.*" He strutted down the aisle.

"See you soon," Lorenzo and Lodovico said in unison.

The train passed Livorno, Cecina, Follonica and Grosseto as it made its way to Rome where Lodovico would be spending a few days visiting friends.

"I still think there could be something wrong with my mother?"

"Not her letters again?" Lodovico shook his head. "How many times have I heard Padre Valentine explain to you that her right arm got weak because of the stroke and it was easier for him to write them. If there were a problem, don't you think he'd tell you? After all, he's a man of God and how long have you known him?"

"He baptized me nineteen years ago."

"Stop fretting, you're starting to sound like Matteo."

"I don't really know much about what her life's been like since I've been gone." He flicked a speck of dirt off the window. "My father hasn't actually seen her in quite awhile and her letters never said that much."

"Padre Valentine says Bruno and Sisina take good care of her and she even has her goddaughter, Francesca, living with her now. I think you've missed your mother more than you realize. As soon as you see you her, everything will be fine."

Why hadn't Lorenzo asked his father more often for permission to return to San Michelle to see his mother? He had always been an exemplary student and a short absence would not have posed a problem. Why hadn't he been more insistent? Perhaps it was because the world of Florence and his new life had entranced him and he didn't really want to return to San Michelle as much as he thought he did.

"It's that damn letter you got last week, isn't it?" Lodovico demanded.

"I wish I knew who wrote it and what it means," Lorenzo said.

"Take it out of your satchel and let me look at it again."

The letter was written on his mother's personal cyanine blue stationery.

"It's strange, you're right about that," Lodovico said. He read aloud. "Come home, Lorenzo. It is time."

"Even if my mother could still write, the style's too florid."

"It's too bad you couldn't have shown it to Padre, he may have had some insight."

Lorenzo folded the letter.

"When you show your father it, I'm sure he'll understand why you left without permission."

"I hope so." Lorenzo put the letter back in his satchel.

They passed Civitavecchia on the coast; the train was close to Rome.

"You haven't seen the Tyrrehenian Sea for along time," Lodovico said.

"Do you know why I chose the aquamarine stone for the jeweled cross?"

"Matteo said it was because the bluish green color was the same as your eyes and your mother's."

"The color reminds me of my home too, Lodovico, the place where I was born."

"That's nice, Lorenzo, I'll tell Matteo."

"Let's find something to eat, Lodovico. Who knows when we'll share our next meal?"

A few hours later, Lorenzo sat alone in a private compartment as the train pulled into Naples; he was relieved that he did not have to disembark and board another one for he had no interest in stepping foot in the city. Even though his studies included law and his father had already told him that he'd be living in Naples in the future, he avoided thinking about this scenario as much as possible. Lorenzo wanted to be an artist and a scholar. Why could his life not belong to him?

The train passed Pompeii, in the shadow of Mount Vesuvius, and headed down a stretch of coastline between Sorrento and Salerno. It whizzed by the towns of Amalfi and Ravello. Lorenzo wanted to visit the blue grotto in the isle of Capri off the coast and explore the Greek ruins in Agropoli. The train turned inland and weaved in and out along the coast. At times the tracks rose to precipitous heights, dramatically close to the edge, then dropped and passed through open forests and alongside stone covered slopes, acres of olive groves, vineyards and orchards. There were flocks of goats and sheep and farms as it cut through the foothills and meandered through the countryside. At Piscotta, the train turned inland again and at Sapri, they had a brief stopover. He boarded another train and a short time later, it left the region of Campania, traversed between two high cliffs, and crossed into Basilicata. When it passed through Maratea with its incredible view of the Gulf of Policastro, Lorenzo knew he was in Calabria. He retrieved an old notebook and as he turned the pages, slowly re-entered the world of San Michelle.

There was the sketch of Bruno that he said made him look "too fat." His drawing of Padre Valentine with his "Roman nose" was next, then Grigio, followed by several of his mother. His strokes were unsophisticated and his renderings amateurish, Verrocchio had been an excellent teacher. Lorenzo was anxious to draw his mother with his new charcoal sticks and white chalk, with the skills he'd mastered; he was convinced he'd capture her beauty.

The cedar trees told Lorenzo that they were close to Diamante. The last sketches were of Caterina. She had been a scrawny girl, usually dirty from working with her father in the garden. Lorenzo still didn't understand how Edoardo could have just disappeared from San Michelle the night of the storm. Padre Valentine was one of the numerous priests that Pope Pius X had summoned to Vatican Hospital to care for the earthquake refugees and he had said that Edoardo's fate was not uncommon. The final sketch showed Caterina's rose birthmark on her left wrist. His mother had been right, they were destined to have a special relationship, which according to Padre had deepened over the years.

Lodovico and Matteo understood that Caterina was a servant girl and that they'd been childhood friends. The last time Lorenzo had seen her was the night of the storm for his father had sent him to Florence almost immediately. It had taken a long time but under Bruno's and Elda's careful watch, she had regained her health. The train passed through Belvedere and Lorenzo put the notebook back in his satchel. Caterina was sixteen years old now; it wasn't only his mother that he wanted to see again. The wording in the letter had been right; it was time for him to come home. The train pulled into Cetraro.

CHAPTER TWELVE

The needlepoint picture of the boy and the puppy hung crookedly on the wall. Why did Armida always leave it that way after she dusted? Caterina adjusted it, if there were more hours in the day, she could do everything for *Mamma* Anna. She went over to the chair. "*Buon Giorno, Mamma.*" Today's the last day of May and it's going to be a lovely morning. Would you like to look out the window?" Anna nodded. It was a minimal movement but the way they usually communicated since she lost her ability to speak eight months ago.

"I can only stay a little while." Caterina opened the drapes then faced her. "I have to water your roses." She straightened the stack of Lorenzo's letters on the night table. "I'll read one to you later." The corners of Anna's lips slid upwards. *Mamma* loved listening to his words and she loved to read them; it was as if her childhood friend was still with her. Caterina wondered if she would recognize Lorenzo's voice, the one she remembered belonged to a fourteen-year-old and she doubted if his man's voice sounded the same.

The statue of the *gobbo* that Mafalda gave her before she died stood beside Padre Valentine's wooden crucifix. Padre had explained that Lorenzo's studies at the academy were so consuming that Santo would not give him permission to leave but Caterina refused to believe that there had never been any time in four years for him to come home. *Mamma* though had always told her that when the time was right, he'd come back. Books would never be as important as people to Caterina but this was because she had lost both her

118

mother and father; perhaps you had to lose those you loved before you valued those who remained.

"There," she said as she placed a lavender stalk on the top letter. "Look at what I'm wearing today." *Mamma* had bought her several dresses last summer and this yellow was her favorites. Caterina lifted *Mamma's* hand to touch the sleeve but her fingers would not bend. "I'll massage rose cream on your hands later." She lay it down on the blanket. Francesca had brought her willow bark yesterday from her walk on the trails and she'd make a decoction tonight for *Mamma* to drink before she went to sleep; it always proved helpful. "Sisina told me that you hardly ate breakfast again this morning. Bruno's worried. I've made you an infusion of cleaver flowers that'll soothe your throat so you can eat a good lunch. Francesca's gone horseback riding so Bruno's going to feed you today."

Caterina held *Mamma* Anna's chin in the palm of her hand and rested the cup on her parted lips; she tipped it and a smidgen of the warm liquid seeped into her mouth. She waited a few moments then repeated the action. "*Bene,*" she said an hour later. "You almost finished it." She wiped her mouth with a cloth napkin and kissed her on the forehead. "Rest awhile." Anna closed her eyes and Caterina left the room.

It was a five-mile walk from the train station to San Michelle. Lorenzo shielded his face with his cap; he wanted his mother to be the first to see him. He approached the incline leading to his family's estate and when he arrived at the top, turned around; his father's fishing boats were anchored in the harbor. Even though the afternoon that had just begun was full of warmth, the memory of the boats that had been smashed against the rocky shores during the storm chilled his blood. In less than an hour, he stood in front of the black wrought iron double gate marking the entrance to the villa. He reacquainted himself with the design of the arch that crossed above him and the oversized initial "M" embellished with golden swirls at each tip, suspended in the middle. Stone pillars, deeply embedded in the ground stood on each side, supported the structure.

He ambled to the villa; the lawn that stretched in front of him was smooth and even with no signs of the gaping holes that had once marred it. A cluster of barns, stables and sheds were in the distance on his right, colts raced against each other in their corrals and sheep and cows grazed in open fields. His boots crushed the fine stones of the circular driveway. The villa was about two hundred feet in front; Lorenzo began to select the colors for the wells in his new palette to create the painting that he'd promised Lodovico and Matteo.

Cobalt blue would capture the sky and titanium white the clouds. The trunks of the oak and pine trees were raw umber; a mixture of ultramarine and cadmium yellow would reproduce the rich green foliage. He'd create the subdued green of the tiled roof by blending blue and lemon yellow; the muted pink walls would be a challenge, he'd experiment with pale undertones to try and replicate this shade. The reddish brown terra cotta pots on the stone platform on each side of the granite steps were filled with ultramarine fuschia plants and the bougainvillea hedges close to the expansive windows of the salon were resplendent with alizarin crimson blossoms. Because of Verrocchio, he had so many more words to describe what he saw.

The curving brick pathway that reminded his mother of the streams winding through their estate made him eager to walk the trails with her again. Up ahead a woman, whose back was to him, was working in a flowerbed, which had been his mother's favorite. She used a spouted tin can and sprinkled water on the earth around the rose bushes. She turned around and he stopped.

A wide brimmed straw hat obscured her features and gardening gloves covered her hands. Her mid-calf length dress was an aurora yellow, the same hue as the sun when a light haze covered it. A breeze moved through the air and wrapped it against her body, revealing broad shoulders, full curves, a trim waist and long legs.

When she removed her hat, the sun ignited the auburn highlights in the lustrous brown tresses that framed her dark alluring features. She took off her hat and gloves and set them on the ground. Even though this woman bore only a slight resemblance to the girl who had shared his childhood, Lorenzo knew that it was Caterina. He stepped forward and she noticed him.

She cast her eyes down to his leather boots, raised them to his brown ochre woolen trousers and olive shirt and settled them on the collar of his tan jacket. Lorenzo's physique bore no trace of the gawky lad he had once been; he too had undergone a transformation. She held her arms by her side. Lorenzo was crestfallen for she did not recognize him. He slipped off his satchel.

"*Mia amica*," he said.

"*Mio amico?*" she asked. A half-smiled shaped her mouth.

"*Sempre*," they said in unison.

Lorenzo offered Caterina his hands but she did not accept them.

"*Mamma* Anna knew you'd come back." Caterina tucked a strand of hair behind her ear; she had wanted this day for a long time but now that it had arrived, she didn't know how to deal with it. Padre Valentine was still in Naples and Francesca hadn't returned from riding, there was no one to help her.

"I'm going to see *Mamma*. Will you come with me?" Lorenzo asked.

Caterina tried to read every night but she had yet to find the words, which could explain all that had happened. She picked up her hat.

"Is there something wrong?"

"The San Michelle you and I knew as children Lorenzo no longer exists, the storm changed everything."

"I'm sorry about your *Pappa*, Caterina. I wish I had been here for you."

He should have been here for *Mamma* Anna.

"Padre Valentine told me everything," Lorenzo said.

Obviously not enough to make you come home.

"What is it?"

"*Mamma* Anna stayed away for over a year."

"*Si*, she was with Eugenio and Francesca in Taranto."

"When she returned, we were happy again."

"Padre told me that too."

"But when she lived with Eugenio..."

"I know. *Pappa* said she had a slight stroke but she recovered completely."

"After Padre brought her back from Naples..."

"What are you talking about?" Lorenzo asked. "*Mamma* was never in Naples."

It had been so long that Caterina no longer knew how to talk to Lorenzo.

"I'm going to see her now."

If Lorenzo had come home sooner, maybe none of this would have happened. "I'll take you but your mother is not as you remember."

Anna shifted her eyes and watched Bruno place a letter on the table next to Lorenzo's.

"It's from Eugenio. Perhaps, he'll tell us when he's going to visit. Francesca will read it to you later."

Eugenio had taken her to Naples in October and that was the last time she had seen Santo; there had been no letter from him in months and she still did not know when he would bring her sons to San Michelle. It had been four years since she'd seem them but Anna had no one to blame but herself. It was wrong for a mother to always wait for her children to visit her; sometimes it was necessary for a mother to go to them.

"The sky's a lovely blue, *Signora*."

Her mind had not yet robbed her of what colors looked like.

"You should be able to see it."

That was too far for her eyes today but she nodded so that

Bruno wouldn't know. Anna hoped that when she had the ability to speak, she'd told him enough times how much she loved him. It was terrible not to have said the things one should have when one was able to but Anna hadn't realized this until it was too late and now all the words that she wished she had expressed were locked up inside her. There were so many of them Anna feared that someday she'd explode.

"I'll get your lunch now, I made *zuppa*." Bruno fluffed the pillow behind her back. "You've got to start eating your breakfast. Sisina was very upset this morning."

Sisina put too much food in her mouth and made her throw up. Then she got angry when she had to clean her. Sisina had never been impatient like this before and Anna wished she could ask her what was the matter. If Anna could talk she'd thank Sisina again for all her help over the past fourteen years; she thought that she'd done this in the past but obviously she'd been mistaken.

"*Ciao*. I'll see you in awhile." Bruno's broad face was close to hers; he had so many missing teeth that Anna wondered how he ate enough to stay fat. She heard the door open then close and knew that he had left the room. She glanced at Eugenio's letter and recalled the summer of 1910 when San Michelle had been restored and after one and a half years away, she had come home.

"I wish I could have said good-bye to Francesca," Anna said. She stood beside Eugenio on the platform in front of the train station in Taranto; Sisina waited behind them with their luggage. Grey smoke billowed from the top and sides of the steam engine and the tender car was filled with coal.

"School was starting in Pisa," Eugenio replied.

"She's so much like her mother."

"You said lovely things about Mariangela."

Francesca called Anna "her Gabriella" the last night they were together.

"Gabriel was God's archangel who announced his presence by sounding his trumpet," Francesca told her. "He was the bearer of good tidings and *Mamma* Anna, you have told me such wonderful stories about my *Mamma*, that I will always think of you as my Gabriella."

"It's not wrong to send Francesca to Pisa, is it?" Eugenio asked.

Passengers boarded the train; it would soon be time to leave for Metaponto.

"Of course not," Anna said. "She's twelve and must learn that there's more to life than dancing the tarantella."

"Even in the leather boots you gave her, she dances," Eugenio said.

"Genoveffa bought her a dress but..."

"That daughter of mine is going to drive her stepmother crazy. She actually prefers men's trousers."

"Don't worry. She's a beautiful girl." Anna folded her hands. "Genoveffa helped me pick out lovely dresses for Caterina."

The suitcase behind her held the dresses. Nella's death had been tragic but Edoardo's disappearance was something that she'd never be able to understand. The girl was alone now and Anna would watch over her; she had been right about Caterina's rose birthmark; they were destined to have a special relationship. Santo had taken her sons away from her; she would never let him do the same with Caterina.

Santo had spent the month of May in Taranto with Anna and when he left he'd told her that for the next two years, he'd be busy with Buccella and doubted if he'd have much time to visit her in San Michelle. It had already been a year and a half since she'd seen Caesare and Benito. Santo had kept her away from Caesare because of the extent of his injuries, Benito, of course, would not leave his side. Anna patted her face with her handkerchief; coal dust had settled on her skin and left a dark residue on the delicate white cloth. A porter approached them.

"He'll take our luggage. Eugenio said to Sisina. "Go with him and meet us in our coach."

Anna rubbed her right arm.

"It's bothering you again, isn't it?" Eugenio asked.

"I'm tired, that's all." Yesterday, she could barely hold her pen and write a letter to Lorenzo. She'd had the stroke shortly after coming to Taranto and the doctor was concerned that she was on the verge of suffering another one. Not seeing Caesare and Benito had been difficult but it was her separation from Lorenzo that had been almost too much for her to bear. Anna tucked her handkerchief into her sleeve.

"The doctor said you'd be fine if you'd stop worrying so much," Eugenio said. He put his arm around her.

"I haven't been sleeping well, I'm anxious to get home." The warning whistle sounded, it was time to board the train. Eugenio helped her ascend the steps leading into the first class car.

"I'll make sure Sisina's attended properly to the luggage," he said. "I'll be back in a few minutes."

The seats in the private compartment were well padded, the floor was carpeted and the large window beside her would afford her a lovely view of the Ionian Sea. Anna made herself comfortable. She pulled her sleeve over her wrist, the skin irritation had spread and Sisina would need to apply another burdock poultice. The doctor had identified it as "psoriasis" but giving it a name didn't change anything. The simple fact was that Anna was almost forty and her body was breaking down; soon she'd be an old woman. Santo said that Caesare was making progress under Fiore's care; if anyone needed a good doctor, it was her son; Caesare was only twenty-two and he had much life yet to live; Anna's was almost over.

A short time later, Eugenio and Sisina entered the compartment; Eugenio sat next to Anna and Sisina across from them. Sisina folded her shawl and tucked it behind her head; as the train eased into a gentle rhythm, she fell asleep.

"Why don't you just tell Santo that you don't want the fishing business in Taranto any longer? You don't like the way he treats your men and you have lots of money."

"Our fathers were brothers, Anna. Have you forgotten?" Eugenio patted her hand.

There had never been a signet ring on his finger.

"I can't do that."

The view of the Ionian Sea was lovely. Anna did not know what the "N" on Santo's signet ring stood for, had never met Buccella nor solved the mystery of the missing ledger. But what did it matter? It couldn't give Caesare his leg, make up for the time she hadn't spent with Caesare and Benito, reunite her with Lorenzo or bring Edoardo back. And of course, nothing could make Santo love her the way he once did.

"Be positive, Anna. Caesare's recuperating; Benito's doing well in the business and Lorenzo's a brilliant student at the academy. I'm sure Santo will bring them to San Michelle soon."

Sisina stirred then settled again.

"When will Buccella have enough money?"

"I don't know. I've never met him and all that I can tell you is that Santo's in charge of a group of men who are trying to merge his fishing operations with a similar business in Naples."

The whistle sounded and the brakes screeched to a halt as they pulled into Metaponto. "The hour passed so quickly," Anna said.

"Come. I'll make sure you and Sisina board the right train to Crotone before I depart. Remember, it goes to Cosenza then Cetraro. I sent a telegram to Padre Valentine and he'll be waiting for you at the train station to take you to your villa."

A little while later; Anna and Sisina stood on the platform in front of the railway station in Metaponto.

"Here are your tickets," Eugenio said. "I hope it won't be too long before I see you and Francesca again." He kissed her on the cheek.

"*Grazie*, Eugenio," Anna thought to herself. She slipped back into the quiet of her mind.

Several minutes had passed since Caterina had gone into his mother's sitting room. Lorenzo waited in the corridor. She had been resting and Caterina wanted to ensure that she was dressed properly before he saw her. Lorenzo reminded himself that Caterina was probably over zealous because she'd lost both of her parents, he had been more fortunate in life for his were still alive. He rubbed the palm of his hand against the bristly stubble on his chin; perhaps he should have taken the time to bathe and shave. The door opened and Lorenzo bolted into the room; he passed Caterina but another woman blocked his path. The woman handed her tray to a servant he recognized as Sisina then stepped forward and for a moment, it was as if he was in the Uffizzi Gallery in Florence admiring a religious painting of an angelic creature. Her hair cascaded to her shoulders in loose ringlets; its color held the rays of the sun. She embraced Caterina, then exited the room without acknowledging his presence; Lorenzo wondered if she were a phantom of his mind. He moved ahead.

Who was the woman in his mother's floral chair? Her feet rested on the stool he used to sit on when they played their fable game; the blankets that draped her lower body reminded him of a shroud. Her hands rested on top of the woolen material; the veins were thin and high, as if they were rivers about to overflow. The fingers were twisted and stiff like the gnarled roots at the base of an old decaying tree. The sleeve of her white nightdress had been pulled up, exposing pasty skin dotted with red crusty sores. A cream shawl wrapped around her shoulders could not hide the emaciated frame of her upper torso. Matteo's cameo brooch was pinned close to the woman's heart and a St. Jude of Thaddeus medal, the patron of desperate causes, next to it.

"*Mamma?*" he whispered.

What remained of her hair hung down in clumps, its pewter gray a color that Lorenzo rarely saw on an artist's palette. Her translucent skin was spotted with the same patches that were on her forearms. He leaned over. "*Mamma.*" He kissed her cheek. "It's Lorenzo." She did not open her eyes. Caterina stood beside him.

"Does she realize that I'm here?"

"Come Lorenzo. Your mother will sleep for awhile longer."

"What happened to her, Caterina?"

"Get some rest first."

"I never meant to stay away so long." He kissed his mother's cheek again.

Caterina took his hand.

"I'm sorry, *Mamma.*" Lorenzo let her lead him out of his mother's sitting room.

Anna waited until she heard the door shut then opened her eyes. Tears welled up and flowed down her cheeks. Even if she had the strength today to lift her hand and wipe them off her face, she wouldn't, for these were tears of joy. Lorenzo had come home just as she had told Caterina; a mother knows her child.

CHAPTER THIRTEEN

Caterina and Lorenzo stood at the base of the steps in the entranceway of the villa. "Why don't you rest, Lorenzo? You've had a long day and..."

"I don't understand, Caterina."

How could he? No one else did.

"*Pappa* told me that it was just a slight stroke. I want to go outside." Lorenzo opened the door and they made their way down the pathway. "And Padre said the same thing."

It wasn't Padre's place to tell Lorenzo. "Your father must have said something about *Mamma's* deteriorating health, especially after Padre brought her back from Naples."

"He didn't and I know absolutely nothing about her going to Naples."

What purpose did it serve for Lorenzo's father to keep the truth from him? "Why did you decide to come home now? Everyone thought you'd forgotten about us."

"Verrocchio was a very strict teacher. All I did was study."

The geraniums in the urns they passed were vibrant. Lorenzo's letters were full of things he did with Lodovico and Matteo. She picked up a handful of soil; it was moist and cool.

"*Pappa* wouldn't give me permission to come back to San Michelle. I asked him several times."

"He gave you permission to come back now so why not before?" Lorenzo couldn't fool her just because she'd never studied at a private academy. "Your *Mamma* missed you more than your brothers. Do you have any idea how many times I read your letters to her?" She brushed he soil off her hands.

"What happened to *Mamma*?"

The wooden bench faced the sea and Caterina sat down. The early evening sky had lost most of its blue and a light breeze brought a welcomed coolness. The lemon and lime trees to the right were thick with leaves and heavy with yellow fruit and white flowers. A flock of noisy seagulls gathered above the rocky cliffs and flew in circle patterns then suddenly darted downwards. Dead fish must have washed up on the shore, Caterina thought. Lorenzo joined her. She shifted her body away.

"If you don't tell me what I should know, who will?" He rubbed his hands as if washing them.

"There's so much to say, Lorenzo, I don't know where to start." The seagulls had disappeared and taken their noise with them. "I don't know everything and there are some things that only Padre Valentine can explain to you."

"Tell me whatever you can."

"In 1910, just as the summer was leaving the earth, *Mamma* returned and brought happiness back to San Michelle. Her right arm was weak so she could only hug me with the other, I remember how pale her face was, but she was still so beautiful. "Caterina folded her hands in her lap. "Even though she had to rest every day, she and Sisina went for carriage rides and they usually took me. She wanted to visit everyone."

" Just like we used to at *Natale*."

"*Si*, Lorenzo. As soon as they saw her, they stopped working. '*Buon Giorno, Signora*,' they said as she passed by their cottages. '*Salve*,' she'd reply. The children ran up to her with flowers. It saddened her that there were so many of us missing. Vito Mabruco and his men had the villa ready for her when she returned but she wanted the flowerbeds and gardens replanted, new trees to replace the ones that had been destroyed and our cottages either rebuilt or repaired. Mabruco worked hard for the next year to make sure everything she wanted was done."

130

"I'll thank Mabruco when I meet him," Lorenzo said.

"He's away but he'll be back at the end of summer."

"Padre said that as time passed, you spent more and more time with *Mamma*." Lorenzo picked up a stone and turned it over as if he were examining it.

"She needed help with her rose gardens and we'd go together to my *Mamma's* grave. When Padre wasn't here, she'd teach me. Did you ever find out at the academy who your saint was?"

"*Non*. I'll ask Padre the next time I see him."

"Padre left after the storm too."

"He told me about Vatican Hospital and the cholera and diptheria victims," Lorenzo said.

"And he spent a lot of time in the south. He said that there were people in Reggio di Calabria who had been buried alive and whole villages disappeared. If *Mamma* hadn't come back, I'd still be alone."

"I'm so sorry about your *Pappa*."

"I wished we could have buried him next to *Mamma*. Ermenigildo searched everywhere but...he found Nicoletta..."

Lorenzo threw the stone on the ground and put his arm around her.

The empty space within Caterina was so big. She had lost her *Mamma* and *Pappa*, if *Mamma* Anna went away it would swallow her and she'd disappear. Her body seemed to melt into Lorenzo's; it would be easy to fall asleep. *Mamma* had been sick the past week and she'd had little rest.

Sisina and Armida crossed the ground and talked to a worker with a hoe.

"Who are those people with Sisina?"

"Armida's a servant who helps her and Interzino, the gardener. Mabruco brought them here."

"Bruno must miss your *Pappa* terribly."

"Even though Interzino's good, he complains all the time about the vegetables."

"I want to see Bruno."

131

"That would be wonderful. He'll be preparing *Mamma's* dinner."

The wind had become stronger and Caterina could hear the waves crash against the rocky beach as they made their way to the villa. "Do you remember when Grigio died?"

"And we weren't sure if he'd get into Heaven because Padre Valentine wasn't there to say prayers."

They still shared memories, Caterina realized; there were some things between them that hadn't changed.

Bruno dusted the cherub in the corner of the gilded wooden frame. *Signora* had given him the mirror and he'd hung it on the wall in his kitchen. "This cherub reminds me of you," she'd told him. Even though illness had changed the *Signora*, when Bruno looked at her, all he saw was her beautiful face. His reflection showed his missing front teeth but considering he was almost fifty, he still had lots left; he could eat almost anything he wanted if he cut it up in small pieces or cooked it until mushy. He missed his chocolate covered figs though and wished he'd eaten more of them. There was tomato sauce on his forehead; he wasn't certain if *Signora* was still able to see him but he wanted to look good in case she could so he wiped it off. He placed his hand on the back of the chairs as he went to the counter; his knees had been sore all day.

The *zuppa* he was cooking for the *Signora's* dinner would never be as good as the soup he used to make with Edoardo's vegetables. Edoardo grew the most delicious reddish-yellow carrots but Interzino's were always dry. Bruno picked up his knife and began chopping an onion. He was glad when his eyes started to burn for if Sisina or Armida walked into his kitchen they wouldn't know he was crying. If only he'd been able to stop Edoardo from going to visit his cousin in Reggio, Caterina would still have a *Pappa* and he'd still have a gardener and he'd be able to cook *Signora* better meals and maybe, she'd get better. Padre told him that what happened to Edoardo wasn't their fault, it was just part of God's plan and they both had to accept it. Bruno stopped liking God after he took Edoardo away and after what God had done to the *Signora*, Bruno was beginning to hate Him. Bruno didn't want to burn in Hell though so he knew that he'd have to talk to Padre soon or his soul would be dammed.

"Would you make me your minestrone with the thin vermicelli in it?"

Whose voice was that? Not Rinaldo's. He put the knife on the counter and wiped the tears off his face. Caterina had brought a tall fair-haired young man into his kitchen. Bruno blinked several times and saw the *Signora's* eyes. "You've come home." Lorenzo embraced him and Bruno rested his head against his shoulder. He was glad that Lorenzo's arms were long enough to wrap around him; Bruno couldn't remember the last time he had been held.

A little while later, Bruno sat across from Lorenzo at the kitchen table and Caterina set a plate of lemon cake slices in front of him. "She bakes the best *ciambellone*." She combed the narrow fringe of hair that circled his head with her fingers. "Your *Mamma* will get better now that you're back." Bruno did not want to waste time asking Lorenzo why it had taken him so long to return; all that mattered was that he was home, the *Signora* would get strong and everything would be almost like it used to be. Sisina walked into the kitchen. "Who's with *Signora*?" Bruno asked.

"Armida," Sisina answered. She turned towards Lorenzo. "I didn't know you were coming to San Michelle, *Signore*."

"I came to see *Mamma*. How is she?"

"Resting peacefully."

"Here, Sisina." Caterina put a slice of lemon cake on a plate.

"*Non, grazie*. I must go." Sisina walked out of the kitchen.

"I'll have that. I'm hungry from cooking all day."

"He's been having a lot of dizzy spells." Caterina pulled the plate away from Bruno. "Padre's going to ask Fiore what to do about them."

Bruno got up from his chair.

"And I've discovered your latest hiding place," Caterina said.

"When will *Mamma* wake up?" Lorenzo asked.

"Soon. Let's go and see her," Caterina said. She stood up and took his hand as they left the kitchen. Her childhood friend had returned.

CHAPTER FOURTEEN

Lorenzo sat on the stool in front of his mother's empty chair; she was still asleep in her bedroom. The early morning air that flowed through the window carried with it the promise of another lovely June day. After she awoke and Sisina had helped Caterina bathe and change her, *Mamma* would spend the day with he and Caterina, as had been the case for the past week. Lorenzo rolled his sleeves up to his elbows; he'd forgotten to change his shirt again.

When *Mamma* opened her eyes that first morning, they had no blue or green. The viridian Lodovico had given him for her portrait was no longer appropriate; there was in fact no paint on his palette to reproduce the dull grey film that clouded them. Even if he experimented with different variations of black and white, it would be impossible to replicate what he saw for he lacked the skill to create a colorless shade. Caterina was right though, *Mamma* could still see, for one moment after she opened her eyes, she smiled.

"*Uno, due, tre, quattro, cinque, sei, sette*! Seven days you've been here and you're always in the way. Get off that stool, it's for *Mamma's* feet, not your ass. You're going to break it, you're not a little boy anymore."

Even though they had only met once when he visited Taranto with his mother almost ten years ago, he did not have to turn his head to know it was Francesca.

"There's so much that has to be done to keep your *Mamma* comfortable and you've hardly been any help at all."

How had her leather boots moved so quickly across the floor?

She was beside him now. The white sleeves of her blouse were puffy like billowing sails on the boats in Cetraro's harbor on a windy day and her vest was covered in beads that reminded him of a rainbow.

"Most of the time, you're just a nuisance." She jabbed her finger at him.

Her high pitched voice still gave him headaches and if she kept this up much longer, Caterina would have to make him a lavender infusion.

"Everyone's too afraid to tell you because she's your *Mamma*."

A feather jutted out from the purple velour cap on her head. What kind of bird did it belong to? She wore looped earrings; Lorenzo had no idea how they managed to stay untangled from the coiled springs of her golden hair.

Francesca slapped her hands against the sides of her trousers; they were men's that had been tailored to fit her tiny frame. "And Caterina, of course, won't say anything."

Lodovico and Matteo would never believe the amount of words that poured out of her heart-shaped mouth. How could Lorenzo have ever thought that she was an angelic creature in a religious painting?

"But I'm not Caterina." Her blue eyes glared at him.

It should be impossible for a petite woman to cause such a raucous.

"Armida has to clean the room now but she can't if you're in it. So, please get out."

"Why can't you be kind to Lorenzo? He's tried so hard to help," Caterina said. She walked over to them. "I've thought of something else that he could do." She straightened his collar. "You could read your letters to *Mamma*."

"That's a good idea," Francesca said. She held her arms akimbo. "Maybe the sound of his voice will help her talk again."

"I'll start today," Lorenzo said.

"There's another problem."

"What now?" Caterina asked.

"I don't know exactly how to tell you this."

"Whisper it to me." She leaned over and Francesca stood on her toes.

"He needs to bathe." She spoke loud enough for Lorenzo to hear.

Caterina averted her eyes for if they met Francesca's, she knew they'd start to laugh and she didn't want to offend Lorenzo. "Tomorrow, you'll begin reading but now you must sleep." She took Lorenzo's hand in hers and grabbed Francesca's with the other. As they approached the doorway, Lorenzo said to Francesca,

"People in the village think that you resemble *Mamma* when she was sixteen."

They exited the room.

"That makes you my brother." Francesca crinkled her nose. "If you want me to be your sister, you have to bathe every day."

"And if you want to be my brother, you have to be a lot nicer to me."

Happiness was filling up the empty space in Caterina.

Most of the men had gone back to the harbor leaving the Central Station tavern almost empty. The Princess Irene would be departing Naples for the United States in the morning and there was much work to do. Santo sipped his brandy; the crumpled telegram he'd received from Sisina a few days ago lay close to Mabruco's glass. She had proven more valuable than either he or Buccella could have ever imagined.

"Do you want me to go back to San Michelle now?" Mabruco asked.

"Next month is fine, Vito. There's no need to change our plans. Verrocchio has assured me that Lorenzo's studies will not suffer and I've ordered Padre to return."

"And you'll be there by the end of August."

"*Si*. There's no reason to worry. It's already the middle of June and Fiore says that Anna can't last much longer. What possible

137

harm can come from letting Lorenzo spend the rest of the summer at San Michelle? I'll deal with things then."

"Armida says he's just infatuated with that servant girl."

"Your sister's been a great help to Sisina." Santo's camarilla was working so well; he took another drink. "She's probably right but when Anna's gone, I'll get rid of her."

Mabruco nodded in agreement then drank the rest of his brandy.

The rose bushes outside the window that Caterina tended were full of beautiful crimson red blooms and would look wonderful in the chapel in his church. Padre Valentine went over to the table by Anna's chair. He'd been able to convince Santo that even though Lorenzo's actions were rash, they had been motivated by concern for his mother. He was relieved that Santo had relented and agreed to allow Lorenzo to spend the summer at San Michelle; he had directed the priest to deliver this message to him.

The air was sour. The flower petals in the crystal bowls that Caterina had placed around the room were not able to dispel the smell of sickness. He picked up the *gobbo* on the night table. After the storm, they were everywhere. The villagers believed that they had angered God, for reasons unbeknownst to them, and in retaliation, He had summoned the creatures that lived underneath the earth to rise against them. Padre Valentine's efforts to explain that the storm was the natural after shocks of an earthquake had been futile; after twenty years the people still clung to their superstitious beliefs. The priest flung the statue through the window.

"Why did you do that?" Caterina asked. "That was Mafalda's good luck charm." She walked towards him.

"If I had known it was hers, I wouldn't have thrown it away."

"That shouldn't matter. I'd never do that to your St. Jude Medal."

"The *gobbo* is not a holy saint. I've told you, pagan practices won't help *Mamma* Anna get well."

"Then why has she been eating more since I put it on the table a few weeks ago?"

"We've discussed this already, Caterina. Fiore explained that there would be temporary relapses but *Mamma* Anna has suffered too many strokes and she'll never be the same; you must accept this. Your superstitious ways don't have the power to alter God's plan."

"But the macerated garlic helps and so does the yarrow tincture and the infusions and decoctions and poultices. And the water I brought back from Acquappesa last spring soothed her skin."

"These are different."

"According to whom?"

"Nature is not a false god."

"And your God is a true God, Padre? After what He's done to *Mamma* Anna, what kind of God is He?"

"It's terrible what happened to *Mamma* but it happens to many people. The *gobbo* is not a deity."

"Why do you get to decide which of my ways are right and which of my ways are wrong? Whenever I pin red ribbons on her nightdress, she sleeps longer."

"You know I have no problems with the red ribbons." They were exactly like the ones Anna used to give the little children at *Natale*, how could the priest object?

"The rose cream I made for you has gotten rid of most of the marks on your face."

The months that Padre Valentine had spent in southern Italy after the storm had exposed him to diptheria and cholera epidemics and taken their toll on his health. His thin frame reminded Caterina of a tree infected with insects, which were eating it from the inside out.

"Yes, all of these things are helpful. It's the pagan rituals that I cannot tolerate." Caterina was as stubborn as her father had been; he could no more stop Edoardo from going to Reggio di Calabria than he could convince Caterina that her superstitious ways were ineffectual. Yet each time this discussion surfaced, Padre Valentine was compelled to try again. If he'd tried harder with Edoardo, perhaps he'd have been able to dissuade him from leaving and he wouldn't have encountered the wrath of the storm; this might have made the difference between Edoardo living and dying. But then again, if Padre Valentine believed that God's plan for them was unchangeable, there was nothing that he could have done to save him. The problem was that after all that had happened, Padre Valentine no longer knew if he believed what he said about God.

"Why won't you admit that *Mamma's* sickness is the work of the evil eye and someone put the *facina* on her when she was in Naples?"

"The evil eye does not exist," Padre Valentine asserted.

"Then what happened to her?" she asked. "You've never explained everything to me."

"That's because I don't know. How often do I have to repeat myself?"

"Well you'd better think of something to tell Lorenzo because he's going to ask you as soon as he sees you."

There was a distance of about six feet between them; Padre Valentine felt as if they were in a duel. He had no one to blame but himself for he'd been the one who'd taught Caterina how to use her mind; he just never expected her to turn it against him.

"When you were away, I poured oil into a dish of holy water from the font in St. Ursula's Church and the water disappeared underneath. It's a sign, Padre; the evil *Mamma* saw in Naples is growing stronger in her, I think the lavender needs Mafalda's *gobbo* to help."

The curtains in the window snapped as a gust of wind flew into the sitting room and swept Lorenzo's letters and the priest's wooden crucifix on the carpet. The lavender stalk rose into the air then dropped back onto the table.

"You see, Padre. The mystics of the wind say I'm right."

"Why are you arguing again?" Francesca asked.

Padre Valentine hadn't noticed her enter the room and hoped that she hadn't seen him throw the *gobbo* out the window.

140

"You two aren't the only ones full of pain."

The priest approached Caterina; she was staring at the angel panel. He wondered if he wore the same look of exhaustion on his face as she did. He pulled her towards him; she did not resist. They held each other and a silent forgiveness passed between them.

"I'll find your *gobbo* and place it on the table next to *Mamma*." She touched his silver crucifix; her eyes expressed gratitude that the priest knew she would not permit herself to speak. "You need to relax, I'll tell Sisina to watch *Mamma* for a few hours, go with Francesca."

The two women left the room.

"June is almost over, when are you going to start spending more time with Lorenzo?" Francesca asked.

They sat on the wooden bench that Caterina and Lorenzo shared the afternoon he returned to San Michelle. Fancesca's blouse was the color of the yellow fruit of the nearby cedro trees.

"Everyone sees the way he looks at you. Bruno says watching you two look at each other is like watching two people drool over a delicious meal."

How would Caterina ever look at Bruno again?

"He's smart but he's absolutely useless." Francesca stood up and kicked a stone with the toe of her boot. It shot through the air and landed a considerable distance from them. Someone who barely weighed one hundred pounds should never be so strong. "He can't even get one infusion right." She sighed and plopped down beside Caterina. "Talking, writing, drawing, books. Handsome too...but otherwise, useless." She lay her hand over Caterina's; it was too small to be a woman's.

"So you think Lorenzo's handsome?"

"His hair's too long but he does have the most incredible eyes. Not that I see them that often of course. I mean they're always looking at you."

A blush warmed Caterina's cheeks that even the refreshing salty sea air could not cool.

"Do you remember last summer when we made slits in our wrists and pressed them against each other so that our blood flowed into each other's veins?"

"When we became blood sisters."

"I'm glad I never had a sister because I might not have liked her; blood can't make you a family."

Like Lorenzo's, Caterina thought.

"It's better that we got to choose each other."

Mamma Anna and Caterina had chosen each other too.

"What was the promise we made to each other?" Francesca asked.

"That because we shared each other's blood, we'd never be separated from each other and our bambinas would belong to both of us."

"If you can trust me with your *bambinas*, you can trust me with *Mamma* Anna. Let me take care of her now so that you and Lorenzo can spend more time together."

Were her feelings for Lorenzo that obvious? How was it possible for Francesca to know what Caterina had only begun to acknowledge?

"Valerio," Francesca whispered.

"The actor you fell in love with in Pisa."

"Because I was fourteen, *Pappa* thought I was too young."

"We'll find him," Caterina said. "After *Mamma* gets healthy again, I promise."

"But I don't know where he is."

The only time Francesca got upset was when they talked about Valerio; Caterina put her arm around her and it was as if she was cradling a young girl.

"*Pappa* pulled me out of school and sent me here, I didn't have time to get a message to him. I've written letters to my friends but no one knows what happened, he left the troupe and disappeared."

"Lorenzo will help us. And Padre Valentine."

The quiet that Francesca needed filled the next while.

"You and Lorenzo have the hunger for each other that Valerio and I once knew. Your blood is in me, Caterina, and I can feel it."

What Caterina felt for Lorenzo was different than what she had known when they were children and sometimes it frightened her.

"It's time for you and Lorenzo to be together."

Caterina knew that Francesca was right.

"I'd forgotten the beauty of the oleanders." Lorenzo examined the flowers on the cluster of shrubs; it was early morning in the first week of July. "Which color is your favorite, the salmon, white or bright yellow?"

"All of them," Caterina said. "Did you know that *Mamma* Anna calls them her "Gabriella flowers" after the archangel Gabriel because they're shaped like the bell of a trumpet?"

There was so much about his mother that he did not know. She'd been getting better since he'd come home so Lorenzo knew that he had time to make up for the lost years. "Come, I want to start sketching." They made their way across the open field.

"What did you do with the sketches you drew of me when I was little?"

"I kept them." He smiled at her in the way that he knew would make her avert her eyes. Caterina blushed easier than the women in Florence did and Lorenzo found this endearing.

"Tell me that Michelangelo story again."

"Which one?"

"The one about the painting you both liked."

"Your favorite." Lorenzo adjusted the strap of his satchel across his body and took her hand. "When *Pappa* sent me to Florence, my teacher would take me to the Uffizi Gallery to copy the works of the great artists that Michelangelo's teacher..."

"You mean Michelangelo Lodovico Buonarroti-Simoni."

143

"*Si*. That his teacher made him copy when he was my age."

"His teachers were the brothers Domencio and David Ghirlandaio and your teacher was Andrea del Verrocchio. Your teacher had the same name as Leonardo da Vinci's."

"Do you want to tell the story?"

"I've had three teachers too, *Pappa*, *Mamma* Anna and Padre Valentine. I disagree with Padre more than I ever did with the others."

"That's because he's your best teacher."

"Describe that painting for me now."

"It was by..."

"Masaccio and it's called 'Virgin and Child with St. Anne'. Go on."

"The three main figures are the *bambina*, Jesus, his *mamma*, Mary and her *mamma*, St. Anne. Mary is clothed in a dark blue robe with a light blue veil covering her golden hair."

"Blue like the Tyrrehenian Sea."

"Mary is sitting down and her hands are wrapped tightly around the baby Jesus on her lap. St. Anne is standing behind them, dressed in a pink gown..."

"Pink like the walls of your villa."

They swung their arms back and forth in the space between them.

"And she has one hand resting on Mary's shoulder and the other poised over the baby's head. They are surrounded by golden angels and there's a halo around everyone's head."

"Circles of gold like the sun. Lorenzo, you told me that you and Michelangelo both loved this painting because of the colors but I think that Michelangelo could have had another reason."

They stood still.

"Michelangelo's mother died when he was six years old and maybe when he saw the baby Jesus on Mary's lap, it reminded him of when he sat on his *Mamma's* lap."

"I never thought of that."

"But you know what I like the most about the Michelangelo stories?"

With one fluid motion, Lorenzo shifted his satchel to the side and pulled Caterina close to him. "His *Mamma's* name, Francesca." He kissed her and a warm flush rose from her neck.

"We're here." She slid her hands up his body and pushed them against his chest.

The shade that colored her face was identical to the salmon oleanders; Lorenzo would paint her portrait with the flower in her hair. He placed his satchel on the ground. "There." He pointed to a spot about ten feet in front.

"How lovely, the flowers that *Pappa* always said belonged to the earth and the sky." She walked over to the star shaped white jasmines.

"Stop there." Lorenzo sat on the ground and took out Matteo's notebook; he balanced it on his knee. "Move to the left." He wanted the first sketch to be perfect. "That's far enough." He tapped his finger on his mouth. "Sit down, tuck your feet under and fluff your skirt."

"Can you smell the flowers?"

"*Sì.* Now arrange your skirt in a semi-circle."

"The fragrance is sweet."

"Brush your hair off your face."

"I'll bring a bouquet back for *Mamma.*"

"Put your hands on your lap. Fold them together." Lorenzo reached into his satchel for a charcoal stick. "Lift your chin...turn it to your right."

"When are you going to start?"

"Hold still." He held up a piece of white chalk.

"I'm not a marble statue; my name's not David."

"Untie your shawl."

The shawl slipped off her shoulders.

"What's the...Why are you wearing *Mamma's* cameo brooch?"

"She gave it to me."

The notebook slid off his knees. "When?"

145

"While you were in Florence."

"But she was wearing it the first time I saw her."

"I pinned it on her nightdress before you came into the sitting room."

"Why?" The chalk fell to the ground and broke in two; he moved towards her.

"I didn't think you could deal with everything at once."

His trousers touched her hem.

"*Mamma* wanted me to have it."

'But I designed it for her. And Matteo made it. Didn't she like it?"

"*Mamma* loved it. When Padre gave it to her, her eyes sparkled like the sea does when the sun shines on it and the surface looks like it's covered with hundreds of tiny white diamonds."

"Then why?"

"*Mamma* told me to take it."

"You told me that she hasn't spoken in months."

"It happened after she returned from Naples, just before last *Natale*."

"What are you talking about?" The beads of sweat that dampened the curls on his forehead weren't the result of warm mid-morning sun.

"I was watching her sleep. I put her hand in mine and her fingers started to move. I thought I was imagining things at first. Then she opened her lips and released a sound but her words were mixed in with short breaths."

"What did she say?"

"Her eyes opened and they were the color of the sea again. She glanced down to where your brooch was pinned; it was a slight movement but I saw it. She wanted me to have her brooch." Caterina laid her hand on Lorenzo's. "Then *Mamma* closed her eyes and disappeared and she's never come back again."

CHAPTER FIFTEEN

The undulating movement of the silk cover on his mother's upper body assured Lorenzo that she was sleeping peacefully this morning. His letters were on the night table. Whenever he'd read them aloud to her, she never took her eyes of his face; his mother knew that he was there.

"Caterina will be pleased that I got her to drink all the chicken broth for supper," Francesca said.

"I hope she has a good visit with Fortunata," Lorenzo said.

"She hasn't spent as much time with her as she used to since you came home."

"I know. I don't think the little girl likes me. I gave Caterina some colored pencils for her."

The door opened and Sisina tiptoed across the carpet. "Lorenzo," she whispered. "Padre Valentine's waiting for you in your mother's sitting room."

"He's been so busy the last two weeks, he hasn't had much time to talk to me." Lorenzo now thought that the priest had been avoiding him. "I want to know what happened to my mother in Naples."

"Padre has told all of us countless times that he doesn't know," Francesca said.

The priest hadn't told him about his mother's illness so why should he believe him about this.

"I'm sure it was Padre who convinced your *Pappa* to let you stay at San Michelle until the end of the summer."

"Would you like me to change the *Signora* when she wakes up?" Sisina asked. "I can get you when she's ready for breakfast."

"*Per favore*," Francesca said.

"I'll send Armida up with a fresh nightgown and clean bed linens," Lorenzo said. "And Sisina, you'll have to stay with my mother. I'll read to her this evening."

"More sketching of Caterina this afternoon?" Francesca asked.

"*Sì.*"

"You must have filled up all of your notebooks."

"Just about. I'm glad that Benito sent me more."

"You haven't sketched any pictures of me yet," Francesca said.

"I will. Soon."

They left the room.

The only sound in Anna's bedroom was the rattle of Sisina's snoring. Anna was thankful that there was nothing Padre Valentine could tell Lorenzo about what had happened in Naples, only Santo and she knew the truth. Her husband would never say anything and it was locked up inside of her; there was no way Lorenzo could ever discover it.

She'd go back to sleep again, perhaps if she rested a little longer she'd be able to move her fingers more, they'd been so stiff lately. Anna knew that she was dying and wanted to hold Lorenzo's hand one last time. When she first heard Sisina and Armida talking, she thought it was a bad dream.

"Is she awake yet?" Armida asked.

"*Non,*" Sisina said.

"What difference does it make anyway?" Armida asked. "When she's awake she can't do anything."

There was hearty laughter; Anna decided to keep her eyes closed.

"Lorenzo told me to bring these to you," Armida said, "and Francesca wants you to wash and change her."

"Ever since Lorenzo came home, I'm getting stuck with doing more and more work," Sisina said. "I'm sick of it."

"It'll be over soon," Armida said. "He can only stay until the end of summer. Then the *Signore's* sending him back to Florence." Footsteps approached her bed.

"She already looks like a corpse and she's barely breathing."

"Have you heard from Vito?" Armida asked.

"*Si*. He asked about you in his letter."

The footsteps walked away.

"Maybe I can finally get someone to marry my brother so I won't have to take care of him for the rest of his life."

Santo had never told Anna that Mabruco and Armida were brother and sister. She wanted to breathe but didn't.

"I'd take care of Vito," Sisina said. "I shouldn't have to clean her up, I'm not a servant, I'm a Buccella."

"Sisina, relax. Fiore said that she wouldn't last more than a year and when she's dead, you get to go back to Cosenza."

Her throat constricted; Anna was choking herself.

"I'll stay here," Armida said. "I need a nap and that chair's so comfortable."

"If Lorenzo asks where I am, tell him that I have a headache and I'm resting."

"He won't ask about you. All he cares about is Caterina."

"*Signore* won't put up with that nonsense once she's gone," Sisina said. "When I live in Cosenza, I'll have my own villa and she could be my personal servant."

"Maybe the *Signore* will give her to you. He tells Vito all the time how pleased he's been with your service."

"Nobody had to tell me to send him the ledgers," Sisina bragged.

"Both the *Signore* and Buccella will reward you."

"I'd like to make Caterina do all the dirty work I've had to do for that one."

A horrible pain filled Anna's head.

"I'll get Bruno to tell Francesca that you've already fed her and she went back to sleep," Sisina said.

Was her head going to explode?

"*Grazie*, Sisina. I hope Mabruco marries you."

"Have a good rest, nobody will disturb you until it's time for her to eat lunch. You can sleep for almost four hours," Sisina said.

The door opened and closed and within minutes, the sound of Armida's snoring filled Anna's bedroom.

Everything was black when Anna opened her eyes and she knew that it was descending on her again, the memory of what had happened in Naples last autumn. She no longer remembered what had prompted her to go there, who had taken her or everything that had actually transpired. All that remained were disjointed flashes and strange images. She never knew what shape the nightmare would take, for every time it took hold of her, it presented a different version of the horror.

Anna walked through a door and entered a room that she had never been in before; the color burgundy was everywhere. It dripped down from the ceiling, oozed out of the walls, gushed forth from the paintings, bubbled up from the carpet and pooled in the corners. The windows were splattered, the drapes stained and the furniture drenched, it was as if the room was bathed in wine; Anna was terrified the color would drown her. She wanted to retreat but something propelled her forward into another room.

She heard Santo's laughter before she saw him. He was embracing a woman with long hair that was black and shiny like the plumage of a raven. It was wild and tangled and fell loose around her naked shoulders; she looked as if she'd just come in from a windstorm. Her eyes were dark with bits of gold and reminded Anna of two pieces of burning coal. Her red lips were full and wet and as inviting as a piece of fresh, ripe fruit. Her burgundy skirt fell low on her wide hips and Santo's hand was fondling one of her large breasts. Anna didn't want to admit that this man was her husband but when she saw the signet ring on his finger, she couldn't deny the truth. When Anna started screaming, Santo stopped laughing.

There was a beautiful angel with auburn hair and mossy green eyes and white skin. Anna thought she'd died and gone to heaven. She was so happy that she was going to see her mother and Mariangela and Nella; Anna had become Gabriella, the fourth angel on the panel. Wait. Now Anna was lying in a bed and the angel was patting her face with a damp cloth. The cool wetness soothed her hot skin. Padre Valentine appeared by her side and took her hand in his; she heard his prayers but couldn't feel his touch.

The angel and Padre disappeared and Santo and the woman with the red lips took their place. Santo started to laugh and the woman took off her blouse. Anna opened her eyes. Her nightdress was drenched in sweat and the gauzy material clung to her body and pressed against the sores on her skin. Armida was awake and staring at her.

"Did *Mamma* ever tell you the name of the fourth angel?" Lorenzo asked.

Padre Valentine turned around. "*Sì.* Gabriella."

"The archangel with the trumpet. The one who announces God's blessings."

What had happened in Naples was not good news. If Padre Valentine thought he still had a soul, he'd give it to the devil if it meant Anna's life could be spared; Satan, however, had claimed it many years ago and the priest had nothing else of value to offer him.

"I want to know what happened to *Mamma* in Naples. It's time, Padre."

Santo had prepared answers to all the questions he'd anticipated Lorenzo might ask and rehearsed them with the priest; if he failed to adhere to the approved script, Santo would expose his secret. The stakes as always were high, and Padre Valentine had to maintain his focus.

"Why don't you start at the beginning and tell me how on earth my mother ended up in Naples."

"Eugenio took her." The first words he uttered were true; this was a good omen.

"Francesca told me that much but I find it hard to believe that she didn't even know her father had come to San Michelle."

"Your mother sent him a telegram in Taranto last autumn that stated she'd received a letter which said Caesare had begun having seizures. She wanted to go and see him but didn't know where he lived and if Eugenio didn't come to San Michelle and accompany her there, she would take the train by herself."

"I didn't know Caesare was having seizures," Lorenzo said. "Show me this letter?"

"I can't; it disappeared."

"Padre, what are you up to?"

"Nothing." Just protecting his daughter and her mother from Lorenzo's father.

"Did my father ever see this letter?"

"*Non.*"

"Did Eugenio?"

"*Non.*"

"And my mother didn't show it to anyone at San Michelle before she left?"

"*Non,*" the priest said. Sometimes the truth was so strange; it looked as if it were false. This was a lesson in life that Lorenzo had yet to learn.

"What was my father's reaction to this?"

"He was upset." Santo hoped that the letter would provide him with a clue as to who had created this mess for him.

The cord around the waist of his cassock had loosened. Padre Valentine felt his bony ribs through the heavy fabric as he tightened it; the garment had become too big. When had he lost so much weight?

"Sisina found the letter my mother wrote telling everyone that Eugenio had taken her to Naples?"

"*Si.*"

"But *Mamma* couldn't hold a pen in her hand, she couldn't have written any letter."

"I know. And even though it was on her stationery, it wasn't her writing. The words were printed in block letters like a young child who was just learning how to form words."

"Show it to me."

"It vanished."

"Weren't you the last person to have seen it?"

The priest had given it to Santo as soon as he arrived in Naples. After Santo had read it; he'd thrown it into the fireplace.

"I'm sorry, Lorenzo, I just don't remember what happened to it."

The priest had intentionally included an apology, so what he said wasn't completely false. It was risky to use words that Santo hadn't selected for him but just because Padre Valentine's life was a lie didn't mean that he had lost his love for the truth. He walked over to the walnut sideboard, lifted the spouted pitcher off the silver oval tray and half-filled a crystal glass with water. He needed to refresh his throat before delivering any more words to Lorenzo.

"Tell me what actually happened in Naples." Lorenzo was standing behind him.

"I don't really know." And he didn't because he wasn't in the room when Anna had walked in on Santo and Fiorina. He put the glass down and faced him. Santo had told him that he had to look directly at Lorenzo for this part, he didn't want his son to think that his father had done anything wrong. "Your father said that when he walked into the entranceway of his house..."

"My father has a house in Naples?"

"He bought it last year for his business meetings." Santo also needed a home for Fiorina; the priest and Santo both had double lives. "Your mother was lying on the floor and your father sent for Fiore."

"My father walked into the entranceway and found her there, collapsed on the floor in the house where he conducted his business?"

"That's what he told me." Santo had also told the priest that Anna ran out of the room after she saw him with Fiorina. When the

153

truth didn't make a situation better, was it wrong to keep it hidden? And if a partial truth was based on good intentions, did it really constitute a lie?

"When did he tell you this?"

"I took the train to Naples and went directly to your father's house. As soon as I got there, his servant told me what had happened and that Fiore had admitted your mother to the hospital; I was to go there as soon as I arrived." The priest didn't have to memorize this, when the truth was simple, it was easy to recall and repeat.

"The servant was expecting you?" Lorenzo asked.

"*Si*," the priest said. "I sent your father a telegram informing him that your mother was coming and that I'd be there as soon as possible." Padre Valentine had known about Fiorina for years; if Anna ever found out, it would destroy her. As long as his actions didn't endanger Ortenza, the priest vowed to do whatever it took to keep Lorenzo safe, this was the least he could do for Anna.

Lorenzo scratched his chin.

"Your father was alone in the house, he hadn't received my telegram yet and he didn't even know your mother was in Naples until he found her there." Padre Valentine's performance so far would please Santo.

"Where the hell was Eugenio? You told me he took her to Naples?"

"He did."

"But he wasn't with her when my father found her?"

"That's what your father told me."

"This does not make sense. I'm not *stupido*, Padre."

That was why Santo and the priest had compiled and rehearsed these answers; Padre Valentine concluded that intelligence wasn't always an asset in people. If Lorenzo weren't bright, duplicity would have been easier.

"Eugenio showed up at your father's house the next day, after Fiore had admitted your mother to the hospital. He'd gone to a hotel like your mother had asked him to do, she wanted to see your father alone, they hadn't talked in a long time."

"And Fiore didn't know what caused my mother to have a massive stroke?"

"*Non.*"

This was the question that Padre had to be the most careful with. He was thankful that Fiore hadn't given him many words.

"Since her first stroke in Taranto, your mother's body was never the same. She's forty-two, Lorenzo, and Fiore said that what happened was simply a matter of time."

"And that's when she lost her ability to speak?"

"Fiore said she never uttered one word from the time he examined her in your father's house to the time he admitted her to the hospital."

"Even after *Mamma* regained consciousness?"

"Not one word. Your father insisted that your *Mamma* never be left alone in the hospital. If she ever said anything, the nurses were instructed to get him immediately."

"My father didn't stay with her?"

"Your father visited her as often as he could." Santo was adamant the priest present him in the proper light; in reality, he had shown up at the hospital intermittently. Santo had a doctor and priest to take care of things; that was why he had bought them twenty-one years ago.

"What about my brothers?"

"Benito didn't leave her side for the first few days but he had to eventually go and attend to Buccella's work."

"Where was Caesare?"

"With Buccella, in Cosenza. Santo instructed Eugenio to stop in Cosenza on his way back to Taranto and tell them what had happened."

"And you stayed in Naples?" Lorenzo asked.

"*Sì,* until Fiore said she was well enough to return to San Michelle, your father insisted that I remain there." Padre Valentine would have remained there anyway; it was his soul that he had lost, not his heart.

155

"And you brought her back here?" Lorenzo asked.

"*Sì.*"

"And my mother has had other strokes since she came back to San Michelle?"

"*Sì.*"

"Why didn't you tell me the truth about my mother's health when you visited me in Florence?"

"Your father would not permit me to do so."

Padre Valentine had answered Lorenzo's questions just as Santo had instructed him; Ortenza was still safe.

"When's he coming to San Michelle? *Mamma's* been back since before *Natale*, that's almost eight months? Where are my brothers? Don't they want to see her?"

Santo hadn't anticipated these questions, the priest had to think fast and be careful at the same time.

"There's nothing you can do about your father or your brothers, Lorenzo, all that matters is that you spend time with your *Mamma*." These words came easy to him; sometimes it made sense to tell the truth.

"Let's go to her now. I'm sure she's awake and would like to see us."

A little while later, Lorenzo closed the door of his mother's bedroom. Padre Valentine had already left. Armida said she'd awakened briefly but fallen back asleep. He walked down the corridor. What Padre had told him earlier didn't seem logical. Eugenio coming to San Michelle without Francesca's knowledge. Two mysterious letters that both disappeared. Lorenzo sensed that the priest had left words unsaid. He descended the stairs. Did this really matter though? Could it make his mother like the way she once was? Perhaps, Lorenzo thought, truth was overrated. He should have come home before but he couldn't change the past. He stepped outside. Padre was right. All that mattered now was that he be with his mother as much as possible. Lorenzo hurried down the pathway; it was almost time to meet Caterina. He vowed never to take those he loved for granted again.

CHAPTER SIXTEEN

The long-stemmed roses that filled the wicker basket on the ground were not alizarin crimson like those Caterina had placed in the chapel in Padre's church last week but vermilion red. In the past she would have described all of them as "plain red" but since Lorenzo had been home, he'd taught her so many new words, she now saw the world with more color than she'd ever imagined possible. The sky was never "blue" anymore, when it was streaked with purple, it was ultramarine, when there were traces of violet, it was indigo and when there were blue and green shades blended together, it was turquoise. Lorenzo even made the dull, gray sky that was a precursor to a summer storm sound beautiful by calling it "manganese blue." Today the sun was brilliant cadmium yellow and the sky, a deep, intense cobalt blue, Caterina never realized how beautiful San Michelle was until she saw it through Lorenzo's eyes.

"Watch out for the thorns, Fortunata," Caterina said to the little girl.

"These are the *Signora's* red roses that turn pink, aren't they?" Fortunata held the stem between the tips of two stubby fingers.

"*Si.*"

"And you brought them because today's Nicoletta's fifteenth birthday." She lay the rose at the base of the white wooden cross. "Who was your better friend? Francesca or my sister?"

"I've been very lucky; I've had two best friends." She planted a kiss on each of her plump cheeks; her olive toned skin was flawless.

"Pretty soon I'll know almost all the letters to print her name."

"You're very smart." Caterina tapped her pug nose and tousled her thick dark curls.

"You're sure you'll have time to teach me today?" Fortunata's pudgy hands played with the tiny pearl buttons that ran down the front of her blouse.

"We have all day."

"You forgot about me last week."

"Lorenzo's going to take care of *Mamma* Anna so that I can be with you."

"You said that before when you didn't come." She pushed her fat lips into an exaggerated pout.

"I'm sorry, Fortunata. He gave us some colored pencils for our writing lesson today."

"How could you forget about me?" Fortunata dropped her head and the flabby folds underneath her chin ballooned out.

It was a terrible truth but Caterina had in fact completely forgotten about Fortunata's lesson. She had been with Lorenzo and lost track of time.

"Do you like Lorenzo more than me?"

"*Non*, it's just that I haven't seen him for years and I missed him."

"So you don't miss me because you see me all the time?"

"Fortunata."

"Maybe I should go away?"

"Never."

Caterina put her arms around the little girl and patted her fleshy back. "I'm sorry. It will never happen again." Fortunata snuggled close and Caterina remembered the pain within her when Padre Valentine had forgotten about their lesson. Fortunata sniffled and moved away from her; the hurt in her eyes was like that of *Mamma* Anna's when Lorenzo was still in Florence. How had she become careless with someone she loved and how had it been so easy for her to forget? Was this something else that Lorenzo had taught her? If so, it was a lesson that she did not want to learn. He was *Mamma* Anna's son and Caterina should not have to be careful with Lorenzo. But then again, he did share Caesare's blood and perhaps he had a trace of darkness.

"Can we put the rest of the roses on the graves now?"

"That's a good idea," Caterina said. She stood up, grabbed the basket by its arched shaped handle and took her hand. They never hurried her for Fortunata's stumpy legs and flat feet didn't like to move fast.

"Fragola, Oresto, Luigi and Giuseppe," Fortunata said as she placed a rose beside each of the crosses.

A whole family gone. Caterina was the only one left in hers; if she died now, there'd be no one of her blood left either.

"*Mamma* misses Fragola." Fortunata waddled to the next plot.

More than anything else, Caterina someday wanted a child of her own. A little girl.

"There's only one rose left, Caterina."

"That's all we need." They knelt down and Fortunata handed her the flower. Would she name her little girl "Nella" or "Anna"? Caterina placed the rose on her mother's grave. How would she recognize the man she wanted to be her child's father? Their love would have to be different than the love she had for *Mamma* Anna, her *Pappa*, Bruno, Padre and Francesca. Fortunata rested a hand on her shoulder and Caterina patted its dimpled flesh. How would she know this kind of love?

It was late but Caterina had promised Fortunata that she'd stay by her bed until she'd fallen asleep. She snapped a lavender stalk off the bush and entered her cottage. It was another warm July evening but Caterina liked the woodsy aromatic smell of smoldering wood so she added a small log to the fire. Their cottage had not been damaged in the storm and the cross that her father had made was in the exact place on the mantle of the fireplace where he had set it fourteen years ago. The woolen blanket, which *Mamma* Anna had given him one *Natale* and that he covered himself with every night, was folded and lay against the wall next to the pile of kindling wood. Caterina had changed things as little as possible during the years she'd lived alone; sometimes, it made her think that her *Pappa* was still here with her.

She blew out the candle on the kitchen table, walked into her bedroom and slipped the lavender stalk underneath the stuffed burlap sack of her pillow. She opened the cedar box and unfolded one of *Mamma* Anna's white lace handkerchiefs. The cameo brooch rested in the palm of her hand.

The cream color profile of the woman Matteo had carved that rose from the hard brown agate background was exactly the way *Mamma* Anna had looked before her illness. She traced the oval frame with her fingertip. Bruno couldn't believe that he'd even separated the wisps of hair in the tendrils around her neck. Caterina folded the brooch in the handkerchief and put it back in the cedar box. Lorenzo was going to design another one for Matteo to make for *Mamma*. He'd said that since *Mamma* had given this one to her, he had no right to take it away. She lay down on the bed but knew she'd have difficulty sleeping: Caterina didn't like being alone as much as she used to since Lorenzo had returned to San Michelle. At the end of the summer when he went back to Florence, the emptiness within her would grow and Caterina was terrified that even Francesca, Padre Valentine, Bruno and *Mamma* Anna wouldn't be able to keep her from disappearing.

Lorenzo stood next to Caterina at the kitchen counter while she stirred the *stracciatella* soup Bruno had cooked for his mother's lunch.

"It's almost cool off enough. I'll have everything ready for you to take to her in a few minutes."

"*Signore*," Sisina said. "Would you like me to make your mother's tea now or wait until after she's had her lunch?"

"What do you think?" Lorenzo asked Caterina.

"After lunch would be better."

Sisina helped Bruno finish preparing Mabruco's lunch.

"Do you like my dress?" Caterina dipped a spoon into a small bowl of finely grated *Parmesan* cheese. Satiny white funnel-shaped Madonna lilies were set on a soft green background.

"It's exquisite. From *Mamma*?"

"*Sì*." Caterina sprinkled *Parmesan* cheese on the soup and the hard dry shreds melted into the broth.

A thin gold braid, which suggested a ray of sun, held her hair back from her face. The delicacy of the dress contrasted beautifully with her strong features and the modestly scooped neckline revealed a light smattering of freckles on her skin that he had never noticed before. Lorenzo wanted to know everything about Caterina. He touched the sleeve; the material was as soft as it appeared.

"Tear yourself away from her and have some of this," Bruno said.

"I'll be right back." He examined the plate of *affettato* on the table. "It looks delicious."

"The *salame's* always been my favorite." He put a thinly sliced piece of cured meat in his mouth.

"You can't get *salame* that good in Florence."

"Tuscans don't know how to make pork sausages as good as us Calabrians. Try the *sopressata*," Bruno said.

"I've missed your cooking, Bruno."

Sisina had cut a loaf of walnut bread into thick slices and was setting them on a plate. Lorenzo took a fig out of a bowl of apples, pears and grapes.

"*Mangiare*. Have a piece of *bruschetta* too. I rubbed the bread with garlic cloves then brushed it with olive oil. The garlic doesn't have as many cloves as Edoardo's did." Bruno picked up a piece of *mortadella*. "I raise the best hogs in all of Calabria."

"Are you talking about food again?" Francesca walked through the back door of the kitchen. "Are you ready Caterina?"

"Just about." She sprinkled more cheese on the soup.

"Why on earth do you have a burlap sack?" Lorenzo asked.

And what's the blanket for?"

"You're so noisy, Lorenzo. Don't you have a picture to sketch in your notebook?" Francesca dropped the sack on the floor beside Bruno and folded the blanket on the back of a chair. "Why do you have on your fancy dress?"

"They were drooling at each other again just before you came in," Bruno said.

"I intend to change before we go," Caterina said.

"Go where?" Lorenzo asked.

"They need their time too," Bruno said. He untied the cord around the sack and plunked a few apples into it.

"For what?"

"What about the other food?" Francesca asked.

"It's right here." Bruno added a few packages wrapped in cloth to the contents of the sack.

"What's in there?" Lorenzo asked.

Francesca peered inside the sack. "That should be enough."

Enough of what? Lorenzo turned around when he heard Caterina's suppressed laughter. "You too?" he said to her. "Why's everybody ignoring me?"

"Because we want to," Francesca said.

"Why don't you ever dress like a girl?" Lorenzo asked. Francesca was wearing heavy twilled trousers and a purple-grey oversized shirt rolled up to the elbows. "Don't your feet ever get hot in those boots?" The smooth leather was a rich terracotta color with a subtle hint of cadmium orange. They came up to her knee and Francesca had tucked her trousers inside them. "And did you even bother to comb your hair this morning?" She had gathered her hair on the top of head into a ponytail and tied it with a piece of twine. It stuck out in every direction and resembled dry stalks of bent straw. Lorenzo had already drawn numerous sketches of Francesca but even when he showed them to Lodovico and Matteo, he knew that they would doubt such a woman actually existed. They had yet to meet someone like her in Florence.

"Are you finished now, Caterina?" Francesca asked.

"Everything's ready." Caterina carried the bowl of soup to the table and set it on the tray. "I hope *Mamma* Anna can eat some of the eggs, *stracciatella* is one of her favorite *zuppas*."

"The *Parmesan* cheese will make her strong," Bruno said. "Why don't you cut a little piece of the *bruschetta* and put it on a plate, maybe Lorenzo can dip it into the chicken broth to soften it."

"I'll do that," Francesca said.

"What a gorgeous rose," Lorenzo said as Caterina placed the vase on the tray. Sisina moved out of the way so he could stand next to her. The chaste white cup shaped blossom was thickly petaled, its foliage a deep, rich green. Lorenzo wanted to do a black and white chalk sketch of Caterina holding the flower close to her face. He'd use his putty eraser to soften the edges and give the sketch an ethereal effect.

"I have an idea, Lorenzo. Why don't you sketch Caterina holding a rose?" Francesca placed a plate with the *bruschetta* on the tray.

"Let's go to my cottage now so I can put on my old dress."

"Now do you see why I don't wear dresses?" Francesca slapped Lorenzo's arm. "They're too much trouble. You never have to change trousers."

"It'll only take me a minute, Francesca, and we've got all afternoon. I'll be back in a few hours, Lorenzo."

"Let's go." Francesca grabbed Caterina's hand and led her out of the back door.

"Sisina," Lorenzo said. "Feed my mother and stay with her this afternoon." He faced Bruno. "I'm going to find out what they're up to."

Lorenzo dropped to his feet and lay flat on his stomach; he waited for a few moments then propped his upper body on his elbows and pulled his torso forward. He slithered silently through the narrow, sheathing blades of grass. The light breeze of the hot July afternoon helped camouflage his movements; Lorenzo did not want Caterina and Francesca to know that he'd been following them for the past hour.

They stopped at the edge of the woods about forty feet in front of him. Caterina spread the blanket on the ground and Francesca placed the sack in front of a nearby tree; they sat down next to each other. Lorenzo came to a halt; it was as if he were immersed in a sea of gold. To paint this scene, he'd blend yellow ochre and brown madder alizarin with just a hint of Naples yellow for the grass and sap green, raw umber and gray for the trees. In order to outline the leaves and branches, he'd use the tip of his bullet-shaped sable brush. He rested his head on his arm and the warmth of the sun lulled him to sleep.

"*Non*! Don't do that," Caterina screamed.

The alarm in her voice jarred Lorenzo awake.

"Leave me alone," she cried out.

Lorenzo jumped up at the same time that Caterina bolted out of the woods. Her hair covered half her face and her hands had hiked her dress above her knees.

"Caterina, I'm here." Lorenzo raced towards her. He scanned the trees but couldn't see what was chasing her. Caterina toppled forward.

"Caterina," he shouted. She pushed herself part way off the ground, her hair now completely covered her face and Lorenzo was terrified that whatever she was fleeing from would overtake her.

Francesca popped up, spun around towards Caterina and gesticulated wildly with her hands. Whatever was going after Caterina, wanted Francesca too, Lorenzo had to save both of them. His heart raced and a cold sweat broke out over his body. All of a sudden something dark leapt out of the woods; tore past Caterina and Francesca and charged towards him.

"Stop," Caterina yelled. She scrambled to her feet.

A sixty-five pound wolf was a short distance in front of him. The animal lowered its head, wrinkled its muzzle, bared its large teeth, fixed its eyes on Lorenzo and emitted a low and throaty growl, Lorenzo wasn't sure if he was going to vomit or faint.

CHAPTER SEVENTEEN

"Why did you frighten Lorenzo?" The wolf trotted over to Caterina. "Don't you ever act like that again." She tapped its nose with her finger. "*Capisco?*"

"I suppose we'll have to share our secret with him now," Francesca said. She brushed grass and dirt off his trousers.

"Are you alright?" Caterina asked.

The situation was surreal and Lorenzo found it impossible to respond.

"Your artist needs to paint some color on his face; I hope he brought his palette."

"Francesca, he's in shock." Caterina patted his cheek.

"He's always in shock."

"That's a one year old wolf." The animal growled and Lorenzo stepped back.

"He's smart," Francesca said. "Not very brave but definitely smart." She giggled.

"I promise, he won't hurt you," Caterina said.

"That's just his way of talking," Francesca said.

"He wants to meet you." Caterina took his hand and tried to make him pet the thick, dark fur around the wolf's neck.

"That's a wild animal." He yanked it away. "What's going on here?"

"We'll go for a walk and tell you our story."

They set off on a trail, Lorenzo was in the middle and the wolf was by Caterina's side.

"Are you feeling better?" Caterina asked.

"I'm fine." Lorenzo's hand trembled as he combed it through his hair.

"A wolf would never hurt you." Caterina patted the top of its head.

"They'll only attack if you try to hurt them," Francesca said. If you're nice to them, they'll be nice to you." She skipped down the trail, twirled around then stopped. "You must have read the story of how St. Francis of Assisi tamed the wolf?"

"Of course." A flush spread across his face. "I know all about wolves."

Francesca did some cartwheels.

"*Canis lupis*, one of the most sacred animals in our history. Romulus, the founder of Rome, was drowning in the Tiber River and it was a she-wolf that saved and cared for him."

"You can listen to his lecture, I'm going to run." Francesca bounded past them and the wolf loped at her feet.

"Padre taught me about wolves from your old textbooks," Caterina said. "Priests used to worship them and it was man who destroyed the relationship that once existed. They began to kill the animals for fun and not because their families needed them for food."

"You're right," Lorenzo said.

"Wolves began to fear man."

"That's why this relationship is so incredible."

"Those are the exact words that Padre Valentine used."

"Padre knows about the wolf?" Lorenzo asked.

"Actually, I think Bruno used those words too."

"Bruno knows?" Lorenzo's mouth was agape.

"Of course." It was good for Lorenzo not to be the one who always knew everything. Francesca returned and the wolf pranced around in front of them. "Everyone at San Michelle loves you." She ruffled its hair.

"Everyone?" Lorenzo asked. The color painted on his face was vermillion red.

"He knows we played a trick on him," Francesca said.

"I think we've had enough fun." Caterina said.

"I assume this means you two are finally going to tell me what's going on."

"*Sì*," Caterina said.

They walked down the trail and the wolf took his place beside Caterina. "It all started last autumn after *Mamma* Anna had left for Naples. Francesca and I were walking on a trail just like this one when the wind brought me a strange sound."

"I didn't hear anything at first but Caterina can do this "seeing with her ear thing" that her *Pappa* taught her so she made me stand still. Then all of a sudden, she hit me on the arm and marched off into the woods. I followed her and she walked over to this old oak tree as if there was a path leading to it."

"Its trunk was massive," Caterina said. "The roots were thick and raised above the ground that..."

"...they looked like the gnarled fingers of an old man." Francesca shaped the fingers of one hand into the image.

"I knelt down on the ground," Caterina said, "and started to brush away some of the branches cluttering the area around the tree."

"Do you remember how much it stunk Caterina?" She pinched her nostrils.

"You almost threw up."

"And the stench burned my eyes."

"I finished removing the branches and unearthed what looked like an opening of an animal's den. I peered inside and heard a sound."

"She let me poke my head in too and it sounded like the whimpering cries of a *bimba*."

They huddled together. The wolf sat on his haunches and the side of his body touched Caterina's dress. "I peered into the opening again and at first all I could see was black but as my eyes adjusted, the scene gradually revealed itself to me. Bits of fur were mingled with patches of blood."

"All of sudden though it got really quiet.," Francesca said.

169

"The crying just stopped."

"Then what happened?" Lorenzo asked.

"I noticed a shape trying to emerge from the shadows," Caterina replied. "It crawled towards the opening and when it was close enough, I stretched out my arms and pulled it towards me."

"It was a messy dirty smelly ball of fur, Lorenzo."

"I wrapped my shawl around it."

"What was it?"

"A wolf pup," Caterina said.

"We couldn't understand why it was all alone," Francesca said.

"Wolves live in-groups and there are usually five pups in a family," Caterina said.

"But no one was guarding this little one." Francesca shook her head.

"I named him, Shadow," Caterina said, "because that's from where he emerged."

Caterina and Lorenzo sat down on the blanket; Francesca stood on the ground a few feet away from them. It was late afternoon when they returned to the edge of the woods. Shadow nuzzled Caterina's hand. "Time to *mangiare*?" she asked. She brought her face close to its muzzle.

"Look what Bruno gave you to eat," Francesca said. She'd untied the sack, unwrapped one of the packages and set it in front of her feet.

The wolf slanted its large ears forward, yelped then raced towards her. His canine teeth ripped the meat apart and his long rough tongue licked the bones clean. Caterina poured water from a canteen into the wooden bowl they'd brought with them and the wolf lapped it up.

"Did you know that he has two layers of fur around his neck?" Caterina sat down beside Lorenzo again. "The top one is stiff and keeps him dry and the one underneath is shorter for warmth."

"Do you want your treat now?" Francesca asked. The wolf sat on his haunches and she gave him a *biscotti*.

"Have you noticed the grey tips and the patch of gold on his legs?" Caterina asked. "Would you paint me a picture of Shadow? Not a sketch but a picture with color."

"Of course," Lorenzo said.

"I'd like one of him sleeping. He covers his face with his tail to keep warm and he looks so sweet." Shadow trotted over to the blanket and lay down, resting his head on Caterina's thigh. Francesca pulled a shawl out of the sack and stretched out in front of them. She used it as a pillow and fell asleep. "When we're outside like this, both Francesca and Shadow love to take a short nap."

"So who else actually knows about Shadow?" Lorenzo asked.

"Well, in addition to Padre and Bruno, everyone at San Michelle," Caterina said. "Mabruco built a small shed for Shadow at the edge of the estate so that he wouldn't frighten the other animals."

"And that's where he stays?"

"*Si*. When he was younger, we had to tie him to a tree but he doesn't wander now." Lorenzo put his arm around her shoulder and Caterina leaned against him. "Fortunata loves to feed him *biscotti*."

"Wasn't everyone frightened of him at first?"

"That's why we kept him a secret for almost two months until Padre came back. Padre was the one who convinced everyone that Shadow wouldn't hurt them."

Lorenzo kissed her on the cheek; she moved her mouth closer to his. "*Dio*," he yelled an instant before toppling backwards. The wolf had thrust his head into his chest.

"What are you doing, Shadow?" Caterina asked.

"Why did you wake me up?" Francesca snapped.

Shadow's face was just inches above Lorenzo's.

"Shadow," Caterina said. The wolf raised his head and backed away. Lorenzo pushed himself up. "Francesca, I think you and Shadow better go chase some butterflies for awhile."

"*Si*." She bounded off and Shadow followed her.

"I don't want to hear one word from you," Caterina said. She covered his mouth with her hand. "Shadow doesn't know you yet."

171

She shifted her body and pulled his arm around her shoulder. "Do you know what *Pappa* used to tell me about Montea?"

"That it's the highest mountain we can see from San Michelle?" Lorenzo replied.

"And that it's as high as the road into Cetraro from your villa is long."

"Only the smaller mountains are on our estate, not Montea."

"Montea belongs to all of the Calabrian people and that's where Dreamer's Rock is too. On the edge of the smaller mountains below Montea."

"I haven't heard anyone mention Dreamer's Rock in a long time," Lorenzo said.

"Don't the people in Florence know about it?" Caterina asked.

"*Non*, Caterina. Florence is a very different world and..."

"I want to see your Florence, Lorenzo. I want to visit the Uffizi and stand in front of the painting that you and Michelangelo loved. I want to touch the David that he released from the marble. I want to walk across the Ponte Vecchio and look at the swirling waters of the Arno River just like Leonardo did. Padre Valentine says there are ships as big as your villa in the Naples' harbor and Francesca told me about a tower in Pisa that leans and looks like it's going to fall over but never does. I've never been anywhere except Cetraro and San Michelle, Lorenzo. I wish I could be like Elda and Sisina and Armida, but I can't. The books I've read have made me restless and I want to see their words for myself."

"Is it safe for us to come back?" Francesca yelled. "Has he calmed down yet?"

They were about ten feet away. "*Si*," Caterina said.

"I want you to see your words," Lorenzo said.

"I've never chased so many butterflies," Francesca exclaimed.

"It's time to gather our things," Caterina said. It was the last week of July and in one more month, Lorenzo would be gone, back to his life in Florence with Verrocchio and Lodovico and Matteo and he'd forget all about her. How could she go back to her life when he was no longer here? Lorenzo had changed everything at San Michelle.

"Get off the blanket, Lorenzo, so I can fold it up," Francesca said.

"Are you alright?" Lorenzo asked.

His hand pressed against the small of her back; it fit the space perfectly.

"I'll take Shadow back to his shed and catch up with you two later on the trail," Francesca said. "Watch how many cartwheels I can do in a row."

They didn't take their eyes off Francesca until she and Shadow disappeared from sight.

"I've never met a sixteen year old woman who's still a little girl," Lorenzo said.

"Francesca's a woman, Lorenzo, and you don't know anything about her."

"Did I say something wrong?"

Her anger had nothing to do with Lorenzo but Caterina needed to release it and he was there. "Do you know the real reason why Eugenio sent Francesca to live at San Michelle?"

"To spend time with *Mamma*," Lorenzo said.

"*Non*. It was because of Valerio,"

"Who's Valerio?"

"An actor studying the character of "Harlequin" the acrobatic clown who was a member of the *commedia dell'arte* visiting the school in Pisa that Francesca was attending. They met and fell in love and when her teacher found out, she told Eugenio who immediately sent her to San Michelle."

"I never would have imagined such a thing," Lorenzo admitted.

"Strange words for an artist." Caterina regretted the spitefulness of her words. "It gets worse." He held her hand and her anger began to dissipate as if he was drawing poison out of her body. "Francesca knew that someday she'd have to marry a man her *Pappa* chose but this didn't bother her."

"Until she met Valerio."

173

"Francesca's determined to marry him but she doesn't even know where he is."

"That's horrible."

"Valerio's the one who taught her how to do cartwheels. Francesca and I are blood sisters, Lorenzo. We feel each other's pain." Caterina pressed her body into his and the residue of anger evaporated.

"Then Francesca's pain will be mine too."

The ground rolled out in front of Caterina and Lorenzo for ten feet to the shoreline of the stream, one of the many that ran through San Michelle. They sat on a fallen tree trunk; a stand of pine trees was across from them. The afternoon rays of the early August sun painted the water as if it were a giant paintbrush, threading it with thin ribbons of blue and grey and green.

"This is where Francesca and I became blood sisters. I counted over one hundred jasmine stars in the sky that night and we fell asleep listening to the waves."

A plump reddish-brown thrush perched on a branch of a nearby oak tree and sounded its loud trill. "It's a gorgeous spot. I can see why you and Francesca came here with *Mamma*."

"Mabruco had his men clean up the underbrush for us."

"I've thanked him several times for all he's done," Lorenzo said.

Shadow sped by Lorenzo, plunged into the stream and began biting the waves. He peeled a strip of bark off the log.

"*Mamma's* barely eaten anything the past few days and it seems that all she wants to do is sleep," Caterina said. "It's been a week now since she's even been in her sitting room."

"It's just a not-so-good period for her. That's what Padre said. She'll get better." Lorenzo hoped that Caterina would not hear the doubt in his words. "I read her a Leonardo fable yesterday. The one about the lion awakening his cubs. "

"She encouraged you to draw right from the beginning."

"The only reason *Pappa's* interested in my art now is because Benito's convinced him it could bring more money into his business."

"I've never understood how you and your brothers could have the same blood."

Shadow's body was pointed directly at Caterina. "He watches you all the time."

"Padre says that Shadow knows I'm the one who saved him and he feels it's his duty to protect me." The wolf rested his head on the ground between his front paws and a few moments later, closed his eyes.

"He finally trusts me." Lorenzo smiled.

"I told you Shadow just needed time to get to know you." Caterina put her elbows on her knees and rested her chin within her hands. "Mafalda told me that because a *Mamma* carries the child within her, she gets to choose which one she gives her blood to. And the one she chooses also receives her soul. That way, the *Mamma* never dies, her spirit lives on in her chosen child. You only have your *Mamma's* blood."

"And you have both your *Mamma's* and *Pappa's* because you were their only child?" Lorenzo asked.

"That's what Mafalda told me."

"Families are strange, Caterina." Lorenzo threw the strip of bark onto the ground. "Leonardo's father, Piero da Vinci, was a lawyer and his mother a peasant girl. They weren't married and as soon as Leonardo was born, his father took him away from her. Leonardo's mother never got to know her own son."

"Michelangelo lost his *Mamma* when he was a young boy. Maybe an artist can only achieve the greatness that is within his blood after they lose their *Mamma's*."

A shiver raced up Lorenzo's spine.

"Who do you like better? Michelangelo or Leonardo?" Caterina asked.

"Leonardo definitely. He could sing, play the lute, draw what was inside our bodies, recite the names of stars, design bridges, paint, sketch and, if he were here with us now, take a lump of clay and mold it into the shape of your head."

"When your *Pappa* sent you to Florence after the storm, you were the same age as Leonardo when his *Pappa* took him there." Caterina walked over to the stream. "Sometimes I think your *Pappa's* family is a lot like the Medici's were in Florence when Leonardo lived there. They ruled the city and got whatever they wanted just like the Marino's do in Cetraro." She bent down and swished her hand in the water.

The incident of Clorinda's drowning returned to Lorenzo.

"Do you know what else I thought of, Lorenzo?"

Her voice stopped the memories before they had completely formed and tainted their time together. She stood up and the sun lit up the auburn streaks in her hair as if it were on fire.

"Leonardo used to wander around Florence and was able to keep pictures of everything he saw in his head and later when he was back in the workshop, he would draw these pictures exactly and people would recognize them." She walked back to him.

"I've always been able to do something like that too."

"What do you mean?" He fiddled with the ribbon around her waist.

"When *Mamma's* flowerbeds are empty, I can look at them and see them as they are in the summer. Even though I haven't seen *Pappa* since I was a little girl, his face is still perfectly clear; if I was an artist, I could draw it and it would look exactly like him. And when Padre teaches me and uses words that I've never heard before and need him to explain and have no use for myself, well, I've never forgotten them."

Lorenzo sat her on his knees and she put her arm around his neck. "You know the real reason why I like Leonardo more than Michelangelo." He nuzzled her neck.

"Tell me again." She twirled his curly hair with her fingers.

"Because the name of his *Mamma* was Caterina. I have something very special that I want to give you." He eased her off his lap.

"What?"

He reached into his shirt pocket and gave her a package wrapped in one of his mother's lace handkerchiefs.

Caterina unfolded the delicate material. It was a jeweled cross with an aquamarine stone in the center surrounded by four iridescent opals. She held it up by its fine linked gold chain and a beam of sun passed through the blue green stone and made it glow. "It's alive, Lorenzo. It has its own light."

"I created the design and selected the stones and Matteo crafted it. Do you like it?"

"The stone's the color of your eyes." Caterina touched his face with the tips of her fingers. "And for the rest of my life whenever I look at this cross, it will be your eyes that I see."

Lorenzo embraced Caterina but he couldn't hold her close enough. He kissed her lips; they were warm but cool compared to the intensity burning within his body. It was clear to him now; Caterina was the reason he had returned to San Michelle.

CHAPTER EIGHTEEN

Bruno hoisted himself up the last step, lumbered down the corridor and entered Anna's bedroom. He shuffled across the carpet then slumped into the chair by her bed. How much longer would his legs be able to carry him? It was mid-morning, and the *Signora* was still sleeping. For the past few weeks, this was all she did. Caterina had been able to get her to drink a cup of chicken broth for supper last night; at least there was something he could cook that she'd eat. Bruno rubbed his knees. Yesterday one had buckled and if Lorenzo hadn't been near him, he would have toppled forward onto the hard floor and smashed his head. Perhaps this would have been a good thing; the *Signora* would never get better and he didn't want to live in a world where she did not exist. Padre Valentine would be stopping by shortly; he'd rest for a few minutes then begin his journey back to the kitchen.

The late morning wind whipped the water into white-capped curling waves that crashed against the rocky shore and broke into pieces that reminded Padre Valentine of tiny shards of glass. If he jumped and experienced terrible torment and prolonged suffering and endured a horrible death, would God forgive him and let him into Heaven? The wind pushed the priest back; it had rejected him. He turned around; Bruno was waiting for him and he needed to return to the villa. Thankfully, Padre Valentine told himself, his friend had never spurned him. He stepped forward. Surely, there was something he could do to redeem his soul and reclaim his place with God.

There had been enough tuna sauce to cover the sliced cold veal; *vitello tonnato* was one of Bruno's favorite luncheon dishes and he was glad that Mabruco had left him some. He licked the sauce off his fingertips; he had blended the right amount of lemon juice and olive oil into the egg yolks. He pushed the empty plate away and pulled the one with a slab of chocolate zucchini cake towards him; he shoved a piece into his mouth. The back door opened and Padre Valentine walked into the kitchen.

"What are you doing? Fiore said you're supposed to reduce the amount of sweets you eat. Are you trying to kill yourself?" He seized the plate and plunked it down on the counter.

"I don't care anymore." The priest sat down next to him.

"Your knees wouldn't give you as much trouble if you lost a little bit of weight."

Why should he have to watch what he ate? When the *Signora* was gone, he wouldn't have to climb the stairs to her bedroom so why did he need strong knees? Without the *Signora*, food would be all that Bruno had and even if he ate everything, it wouldn't fill him up and make him stop missing her. What Padre Valentine felt for God was nothing compared to what Bruno felt for the *Signora*. The truth was Bruno wanted to die. Not right now but one minute before the *Signora* so he wouldn't have to experience the pain of losing her. He'd die then a minute later be in Heaven. Grigio would pull the cart with him, Nella and Edoardo to the gates where the *Signora* would be waiting; Bruno would help her up into the front seat and the *Signora* would sit beside him. They would enter paradise.

"I know you're upset about the *Signora* but there's nothing else we can do. Her time is soon. We must accept that."

"There can be no San Michelle for me without the *Signora*."

"You can't talk like that, Bruno."

"But I just did."

"What would happen to Caterina if you weren't here?" Padre Valentine asked.

If Caterina ever discovered that he had failed to stop her *Pappa* from leaving, she'd blame him for his death and no longer love him. Bruno couldn't bear the thought of losing both the *Signora* and Caterina. At least when he died; the secret would be buried with him for Padre would never tell Caterina because he had the same fear. "You could take care of her."

"Stop this." The priest put his hand on Bruno's arm; he bruised easily now and there would be a mark on the skin tomorrow. "Do you understand me?"

"Of course, I just don't agree with you, Padre."

Sisina walked into the kitchen. "The *Signora's* awake."

"I'll go to her," Padre Valentine said. He walked over to the counter, put the plate in front of Bruno and left the kitchen.

Bruno pushed the cake away. He wasn't hungry anymore.

The tip of a lavender stalk poked out from underneath Anna's pillow; Padre Valentine repinned the St. Jude medal to the top of her nightdress. "Hello, Anna." There was no response. He wanted to touch her hand but didn't dare. The psoriasis had worsened just as Fiore had predicted. Dry, scaly material had built up underneath the nail beds and separated them from the skin. The joints between her fingers were inflamed and the tissue had become stiff and unyielding. Red oval patches with silvery scales covered her skin.

Padre Valentine folded his hands against his silver crucifix. "*Saint Jude, glorious apostle, faithful servant and friend of Jesus. Pray for me, your servant, Anna, who is so miserable. Make use, I implore you, of that particular privilege accorded to you to bring visible and speedy help where help was almost despaired of. Come to my assistance in this great need that I may receive the consolation and help of heaven in all my sufferings. I promise you, O blessed Jude, to be ever mindful of this great favor and do all in my power to encourage devotion to you. Amen. Saint Jude, pray for us and for all who honor you and invoke your aid."* The last sentence was not just dedicated to Anna.

The *gobbo* was on the night table; Caterina had moved it here because Anna rarely spent anytime in her sitting room anymore. He walked out onto the loggia that extended from the bedroom. There was a roof above the open gallery supported by columns on each side. Padre Valentine leaned against the half wall; a black-headed gull was suspended in the air a few feet in front of him. Its black tipped wings, white under part and dark spot behind its eye were clearly visible. The wind was so strong, that the bird could not move forward or backward. It was powerless against the force that held it, just like Padre Valentine had been ever since he agreed to the pact with Santo twenty-one years ago.

The priest reentered Anna's room. His cassock brushed against her chair as he took his place beside her bed. The first few days after her stroke in Naples last autumn, Fiore wasn't certain if she'd survive. Ortenza didn't leave her side and Fiore said her vigilance made the difference. "That was my daughter, Anna," he whispered. "The young woman who nursed you, her name's Ortenza. Do you remember waking up and calling her "an angel"? You thought you'd died and were in Heaven. You asked for your *Mamma* and Mariangela and Nella." Ortenza had given Anna almost another year of life, enough time for her to see Lorenzo again. If that was the reason Ortenza had been born and why he had made the pact with Santo, the price that Padre Valentine had paid was worth it. "I promise you, Anna, I will take care of Lorenzo." He made the sign of the cross on her forehead. "And I will make sure that no harm ever comes to Caterina." Padre Valentine sat down in the chair, repeated the promise he'd made to Anna over and over again then, after a short while, walked out of the room.

Was it day or night? Anna didn't know for her eyes could

181

barely see through the grey color. Where had the fat man gone? She liked his face. She wished that the girl with a purple feather growing out of her head would dance again too. A priest had visited but Anna's hearing must have gone array because she thought he said that he had a daughter who was a nurse taking care of Lorenzo. Priests didn't have children and she didn't know anyone called Lorenzo. Anna's right arm and leg no longer moved and now her entire left side didn't work either. The last time someone had given her tea, she thought she was going to drown.

Anna didn't really want to die; it's just that she no longer wanted to live. Her mind was almost as broken as her body. Who was the handsome fellow in the white shirt walking along the beach? He had such a dazzling smile. The two boys playing on the deck of the fishing boat were so sweet. If she knew their names, she'd say hello to them.

Most of all though, Anna wanted to see the young woman with the mark of the rose on her wrist and the young man who had the eyes of the sea. They loved each other; she'd seen them embrace. And Anna knew they loved her, she could still feel their kisses on her forehead. When she took her final breath, Anna hoped that it would be their faces that her mind last remembered.

Lorenzo handed Sisina his mother's dinner tray; the cup was half-filled with chicken broth. Caterina sat on the edge of the bed. "At least *Mamma* ate more than she did today for lunch," Lorenzo said.

"Is there anything else that I could bring your *Mamma*, *Signore*?" Sisina asked.

"A cup of tea with your *millefiori* honey would be wonderful," Caterina replied. She drank almost all of it yesterday at breakfast." Sisina left the room.

It had only been a few sips, Caterina acknowledged, but it was more than she had the day before and it was reason enough for celebration.

"Which letter are you going to read, Lorenzo?" Caterina asked.

"*Mamma* liked the one about how you won your fencing match." She brushed a strand of hair off his mother's forehead.

In the past two weeks, her skin had become so taut that the skull beneath was clear, sometimes she resembled a living corpse. "I remember her smile." Would he ever see it again?

"Move the vase closer in case *Mamma* opens her eyes," Caterina said. "The rose is starting to turn pink."

The rounded base of the glass vase slid easily across the smooth surface of the night table.

"And open one of the doors to the loggia; if there's a breeze, it'll bring the scent of flowers into the room."

The warm evening air brushed against Lorenzo's face. He leaned against the half wall; Armida and Mabruco were standing in front of the cliffs overlooking the sea. A breeze carried the scent of flowers past him into his mother's bedroom, Caterina had been right. In three weeks, he was supposed to return to Florence. Lorenzo did not want to leave San Michelle but he did not know how to stay. *Mamma's* time was soon, Lorenzo realized that, but his time with Caterina was only beginning.

How could he look at Michelangelo's "David" and not remember Caterina's yearning to see the statue? The Arno River would remind him of the stream where he'd given her the jeweled cross. And every time he and Matteo made a cameo brooch, Lorenzo would recall the story of his *Mamma* giving Caterina their first one.

Pappa would never approve of Caterina or even understand his feelings for her. Lorenzo stepped back from the railing. Caterina belonged to *Mamma*, *Mamma* had been right about her rose birthmark. And when *Mamma* was gone, Caterina belonged with Lorenzo. There was no doubt in his mind that this was how things were meant to be, the only doubt within Lorenzo was how it could all happen. He walked back into his mother's bedroom.

Caterina was massaging rose cream on his mother's hands; her fingers had frozen into a claw like shape. They'd never be able to hold hands like they did when he was a little boy.

"I think I feel a little movement."

He kissed Caterina on the cheek and his mother's eyes opened.

"I told you *Mamma* would get better."

"*Amare, Mamma,*" Lorenzo said. She closed her eyes.

"At least she knows we're here. Read a letter now."

He lifted the lavender stalk off the pile of his letters and sat down in the chair. Lorenzo didn't share the optimism in her words but why should he be the one who took away Caterina's last vestiges of hope? He shuffled through the letters and randomly selected one dated July 23, 1912.

"Dear Mamma,

Today was glorious and Verrocchio gave us the afternoon off from our classes. Lodovico wanted to visit "Casa Buonarroti" so that's where we spent most of our time. Matteo, of course, came too.

Michelangelo's house is on "Via Ghibellina" in the very heart of Firenze, Florence's real name. He bought the house and his family has kept it for almost three hundred years. There are marvelous frescoes by Jacopo Vignali in some of the rooms as well as a reliquary of St. Agatha. I stood in the same courtyard that Michelangelo did! Isn't that incredible, Mamma?

My classes have been going very well. In another two years, I will be finished my studies and qualify as a lawyer. I know this will make Pappa proud. I must go now for I have much to do. I'll write again soon.

Amare Mamma,

Lorenzo"

Where had he gone that was so important he didn't have time to ask his mother even one question about herself? Lorenzo couldn't remember. *Mamma* had been his first teacher; why had he not shared all the new words he'd learned in Florence with her at a time when she needed to hear them the most? He crumpled the letter and tossed it aside.

Caterina came to him and eased herself onto his lap. She cradled his head and he buried it within the soft valley of her breasts. How had she known that he needed to be held? She caressed his hair and gave him the touch that he craved to feel. The beat of her heart pulsed and stirred up an element deep within him that no other woman had ever moved before. When had it become unnecessary for them to use words to speak? And when had their understanding of each other shifted to this new dimension? Lorenzo was an artisan of words yet he had none to define what it was that existed between them now. Caterina brought his face to hers and when their lips met, Lorenzo knew that they had crossed into a different realm. There was no way of going back to what was once between them; everything had irrevocably changed and Lorenzo knew that the excitement and eager anticipation within him was matched by that within Caterina.

CHAPTER NINETEEN

Caterina snapped a stalk of lavender off the shrub. The sun had begun to rise above the cottages and promised another warm day. She handed it to Francesca. "Did you see the sunset last night? There was a transparent wash of orange over the chrome yellow; it was spectacular."

"You're starting to sound like Lorenzo. He's probably been waiting for you at the stables for hours."

"I want to leave as soon as possible. I'd like to get to Dreamer's Rock by noon," Caterina said.

Francesca tucked the stalk behind an ear.

"Don't forget to put the lavender underneath *Mamma's* pillow," Caterina said.

Mamma slept more and more every day and for the past week, all she drank was chicken broth. The final week of August had just begun and Lorenzo would be leaving for Florence soon; *Mamma* had to start getting better, there wasn't much time left.

"I still don't understand why only first born sons can climb to Dreamer's Rock and spend the night there with their *Pappa's*," Francesca said. "We don't have a ritual like this in Apulia."

"It's to mark his passage into adulthood. My *Pappa's* family believed in this ritual too but applied it to all first born children, not just their sons."

"And that's why he took you there?"

"*Si*. The summer before the storm." Caterina waved at Armida

186

and Interzino as they passed by in a cart on their way to the villa. "Most Calabrian families don't share this belief."

"Which is why you've kept it a secret."

"*Sì.*"

"And that's why you won't tell me what happened to you at Dreamer's Rock?"

"Not until I've told Lorenzo." Shadow trotted around the corner of the cottage and sat on his haunches beside her. "Now recite what you're going to tell anyone who asks where Lorenzo and I are today and tomorrow."

"How many times are you going to make me repeat this?" Francesca flopped backwards onto the ground with dramatic flourish.

"Only once more."

"You're going to do Elda's chores then cook supper for Elda and Ermenigildo because Elda hasn't been feeling well lately. Then you're going to spend the rest of the evening with Fortunata." Francesca sat up and touched the tip of Shadow's nose with hers; the wolf pulled his head back. "Teaching her letters and writing."

"Continue," Caterina ordered.

"Lorenzo's going to be painting and sketching scenes of the coastline and Cetraro for Lodovico and Matteo." She slapped the palms of her hands together. "Are you happy now?"

"*Non.* What am I going to be doing tomorrow?"

"Helping Elda dry herbs."

"And *Mamma?*"

"There are lots of us to watch *Mamma.* Me, Padre, Bruno, Sisina and Armida." Francesca stood up.

"You'll have to watch Bruno too. He's been having more dizzy spells lately."

"Why can't you tell me why you have to take Lorenzo to Dreamer's Rock?"

"I will tell you as soon as we come back."

"Lorenzo's such a nuisance. I'll see you tomorrow around dinner."

"When I was little, *Pappa* took Caesare and Benito hunting wild boar in the mountains below Montea near Dreamer's Rock." Lorenzo angled his body in the saddle towards Caterina as they approached the gates of San Michelle.

"But that's not the reason you're anxious to explore the area?" Caterina asked.

"*Non.* One of my teachers who'd been there said it was beautiful "especially for an artist." Beech, pine, spruce and turkey oaks cover the slopes and the area is full of roe deer, martens and wildcats." He patted the strap of his satchel strung across his chest. "I'm glad I brought my notebooks."

"My *Pappa* loved the birds the most: the peregrine falcon, eagle owl and goshawk. We spent the night at the base of Dreamer's Rock the summer I was eleven."

"I'm glad you suggested we visit the area. *Pappa* never had time to take me and because I wasn't the first born son, there was no need for him to do so."

"Did you ever find out what happened to Caesare at Dreamer's Rock?"

"*Non.* It's a secret between him and *Pappa.* Not even Benito knows."

They passed through the gates and headed in a northeast direction. In one week, Lorenzo was supposed to leave San Michelle. He knew there was a way for him to take Caterina to Florence; he just hadn't thought of it yet. They rode along in silence.

"I can see Dreamer's Rock," Caterina said. "There, in the distance."

A breeze lifted her long dark hair and it floated above her shoulders. She was wearing the yellow dress she'd had on the afternoon he'd returned to San Michelle; a cream colored shawl covered her shoulders. The horse's coat was off-white. Lorenzo watched with disbelief as the line of separation disappeared between them and their forms melted into one; they were transformed into a mystical creature. She smiled; this ethereal creature called Caterina was an enchantress, who had cast a spell that would forever hold him. Lorenzo had neither the desire nor the capacity to escape; he was destined to spend the rest of his life with her. The solution was clear now; tonight, at Dreamer's Rock, he would ask Caterina to be his wife.

A short time later, Lorenzo pulled the reins and brought his horse to a halt. The cluster of low-lying mountains and the narrow winding river bore a remarkable resemblance to the background of the Mona Lisa. Dreamer's Rock was the perfect place for them to mark the beginning of their new life. They dismounted. Lorenzo untied the blanket and supplies bag and poured oats on the ground. Caterina tethered the horses to a tree and filled the pail with water from a nearby stream.

"It's getting late," Caterina said.

"There's plenty of time before dark to make camp."

"Let's start up the trail now."

"What did you say?" Lorenzo asked.

"We have to make camp at Dreamer's Rock," Caterina answered.

"Only a father and a first born son can climb the trail and spend the night there." Lorenzo moved towards her. "The mystics live on Dreamer's Rock. You know the ritual. Our people are the same."

"We are both Calabrian, Lorenzo, but we are not the same; our blood is different." Caterina turned away. "Some believe that it can also be a father and his first born child."

"What are you saying?"

"*Pappa* and I climbed the trail and spent the night on Dreamer's Rock."

"That's impossible," Lorenzo said.

"It was the summer before the storm when I was eleven years old. And the mystics came to me."

"You spent the night on Dreamer's Rock with your *Pappa* and the wind brought the mystics to you?"

"*Sì.*"

"And the mystics gave you the knowledge and insight that a first born son would receive?"

"*Sì.*"

"I've never heard anything like this before."

"I would never lie to you, Lorenzo."

As unbelievable as Caterina's words seemed, Lorenzo knew that they were the truth; there was no duplicity between them.

"There's more that I must tell you." She brought her body into his; their shapes fit so perfectly; it was as if they were half of the same mold. "The wind did not just bring me knowledge and insight." She traced his bottom lip with her finger. "It whispered your name to me too."

"My name?"

"The mystics have blessed us, Lorenzo. That's why I brought you to Dreamer's Rock." Caterina kissed him. "They told me that we belong together." There was no other man but Lorenzo who could be the father of her child.

Ledges jutted out and sliced the narrow path. It twisted and turned and they grabbed onto branches and outcrops of rocks to prevent them from slipping on the stones that broke up the uneven ground. Isolated groupings of trees rooted in rock peppered the slopes; their hold was tenuous and it was a wonder that they managed to survive.

"We're here," Caterina said about one hour later.

She stepped onto the clearing and Lorenzo gave her their sack of provisions. She walked across the hard earth into the opening of a cave carved out of the side of the mountain. He looked down from a rocky precipice and estimated that they had climbed 1,000 feet. He gathered dead branches and dry twigs and as the last rays

of the sun disappeared, entered the cave with the kindling. Within
a few minutes, a red-yellow spark flashed from the two sticks
he was rubbing together and ignited a flame. Caterina spread a
blanket on the other side while he added wood; the fire came to
life. Its red tongues lengthened and thickened and absorbed all
the yellow; they matched the highlights of Caterina's hair and the
two became one hot burning mass of color. The features of her face
adopted a luminescent quality and once again, she underwent a
transformation. How could there be so many women within her?

"Caterina." Would his husky voice frighten her? Would she
recognize it as his?

There were many men within Lorenzo too and he wanted
Caterina to be intimate with all of them.

Lorenzo crouched low and slid around the fire. She nudged
towards him. Expectingly. He grabbed the back of her head and
pulled her face towards him. She offered no resistance; willingly, she
gave him her lips and he covered them with his mouth. She shoved
her body against his and they spilled onto the blanket. He raised
himself over her and the reflection of the flames lit her beauty with
a wildness that he wanted to capture. He undid her buttons and
she ripped off his shirt. She pushed herself up and slipped her dress
from her shoulders; Lorenzo cupped her breasts with his hands. She
fumbled around the waist of his trousers and together, they tore
them off. They fell backwards and their legs entangled with each
other.

Lorenzo's mouth moved down her body. Caterina had never
felt his touch before yet there was no strangeness to it now; she
guided him to where she wanted his warmth and he awakened
in her a part that she had not known existed. She felt him and
together, their movements created a new rhythm. There was no fear,
no doubt, no hesitation and no boundaries; her need to become
one with him was as great as his need to enter her. The separation
between them decreased until there was none and they were finally
together, as was always meant to be.

The sun had barely risen and Caterina was sitting outside on a blanket. The rocky side of the mountain that held the cave where they had spent the night was behind her. Lorenzo unbuttoned almost all the tiny white buttons on her dress. "You missed that one." He kissed a freckle on her chest and she twisted a curl of his hair around her finger; his lips were wet against her skin. She shivered but it was not a flash of fear that raced through her body. She slipped a hand through his opened shirt, the muscles of his chest were hard and once again and her need for him surfaced.

"Wait just a while." He pulled back.

How this was possible, Caterina did not know. Could he ever completely satiate this yearning within her?

"This is the first morning of our new life and I'm going to sketch a picture of my wife for our bedroom in Florence."

"Tell me about our new life once more." She would set aside her desires until she heard this again.

"After Padre Valentine marries us and you are my wife." Lorenzo moved back a few feet and adjusted the notebook on his knees. He picked up a charcoal stick and began to sketch.

"And you are my husband." Caterina loved the way those words shaped her mouth; she would never tire of saying them.

"We will live in Florence."

"With *Mamma* Anna."

"*Si*," Lorenzo said.

"We will find her a new doctor and she will get well."

"Hold still for a few more minutes."

"Francesca will be with us too."

"Lodovico and Matteo will help us find Valerio."

"Verrocchio will find me a teacher," Caterina said.

"I will take you to the Uffizzi Gallery to see the painting Michelangelo and I both love."

"We'll walk along the Ponte Vecchio and look at the swirling waters of the Arno River like Leonardo did."

"I'm almost finished."

"And we will have *bambinas*."

"You're convinced that our first will be a little girl?" Lorenzo asked.

"*Si*. And you're certain about her name?"

"I am the father so I get to chose. I will name her Caterina Rosa."

"Shadow will come with us and play with our *bambinas*." Her desire would no longer be quelled. She undid the remaining buttons on her dress and it fell to her waist; the coolness of the fabric could not lessen the warmth of her skin. Lorenzo moved towards her and she peeled his shirt off his body.

"*Mio amare*," she whispered.

"*Mia amare*," he replied.

"*Sempre*," they said in unison.

The wind whipped Caterina's hair and covered her face; it outlined the curves of her body underneath her dress.

"Be careful," Lorenzo said. He yearned to touch her again; there were hidden places that he'd yet to explore. "You're too near the edge."

Caterina stood barefoot on the precipice that jutted from the clearing. She stretched her arms straight out at the shoulders and extended the fingers of her hand. She turned towards him. "The mystics are here and they're saying your name to me again." She faced the opened space in front of her again. "They tell me that I will love Lorenzo Marino forever." She arched her back and tilted her chin towards the sky. "I am the woman in the wind."

"There, I'm finished. Now get off that ledge."

She spun around and raced towards him. "I want to see the sketch. I know it will always be my favorite."

"I will sign my name and date it so that even when we are old, we will remember today."

"I'm going to wrap it in one of *Mamma's* handkerchiefs and keep it beside my heart for the rest of my days."

Lorenzo held her close but it was not close enough and he

wished that she could crawl inside him so that he'd know she'd always be safe.

"I told Francesca that we would only be gone for one night. It's early morning and we'll have to leave for San Michelle soon."

"We still have time." Lorenzo led Caterina back into the cave.

CHAPTER TWENTY

The early morning light shone through the window; Bruno had fallen asleep again at the kitchen table. He lifted his head a fraction above his arms; the bowl of fruit on the counter was fuzzy. Perhaps he'd had too much wine with Rinaldo last evening. He rested his head on his arms. They'd had a wonderful time. His marinated *ceci* beans had been tasty and Rinaldo had two large servings of *zucchini ripieni*. Bruno shifted his legs; his feet were so swollen that he didn't think his shoes would fit. The burning sensation in his throat had returned and his chest felt tight. He'd eaten so many *scallilis, tordillis* and *genettis* but they were so good, how could he resist? Bruno wiped his forehead; he was sweating. If he had more energy, he'd walk across the room and open the door so that a breeze from the sea would cool the air. He closed his eyes. The sharp pain cut through his body so suddenly that he did not even feel it. For one brief moment, it was dark then the light returned.

"Bruno," Edoardo called out. Grigio was pulling a carriage and he and Nella were sitting in the front seat.

The carriage stopped and he patted Grigio's muzzle. The old workhorse nuzzled his pocket and Bruno reached into it and found a carrot.

"We must go," Edoardo said. "The *Signora* will be coming soon."

"I'm so happy that I'm going to see her again," Nella said. "And Bruno, we've been watching how good you've been to Caterina."

"She's *bellissima*," Bruno said. He climbed into the back seat; his knees were no longer sore. "And Lorenzo loves her very much."

"Here are some chocolate covered figs," Nella said. She handed him a paper sack.

Bruno ran his tongue over his teeth; they were good and strong. He bit into the fig; the chocolate in Heaven was even more delicious than the chocolate on earth. As soon as he saw the *Signora*, everything would be perfect; Bruno knew that he would love being dead.

Padre Valentine closed the door to Anna's bedroom where he and Francesca had spent last night. When Francesca told him that Caterina was with Fortunata and Lorenzo was sketching, he suspected that something was amiss for they would never do these things; Anna's health was beyond precarious. It had taken him awhile to prod the truth from Francesca. The priest never suspected that they'd spend the night at Dreamer's Rock; he'd underestimated their love. He proceeded down the corridor and made his way to the kitchen.

The morning had begun on a bleak note and the hours that followed had darkened it in a way that Padre Valentine could never have anticipated; it was early evening and he would be glad when this day was over. He shut the back door of the villa and trudged to the stable. At least death had come quickly to Bruno and he had not suffered; the priest was thankful for God's small mercy. Padre would attend to Bruno's burial tomorrow; in the interim he'd given Rinaldo and the other servants orders not to tell Francesca that Bruno had died for she needed all her strength for Anna. The priest touched his silver crucifix. With Bruno's passing, he had inherited the mantle to safeguard Caterina. Anna's time was imminent and soon he would have the responsibility of protecting Lorenzo. Padre Valentine would not renege on these promises. Was his life at another turning point, just as it had been when he agreed to Santo's contract? And if so, what price would he have to pay this time?

"You've barely spoken a word and we're almost back at San Michelle," Lorenzo said to Caterina. She turned in the saddle; her face was a miasma of shadows, her features only partially lit by the early evening sun and, for an instant, Lorenzo thought that she was an old woman who had not known kindness for years.

"Are you all right? Here, have a sip of water." He handed her his canteen, almost dropping it in the gulf between them.

"*Non grazie*. I'm just tired."

"It won't be long before we'll have our new life." Caterina turned away.

The gate to San Michelle appeared in the distance and the initial "M" gradually took shape. They crossed onto the estate, passed by the villa and the edge of the enclave. Lorenzo had decided to design a gold gimmal wedding band for them; the twin interlocking rings joined by a pivot were first created by the jewelers of the Renaissance and would symbolize their love. He dismounted, slid the door open and led his horse into the stable that Mabruco had built after the storm.

"Tell me, Lorenzo." Caterina passed over the threshold and held the horse's reins at her side. "Exactly how will it all happen? Everything we talked about at Dreamer's Rock. All the plans we made for our new life in Florence. How will we actually be able to leave San Michelle with *Mamma* Anna?"

So this was why Caterina had been quiet; her mind had been too busy thinking to talk.

"I'm a servant girl. Have you forgotten that?" She stood in front of him. "Your *Pappa* will never let you marry me."

"You will be my wife, Caterina. With or without my father's

approval, I will marry you." He put a hand on each of her shoulders. "I will talk to Padre today and everything will be fine." She nestled her head in the crook of his neck. Caterina's words echoed his fears for the truth was Lorenzo didn't know how things would work out; he only knew that they had to. Sometimes, the world of ideas was easier to deal with than reality. Lorenzo and Caterina would have to leave San Michelle as soon as possible for if his father discovered their plans, he wasn't certain that even Padre Valentine would be able to help them.

"Let's put the horses in the stalls and go see *Mamma*." He placed his canteen on the rung of the ladder that lead to the hayloft above then unbuckled the cinches of the saddle and grabbed its horn and cantle.

"Do you want me to help you with the horses?"

"Padre Valentine?" Lorenzo asked. He turned around.

"How did you know we were here?" Caterina asked.

"*Mamma*?" Lorenzo said. He put the saddle on the ground. "Something's happened to her?"

The priest entered the stable and sat on a bale of hay. Lorenzo and Caterina approached him at the same time. He leaned against the boarded wall and spread his cassock around his feet. The movement of the cloth stirred up grains of sand on the ground; they rose in clouds and settled around the hem, adding shades of grey and brown to the garment's black color.

"What's wrong?" Lorenzo asked. The darkness under Padre Valentine's eyes was deeper than that of his cassock. "It's *Mamma*, isn't it?" The priest did not answer his questions but there was no need for Lorenzo to repeat them; he knew what the words did not say.

"Kneel my children and bow your heads."

Lorenzo and Caterina did as he said.

"*Pater noster, qi es in caelis, sanctifectur nomen tuum...*" After he spoke the final words of "The Lord's Prayer," he said, "I will marry you and Lorenzo and I will do everything I can to help you have your new life in Florence. As *Dio* is my witness."

"Padre," Lorenzo said.

"We'll talk later. Both of you must go to *Mamma* now."

They settled the horses and left the stable.

"Now Sisina, won't Santo be interested in that?" a male voice asked from the hayloft.

"*Si*, Vito," she responded. "He will not be pleased."

"He'll be back later today and I'll tell him right away," Vito said. "He'll be angry but there's nothing we can do about it now so let's enjoy ourselves for a while."

"I agree." Sisina laughed. "I've missed you, Vito."

Lorenzo opened the door and Caterina walked passed him into his mother's bedroom.

"You're back." Francesca rose from the side of the bed and stepped towards them; Lorenzo had never seen her movements hold no life. The two women embraced and he shifted his stance to give them privacy. He scanned the bedroom, what good was all this luxuriousness to his mother now? Silk covered walls, the painted verde gris finish on her bureau plat, leather embossed surfaces, floral patterned drapes and bed coverings that matched perfectly. In the end, what did it matter? Caterina guided Francesca to a chair in the corner. He went over to them.

"Ah," she said. "You and Lorenzo?"

"Rest now," Caterina said. She kissed her forehead and Francesca closed her eyes; Lorenzo covered her with a blanket.

They sat on the edge of the bed; Caterina was across from him. The gauze like curtains that draped the window behind her were still and the space outside was dark. He was thankful that the covers were over his mother's hands for he wanted his last memory of them to be that of what they once were. The scooped neckline of her white nightdress was edged in lace and reminded him of her handkerchiefs. He looked at his mother's face, but only for an instant.

Who was she? Lorenzo asked himself. The woman lying on the bed. Where did *Mamma* go? His letters were in a pile on the nightstand; a lavender stalk rested on top and they'd been tied together by a red ribbon. The *gobbo* statue and Padre Valentine's wooden crucifix were in between them and the walnut cassone his mother had used as a jewelry box. Elaborate swirls were engraved in the dark wood and there was a faded coat of arms carved on the top. It had belonged to his grandmother but Lorenzo wasn't sure if her name had been Avanina or Giovanna. Why didn't he know this? Surely his mother must have told him. Had he simply forgotten to tell his mind to remember it? Caterina stroked his mother's cheek. Lorenzo would not allow the strangeness that had marred his relationship with his mother to afflict what he would have with his wife. Nothing would ever come between him and Caterina; he vowed to be a better husband than he had been a son.

Time passed and the first rays of the new day shone through the window. Padre Valentine entered the room and stood beside him. He blessed himself then began, *"Almighty and Everlasting Dio, preserver of souls...grant Thy healing of Thy servant at the hour of its departure from the body..."*

Francesca awoke and joined them. Caterina sprinkled lavender petals over *Mamma's* body and Lorenzo placed his hand on top of the covers directly over his mother's; he hoped that she knew he was there.

Anna felt warmth spread through her fingers, radiate up her arm, cross her shoulder, pass down her torso then settle around her heart. She heard a trumpet sound in the distance. The young woman with the mark of the rose on her wrist and the handsome young man with the eyes of the sea were holding hands and walking towards her; Anna was happy that she was finally going to meet them.

Lorenzo blessed himself as Padre Valentine concluded his prayer; Caterina sprinkled the last bit of lavender on the pillow and Francesca leaned against her. *Mamma* exhaled a breath and slipped away. A rustling sounded; the drapes in the window fluttered as the breeze bathed the room in the sweet fragrance of roses. "Peace," Lorenzo whispered. "*Mamma*, you are at peace." Stillness cloaked the four of them for so long that it was as if they'd become figures in a tableau.

At first it sounded as if someone was rapping on the windowpane but when Lorenzo looked, there wasn't anyone at the glass. He turned his head; the door was open and the sound was getting louder. Was it footsteps that he heard walking down the corridor? All of a sudden, the scent of roses evaporated from his mother's bedroom and his father appeared in the doorway.

Caterina kissed *Mamma* Anna's forehead and it was already cold; the emptiness within her began to grow. She heard Lorenzo's boot click down on the hardwood floor. He was facing the door. She stood up. Caterina hadn't seen Santo Marino since the storm and couldn't believe how much he'd changed in five years.

His dark hair had receded and it was as if someone had drawn a connecting line between the top of each ear, the space in front of which was completely bald. She remembered the dark eyes and thin mustache but not the jowls that hung from his chin. Caterina and Lorenzo glanced at each other and Santo's jaw tightened; he knew about their love. Padre Valentine touched his silver crucifix; he too realized what had just happened. Caterina grabbed Francesca's hand and it was as cold as *Mamma's* forehead. The emptiness within her grew bigger.

Santo strode into the room, attired in a classic black suit and white shirt; it was as if he planned to make an important announcement. Except for the signet ring, he wore no jewelry. Santo stopped in front of the footboard and looked at *Mamma*

Anna. Caterina searched his face but found no sorrow or sadness. How could a husband have no feelings for the woman who had borne him three sons? Caterina needed Lorenzo to hold her. Benito pranced into the room and Santo smiled.

His suit was similar to his father's but cut to accentuate his lean body and fashionably appointed with a reddish colored cravat and pocket fluff, gold cufflinks and matching tie clip. He wore the same signet ring as Santo. His leather shoes were adorned with a gold ankle buckle; he was dressed as if he were going to a party. Benito took his place beside his father. He had yet to acknowledge Lorenzo. His eyes fell upon *Mamma* Anna and the fine lines of his handsome face contorted. Benito cleared his throat and fixed his stare above the headboard of the bed. Even though Benito bore a startling resemblance to the way Caterina remembered that Santo had once looked, there was one unmistakable difference between the two men, Benito's love for *Mamma* Anna was undeniable; he was still her son.

"Ben...tho," a thick voice that Lorenzo did not recognize called out.

"Come, Caesare," Benito said. He waved his hand.

Almost five years had passed since Lorenzo had seen his brother; Caesare took a step forward and Lorenzo was grateful that his father had kept him away from his mother; sometimes it was better to remember people as they once were. Perhaps there had been kindness in his father's action.

There was a wooden peg affixed to Caesare's right leg above the knee and every time its blunt base struck the floor, it made a thudding sound. Lorenzo flinched as if he were being hit; his father glared at him and Lorenzo averted his eyes. Benito walked towards Caesare.

Caesare was dressed in heavy brown trousers; the right leg hemmed and fitted to accommodate the top portion of the peg. He wore a plain blue shirt with sleeves rolled up to the elbows that revealed massive forearms. His first steps were taken with assurance but it soon became apparent to Lorenzo that there was something off-balance about his gait and irregular about the rhythm with which his arms moved. Benito put his hand on Caesare's arm then looked at Lorenzo for the first time since he'd enter the room; the bond between them was stronger than ever. They stood in front of the footboard of their mother's bed. Caesare turned his head towards Lorenzo and it seemed as if it were another moment before his eyes followed. His nose was still flat, his hair dark and chin length and the skin on his face had retained its natural coarseness but his cheeks were now marked with deep and irregular shaped indentations. Caesare showed no signs of recognition; Lorenzo was a stranger to him. He turned away. Lorenzo had not only just lost his mother; he was finally being forced to accept what a part of him had always known. Lorenzo had never belonged with his father or brothers and with his mother's passing, he had no more family and he too was an orphan, just like Caterina. If Lorenzo lost her, he would be completely alone and that was something more than Lorenzo knew he could bear.

Padre Valentine pressed against him; his mouth was speaking silent words. When had the priest started to pray again? Caterina's arm was around Francesca's shoulder. Francesca had only met Caesare and Benito when she was five and his family had visited hers in Taranto. Benito's eyes were lingering on her just as they did on the women Lorenzo had seen him with in Florence; Francesca shrunk back and it was as if Caterina was protecting her from harm.

"Ben...tho," Caesare said. He pointed at his mother and shook his head.

Benito placed his hand on his brother's back. "*Mamma*," he said. "*Mamma*."

CHAPTER TWENTY-ONE

"I want to be alone with my wife," Santo said. "Padre Valentine, you are to stay and help me pray." But the prayers wouldn't be for Anna; Mabruco had told him earlier that morning about the stable incident. Santo didn't have time to deal with everything now but there were a few issues that he planned to settle with the priest. Padre Valentine had violated the agreement they had made twenty-one years ago; as soon as Anna was buried, he would suffer the consequences.

"Benito, wait for me in the corridor with your brothers." Santo had never expected things to develop as they did but then again, Lorenzo always had too much of Anna's blood in him; his feelings for the girl weren't a total surprise. At least the timing of Anna's death had been convenient and it would be easy for Santo to get his son's life back on track.

"Francesca," Santo barked. She grabbed Caterina's hand and he smirked. Santo was glad that she was easily intimidated; Benito wouldn't have the same problems he'd had with Anna. "I will talk to you later." There was no need for him to acknowledge the servant girl; Anna was dead. "Go now." They scurried past him; the door shut and Santo faced Padre Valentine.

What was the cause of Benito's icy silence? Lorenzo watched him walk down the corridor; when he had visited in Florence,

204

they'd enjoyed each other's company. Why had he yet to exchange a word with him? And where was Caterina? How had his father known about their love? He wanted to reassure her that nothing could come between them. At least she and Francesca were together; maybe they had gone to find Bruno. How could anyone tell Bruno that "his beloved *Signora*" had left San Michelle? Lorenzo had been with *Mamma* when she passed onto the next life and he found it difficult to believe that he would never see her again. It was only twenty-four hours ago that Lorenzo and Caterina were at Dreamer's Rock and he was drawing the sketch she'd named "The Woman in the Wind." Too much had happened for one day to hold.

Caesare sat down on a green velour Roman style bench. His natural leg was bent at the knee and flopped casually to one side; the wooden peg on the other extended straight out so that if someone were attempting to pass, they would have to step over it. It was rodlike in shape, tapered to a rectangular base and reminded Lorenzo of the two-edged rapier favored in the mock dueling matches he had participated in at the academy in Florence.

The signet ring Caesare wore was identical to his father's and Benito's but its square shape rose higher than the others did because of the thickness of his finger and the size of his hand. Lorenzo had first noticed Benito wearing one three years ago, after he'd celebrated his twenty-first birthday. Why had he never asked what needed to be done to merit these rings? Was it because he did not want to know?

Benito had stopped in front of a demi-lune table to examine his image in the rectangular mirror that Lorenzo used to look in when he was a little boy. Benito leaned closer and knocked against the Limoges vase displayed in the center. It had been one of his mother's favorites; she loved the purple flowers painted on its fine porcelain surface. The vase swayed to one side but Benito caught it before it toppled over; he moved it out of his way. He inspected his flawless olive-skinned complexion and started humming.

How could that be, Lorenzo asked himself, when such a

short time ago, he'd been so distraught over their mother's death? How could his emotions shift so easily? He spoke his first words to Lorenzo without looking at him. "Verrocchio has told *Pappa* that in six months, you will be finished your studies in law."

This was a fact, Lorenzo silently concurred.

"*Pappa* will then introduce you to Arduino Buccella and you will be moving to Naples and working with me." He adjusted his cravat.

It didn't matter what his father wanted anymore, Lorenzo's new life would be with Caterina and they would be living in Florence.

"There's a new fashion house that I've taken quite a liking too." He flicked a piece of lint off the shoulder of his suit with the tip of a manicured fingernail. "The designer is quite in tune with a man's form. He knows how to celebrate it, as well as your Michelangelo could." He glanced at Lorenzo.

The reference to Michelangelo was intended as an affront; Lorenzo did not appreciate Benito's comment.

"He made this suit specifically for me. A wonderful fit. Don't you think?" Without giving Lorenzo time to respond, Benito pirouetted then stepped towards Caesare. "Even you, my brother, the great Vincenzo Valentino could make look good!" He cuffed Caesare on his ear and Caesare jumped up to mock fight Benito. He knocked the bench against the wall, scratching it with its pointed edge.

"*Non, non,*" Benito protested playfully, blocking Caesare's fists with his hands. "Now look at what you did." Caesare turned his head then looked back at him, there was no response registered on his face.

"*Pappa's* going to have our villa redecorated anyway before he moves back." He messed Caesare's hair with his hands. "It doesn't really matter."

"*Pappa's* moving back to San Michelle?" Lorenzo asked.

"*Si.* He decided a few months ago."

"I don't understand." Lorenzo heard the door open behind him.

"You will understand everything later," Santo said. He stepped into the corridor. "I don't have time to explain things to you now." Padre Valentine stood beside him. "First, we have to attend to your *Mamma*. The funeral will be held in three days and Padre will take care of the service. Benito, you are to select the burial site, ensure it is readied and a proper monument is ordered. Lorenzo will help you and of course, Caesare, if there is anything that you think he can do. Tell Sisina and Armida to prepare your mother's body; Francesca will help them." Santo waited an instant. "And of course, there's no need for that servant girl to ever be in our villa again." He did not want to look at Lorenzo's face for he feared he would slap it."Now go," Santo said dismissing them all. "I have to meet with Mabruco."

The procession made its way down the corridor: Padre Valentine was beside Santo, Benito and Caesare followed, then Lorenzo. The choppy rhythm of Caesare's gait was an unnerving juxtaposition with the fluid grace of Benito's movements and unnerved Lorenzo. Benito returned the flower vase to its regular spot as he passed the table where he'd preened himself earlier. How could he share their blood? Lorenzo slowed his pace; he wanted to stay as far away from them as was possible.

It was early evening when Padre Valentine pushed the wooden cross that Ermenigildo had made into Bruno's grave. It had been a terrible day but why should the priest have expected anything else? How could the day on which Anna died and Bruno was buried be destined to be anything but terrible? It was hard for him to conceive of a San Michelle without Anna and Bruno; perhaps there wouldn't be.

Word of the passing of both Bruno and Anna had spread quickly through San Michelle and Cetraro; Anna's death had been expected, hence the sadness was somewhat mitigated. The priest picked up the bouquet of wildflowers that Elda had lain on the earth several hours ago; the hot sun had wilted them. He placed them near the cross. The simple ceremony he'd performed that afternoon had brought little solace to the servants and workers in attendance; Bruno's death had caught them all by surprise and it would be a long time before its permanence was realized. How could he ever go into the kitchen again?

At one time his life had held such promise; within the past few hours, everything had come crashing down. How had Santo found out that he was going to marry Caterina and Lorenzo and that they were planning a new life together in Florence? Santo had confronted him with his betrayal that morning; his words had been few yet their impact strong. The stakes for transgression had always been clear to the priest and all that Santo had given him was time for he needed him until Anna's funeral had concluded; he would take no action until then. Padre Valentine had two days to devise and execute a plan that would enable him to honor the promises he made to keep Caterina and Lorenzo safe from harm. There were so many problems that he needed to resolve.

How could he prevent Santo from revealing the truth of his identity? Ortenza's mother would be ruined for she and the priest were still legally married. Her husband would forsake her, there would be a scandal and Ortenza and the other children would be pariahs. Even Fiore would be vilified for he had been a willing accomplice in Padre Valentine's duplicity. What the priest had hidden for so many years was unraveling and he didn't know what to do. Why did the truth always have to surface when it was inconvenient to the liar?

He would have to contact Fiore tomorrow. Santo was indebted to Fiore because he had saved Caesare's life and Fiore had not violated the agreement and Santo still depended on him to deal with Caesare's ongoing health problems. Padre Valentine knelt down. Yes, this was definitely the solution. Why hadn't he thought of this before? In the end, it would be Santo's love for Caesare that would protect Ortenza and her mother from ruin.

But how could he marry Caterina and Lorenzo and help them start a new life in Florence? He still didn't have a solution; Padre Valentine wished there were a saint whom he could appeal to for mercy but even St. Jude would consider this situation too desperate for salvation. He had failed Edoardo; he could not fail his daughter. If God still welcomed him in His kingdom, Padre Valentine would offer his life in exchange for Caterina and Lorenzo's safety and happiness. He folded his hand in prayer.

The sun had almost set by the time Padre Valentine completed his prayers over Bruno's grave; he was glad that this day was in its final hours. He began his journey back to the villa.

"Padre," Lorenzo called. "Mabruco said you were here." He grabbed the priest's arm. "Where's Caterina? I haven't seen her since this morning and Francesca doesn't know where she is either and Benito won't let me out of his sight."

His hair was dull and hung limp as if it was too tired to hold its color and the curls were no longer interested in forming their shapes. The shadows underneath his eyes looked like those he'd created with charcoal sticks on his sketches. A pencil thin line flowed out from the tip of each nostril and bracketed his lips; the priest feared Lorenzo's skin was going to split open and his mouth would fall out. He would have to be gentle; Lorenzo had become accustomed to a life of deference and indulgence while living in Florence and what he had experienced in the past day and a half was not something he knew how to bear.

"I took Caterina to Shadow's shed while Caesare was digging Bruno's grave. Shadow's with her."

"Why couldn't she stay in her cottage?"

Even though Santo had told the priest he'd take no action until after Anna's funeral, Padre Valentine was uneasy. Santo did not know about Shadow and the shed was located on a part of San Michelle that had never been put to use; she'd be safe there.

"My father knows about us. That's what's wrong. How could

209

that be Padre? How did he find out?"

"You wear your love for each other on your faces," Padre Valentine said. "That is all your father knows." There was no need for the truth to be revealed to Lorenzo; this was another situation where knowing the truth lacked merit and served no purpose. Besides, if the priest didn't understand how Santo had discovered everything, how could he possibly explain it to Lorenzo?

"Caterina was right. My father will never let us get married."

"I've devised a plan."

"What plan? Tell me." He licked his lips; they were dry and cracked.

The priest would have to talk slowly. Lorenzo had to understand what he was about to say for the circumstances provided no provision for confusion or misinterpretation. "I will marry you and Caterina at sunrise on the day after your mother's funeral at your favorite stream."

Lorenzo watched the priest's mouth as if he needed his eyes to help his ears hear Padre Valentine's words.

"Shadow's shed is close by and that's why I moved Caterina there. On that morning, I will bring Caterina and Shadow to you. You and Francesca will meet us there."

"How?"

"Pretend to be going out for an early morning ride. No one will suspect anything."

"Then what?" Lorenzo asked.

"I will marry you and the three of you are to go to Diamante. There's an old priest there who will help you."

"Why?"

"He knew your grandmother and I can trust him. I'll telegraph him tomorrow." He put his hand on Lorenzo's arm. "Do you understand?"

"*Sì.*"

"Your father's expecting me and I must get back to the villa now. Do not do anything to antagonize him or Benito. I will tell

Francesca everything. Caterina's safe until your mother's funeral is over."

"How do you know that?"

Because Santo had told him. "I know your father, Lorenzo." He was glad that Lorenzo didn't. "We have time on our side."

"Can't I see Caterina now?"

"*Non*. I will go tomorrow afternoon. Your father knows I need time alone to prepare the prayers for your mother's funeral."

"Padre, I could not bear..."

"Everything will be fine. I promise you." The priest put his hand on Lorenzo's shoulder. "The love you and Caterina have will last a lifetime."

"Shut the door." Santo stormed into his sitting room. Benito closed it then stood in front of the fireplace next to his father. "Where's Caesare?

"After he finished digging Bruno's grave, I took him to the harbor. He's been out on the fishing boats all day. I'll get him in a little while."

"And Lorenzo?"

"Mabruco told him that Padre Valentine was saying prayers at Bruno's grave and he went to see the priest."

"Bring both of your brothers to me later. I'll be in my office. We'll all have a drink together."

Benito nodded.

"Tell me about the servant girl."

"She's in the wolf's shed. Mabruco followed the priest."

"Look at the notebook Sisina found in Lorenzo's bedroom." Santo nodded at the table between the chairs behind them. Benito flipped through the pages one at a time. "To have fun with a servant girl," Santo said, "I have no problems with. After all, she is a beautiful young woman and it's easy to understand Lorenzo's taste for her." He picked up the poker leaning against the fireplace.

"To plan on marriage and moving to Florence and neglecting the responsibilities of blood is more serious but still not an insurmountable problem." He shoved the pointed tip of the metal rod into the fire. "But to fill a notebook with provocative sketches that others could find and blackmail our family with is an entirely different matter; it creates the possibility of a complication that we do not need." He glanced at Benito. "You understand why no one must ever have power over you?"

Benito smiled.

"Your brother has much to learn; he's far from being ready to assume his place in the business. I have allowed him too many diversions in Florence but things will change as soon as your mother's been buried."

"There's a page missing," Benito said. He closed the notebook.

"Sisina's going to search Lorenzo's room tonight. We must find it." Santo stoked the fire. "There must be no evidence that could bring shame to the Marino name. In time, Lorenzo will realize that I am only protecting him. I will find him a wife that will move our family forward."

"As you have done for me with Francesca?"

"Her blood is good. Eugenio's too kind with his men but his loyalty is beyond reproach, his fishing businesses are lucrative and he's amassed a sizeable fortune."

"And Buccella approves?" Benito asked.

"Of course."

"What would you like me to do?" Benito slapped the notebook against the palm of his hand.

"The girl has some kind of hold on your brother," Santo said. "It will pass, these things always do. I'd promised Sisina that she could have her for her villa in Cosenza but I'm not sure if that's the solution." The flames in the fire shot up. "Lorenzo may think to look for her there." Santo rested the poker against the fireplace. "It must be impossible for him to find her." He took the notebook from Benito. Santo did not want to kill Caterina for he feared that such action could bring more havoc to his life than what she had already created. "After your mother's funeral, you and Caesare will take her to Naples and give her to Buccella's men. They will see that she disappears." Santo tossed the notebook into the fire and watched it burn. "I will make the necessary arrangements." When the notebook had been reduced to ashes, he put his hand on Benito's arm. "You're a good son. I'll see you later."

Caterina lifted the edge of the canvas flap and peered through the narrow opening of the shed; there were no stars in the evening sky to light the ground in front of her. If not for the single flame of the candle burning in the corner, she feared the darkness would swallow her and Shadow. She closed the flap and rested her head on the wolf's shoulder. Their plans had already gone astray. *Mamma* Anna would never share their new life in Florence and Caterina was terrified that it was a sign that nothing else would work out for her and Lorenzo.

Only three nights, she thought to herself, tonight, tomorrow and the night of the day on which *Mamma* was to be buried; then she would never be apart from Lorenzo again. Soon they would be married; Padre had planned everything. Caterina pressed her hand against her chest. She had wrapped the cameo brooch, the jeweled cross and the sketch in a handkerchief *Mamma* Anna had given her and tucked it inside her blouse. She closed her eyes and returned to Dreamer's Rock. She was standing on the edge of the precipice. Caterina was the woman in the wind and the voices of the mystics came to her again.

"You will love Lorenzo Marino forever," they said.

Shadow growled and the muscles in his body tighten. The voices faded and the emptiness within Caterina began to grow.

CHAPTER TWENTY-TWO

Santo waved at Caesare from the back doorway of the kitchen as his son filled a large basket with vegetables from the garden.

"Would you like anything else for lunch, *Signore*?" Sisina asked.

"A cup of tea with *millefiori* honey. *Per favore*." He laughed as Caesare juggled eggplant.

"*Pappa*," Benito said. "Come and look at this one; it might be suitable for *Mamma's* tombstone." He was reviewing sketches Lorenzo had completed that morning.

"A plump cherub with curly hair holding a single long stemmed rose," Santo said.

"I thought that it could sit on top of the tombstone," Lorenzo said.

"Perhaps," Santo said. The cherub reminded him of Caesare as a baby.

"Verrocchio could find us a beautiful piece of marble and Lodovico would love to carve it for our family," Lorenzo said. "We could start as soon as I return to the academy next month. I could prepare more sketches and you could chose one at dinner."

It was as if Santo was looking at Anna's eyes. "*Si*. A good idea." He walked over to the window and Sisina set his tea on the counter. "How are the preparations coming?"

"Francesca's ironing the *Signora's* dress. Everything's going well," Sisina said.

"*Bene*."

"I'll go back to Francesca now."

"*Grazie*," Santo said. He was very pleased that Mabruco had decided to marry Sisina. What would he give them as a wedding present? It had to be special after all that they had done.

"What's Caesare doing now?" Benito asked. He stood beside him.

"Throwing potatoes at the seagulls."

"Come and see this, Lorenzo," Benito said.

"He almost hit one," Santo said. The three of them laughed.

"You should have seen all the fish Caesare caught this morning," Benito said. "But he didn't like the way Rinaldo cooked them."

"When Fiorina and I move to San Michelle, I'll bring a cook," Santo said.

Lorenzo returned to his sketching and Santo watched him. "What are you drawing now?" His hair was the color Anna's had been when he'd first met her. It was too bad that he'd outgrown her but Buccella had been right all along; one wife could never meet the needs of such an exceptional husband. At forty-seven, Santo assumed that Fiorina would be his last wife but, if she became tedious, he'd find another. How long would Francesca amuse Benito before he was forced to take similar action?

"He could make us a lot of money," Benito said. "He and Matteo have created exquisite cameo brooches that could be the first piece in an exclusive line of jewelry for our business."

"Show me them after you come back from Naples and things have settled." Santo sipped his tea.

"Of course." Benito walked over to Lorenzo and placed a hand on his shoulder. "That's amazing. How can you sketch so quickly?"

All of a sudden, the cup dropped from Santo's hand, struck the counter and smashed into pieces; hot muddy liquid streamed onto the floor. "Benito," he screamed, then ran out the door.

"What happened?" Lorenzo chased his father and brother.

Caesare was on the ground; his arms and legs had stiffened and his eyes were rolled back so that the iris had completely disappeared. Benito turned his head to one side then held it flat against the ground; his father shoved a handkerchief between his upper and lower teeth.

"What's wrong?" Lorenzo knelt across from Benito. It was as if an earthquake was buried inside Caesare. His wooden peg twisted and turned and Lorenzo thought it was trying to detach itself from Caesare's thigh; he slid away so that it wouldn't strike him.

"Get him a blanket," Benito said.

He held Caesare's shoulders down but his lower body continued to erupt in a spasm of kicks and jerks and Lorenzo feared Caesare would rip himself in half. He ran back into the villa and when he returned a few minutes later, the convulsions had stopped.

"Cover your brother," Santo said.

The smell of urine floated up as Lorenzo lay the blanket on him.

His father removed the handkerchief from Caesare's mouth. "He didn't bite his tongue this time but the attacks are getting more frequent."

"What's the matter with Caesare?" Lorenzo asked.

"Your brother has had seizures for over four years because of the injuries he suffered the night of the storm." He wiped the perspiration off Caesare's forehead.

"Why didn't you tell me?"

"What good would it have done?" He cleaned the spittle that had drooled from Caesare's mouth. "You and your brother never got along."

His father's words held no surprise so why were they difficult for Lorenzo to accept?

"There's no fever this time," Benito said.

"And the seizure didn't go on as long as usual," Santo said. "Perhaps the sea air was helpful." He loosened the collar around Caesare's neck.

Lorenzo knew he never fit with his father and brothers and now it was clear; they felt the same towards him. Why was there something in this revelation that filled him with both hurt and shame? In the family he and Caterina would create, all their children would belong; their love would leave no one on the outside.

"That's why I kept him away from your mother all these years. I wanted to wait until the seizures stopped before she saw him again." Santo stroked his son's hair.

"It would have been too much for *Mamma*," Benito said.

Was this the real reason they'd kept Caesare away? They'd hidden the truth about his mother from him so why should he have faith in these words? Too many things were happening in his life and Lorenzo needed to hear Padre Valentine tell him once again that Caterina was safe.

"Can't Fiore cure him?" Lorenzo asked.

"The new medication worked for awhile," Benito said.

"When you're in Naples, take him to Fiore," Santo said. "Perhaps it just needs another adjustment."

"*Si, Pappa.* I'm sure you're right."

"Has he gone to sleep?" Lorenzo asked.

"For a little while. When he wakes up, he usually doesn't remember what's happened."

"I'll stay with him," Santo said. "You have to make sure your mother's burial site is ready for tomorrow."

"I had a hard time controlling him last week after his attack," Benito said.

"But he had been drinking."

"I can stay with you, *Pappa*," Lorenzo said. Why did he want to help? Was there still a trace of love in his blood?

"It would be best if you weren't alone," Benito said.

"You're right," Santo agreed.

"Lorenzo, if there are any problems, send one of the servants for me. And when he wakes up; help *Pappa* bring him to his bedroom. Caesare should lie down for a little while. I'll come back in a few hours." Benito walked away.

Caesare groaned.

"*Pappa's* here, Caesare. It's alright." Santo stroked his face.

In a few days, Lorenzo would have a new life and the time

to know his father and brothers would have passed. Why did this realization sadden him? Was there something innate about a family's love? Could nothing ever completely eradicate it? Lorenzo rubbed his brother's arm and his father smiled.

The afternoon heat had changed from hot to stifling; Padre Valentine had only covered a short distance from the villa and he was already thirsty. He stopped and drank some water from his flask. A haze of sun coated the cluster of cottages in the distance and even though the priest knew the buildings were there, the misty vapor obscured them and at times, they seemed to evaporate and disappear from site. Their lack of permanence was disconcerting for it was as if he no longer completely lived in the real world.

Padre Valentine folded his hands as if to pray, but the action was feigned; he scanned the grounds and searched the woods ensuring that he hadn't been followed. He had seen no one since his meeting with Santo two hours ago and yet felt as if he was being watched. He moved forward and the wolf's shed came into view; the small clapboard structure stood close to a stand of oaks, the brown toned wood blended with the tree trunks. The priest covered the remaining distance quickly; Caterina was waiting for him.

Caterina pulled the canvas flap to one side at the same time that Padre Valentine bent down; she'd been in the shed for a day and a half and hadn't seen the priest since yesterday morning. "Shadow detected your scent when you were probably a mile away. Did anyone see you?" She moved back and the soles of her shoes struck the rear wall.

"*Non.*" His shoulders rubbed against the frame as he crawled inside.

"You're certain that you weren't followed?" She sat on the floor and Shadow lay beside her.

"Santo lets me come and go as I please." He crunched his body into a sitting position and faced her. "He understands my need to be alone and pray." He patted the wolf's head. "Why do you ask? Have you seen anyone?"

"*Non*. I've rarely left the shed." But the wolf had whined for hours last night; Caterina knew that someone was watching them. "How's Lorenzo? Have you talked to him since yesterday?"

Padre Valentine put his hand on Caterina's shoulder; her breath was sour and the color of summer had faded from her skin.

"Aren't you listening?" A stalk of lavender was tucked inside her blouse.

"Lorenzo's fine."

"What's he doing?"

"Santo's ordered him to stay with Benito and they're making preparations for *Mamma's* funeral."

"And Francesca?"

"She has to stay with Sisina but she's fine." The sack of food he had brought her yesterday remained unopened in the corner. "You haven't eaten anything? Have a drink of water." The priest gave her his flask. There was dirt underneath her fingernails. Caterina wiped her face with the back of her hand; its skin was smudged.

"Did you bring the *gobbo*?" Caterina asked.

Padre Valentine pulled the small statue out of his pocket.

"You must marry us tomorrow morning." Caterina grabbed the *gobbo*. "At sunrise before *Mamma* Anna's funeral. And we have to leave for Diamante tomorrow night after *Mamma's* funeral."

"*Non*. I will marry you and Lorenzo as planned. Sunrise on the day after *Mamma's* funeral. Then you will leave for Diamante."

"There's something wrong. Santo knows that Lorenzo and I love each other." Shadow edged closer to Caterina.

"Of course Santo knows. Something as strong as your love for each other could never be hidden."

"Padre, listen. Santo knows everything that Lorenzo and Francesca are doing yet you go about freely. Doesn't that seem strange to you?" Caterina touched his silver crucifix. "I don't know what's going on but I don't trust him. He abandoned *Mamma* Anna. He's not a man of honor like you." She wished that she knew the words to convince Padre Valentine she was right. "The only reason Santo has given you your freedom is because there's something in it for him. He would do anything to keep me away from Lorenzo." She placed the *gobbo* between the wolf's paws.

"Nothing could ever stop Lorenzo from loving you, Caterina." Padre Valentine placed his hand over hers. Some things were impossible to change but she was right; Santo would never permit them to marry. What difference would it make if the priest married them a day earlier than originally planned? If it helped ease Caterina's pain, he would do as she had asked. "I will marry you and Lorenzo tomorrow morning at sunrise before *Mamma* Anna's funeral. And tomorrow night, you will leave for Diamante. I will tell Lorenzo and Francesca and make the necessary arrangements." Caterina began to shiver. "This will be your last night alone. Tomorrow evening, you and Lorenzo will be on your way to a new life." The priest covered Caterina with a blanket and the cold that was within her body passed into his; he too began to shiver.

Santo walked into his sitting room; Rinaldo had stoked the fire and set two glasses of brandy on the table between the two chairs. It was late afternoon and Benito would be returning from the burial site soon. He stood in front of the white marble fireplace with its elegant columns on each side; the bronze statue of *Gattamelata* sat in the middle of the mantle where he had placed it years ago. There had been so much promise in Caesare but it was time to accept the fact that it would remain unfulfilled; a part of Santo always knew his oldest son was doomed.

Shortly after Caesare had murdered Clorinda, they spent the night at Dreamer's Rock but there had been no wind and the mystics had not come. At first this troubled Santo; three years later

Caesare won the Palio and Santo thought everything would be, as it should. Then the storm struck and his fears came to fruition.

An exquisite chandelier with the rock crystal girandoles from Murano hung from the finely carved gilt wooden ceiling; the blue background in the ceiling matched the color of the silk damask walls. Anna had decorated this room beautifully. He sat down in the chair; Santo's life had almost been perfect. The door opened.

"Good afternoon, *Pappa*," Benito said. "How's Caesare?" He sat down in the other chair.

"He slept for over an hour after you left. Lorenzo stayed with him and the men took him fishing a while ago. He'll be back for dinner."

"How was he when he woke up?"

"Agitated but I was there and that settled him." Santo crossed one leg of his neatly pressed trousers over the other and watched the reflection of the fire flicker on the shiny surface of his ebony leather boots. "Lorenzo's sketching; he should be here shortly." Santo reached for a glass of brandy.

Lorenzo approached his father's sitting room; he was holding the notebook with the sketches that he had done for his father. The door was ajar and his father and Benito were talking. He placed his head close to the opening and listened to their conversation.

"I've everything arranged for the morning after your mother's funeral," his father said. "Before sunrise, go to the shed and get the girl. Kill the wolf. I don't want a wild animal on my estate. There will be a private car on the early morning train set aside for you. By the time Lorenzo wakes up, she'll have disappeared. I'll tell him that you've taken Caesare to see Fiore. Do you have any questions?"

"*Non*," Benito said.

"We'll watch Caesare until then. If he has another attack and you're worried about controlling him, Mabruco will go with you to get the girl instead; I don't want another mess like Clorinda."

Where was Padre Valentine? Lorenzo had to find him. He

dropped his notebook. Sisina was walking down the corridor; he'd ask her for help.

"Lorenzo should be here soon," Benito said. "When will you bring Fiorina to San Michelle?" He sipped his brandy.

"Next month," Santo said. "She's anxious to start our new life."

"And Padre Valentine will baptize Gaetano, my new little brother."

"Another Marino son for our business." Santo placed his drink on the table. "Then I'll deal with him."

"What are you going to do?"

"I haven't decided. Nothing will harm Fiore but I can no longer trust the priest."

Benito placed his glass on the table.

"There's no need to hurry; I'll get Fiorina settled here first," Santo said.

"Do you think she'll want to paint this room burgundy?"

"She'll probably want to paint the whole villa burgundy." Santo laughed. And so did Benito.

Padre Valentine stepped down from the carriage in front of the villa. "*Grazie*, Mabruco. The priest's probably too feeble now to come all the way from Diamante to the *Signora's* funeral but I thought that he should know."

"I'm sure he'll say special prayers for her in his church," Mabruco said.

"It was very kind of you to take me to the train station; I know how busy you are."

"The *Signora* was a lovely woman; she'd want me to help you Padre." He flicked the reins on the horse and the wagon pulled away.

The telegrams he had sent the old priest and Fiore explained everything that had happened; all he had to do now was find Lorenzo and tell him their plans had changed. Padre Valentine ascended the stairs and entered the villa; Sisina was standing in the entranceway.

"I've been looking for you," Sisina said.

"Is there something wrong?"

"*Signore* Lorenzo wants to meet with you. He just went up to the *Signora's* sitting room."

"I'll go there now. Could you please tell *Signore* that I'll meet him in his office in a little while?"

"Of course, Padre."

"Here's Lorenzo now," Santo said as the door to his sitting room opened.

"I'm anxious to see his sketches," Benito said. "You should try and chose a design. It would be nice to have *Mamma's* monument completed before *Natale*."

Sisina entered the room. "This was lying outside." She handed Santo the notebook. "And the door was open."

"That's Lorenzo's," Benito said.

"He was listening to your conversation," Sisina said. "I was walking down the corridor and when he saw me, he dropped it on the floor."

"Where's he now?" Santo asked. He handed the notebook to Benito.

"With Padre Valentine in the *Signora's* sitting room."

"*Grazie*, Sisina. Once again, you've proven your worth," Santo said. "Benito, we will have to change our plans."

CHAPTER TWENTY-THREE

Padre Valentine whirled around and faced Lorenzo; the cassock's heavy material swished about his reed like frame and threatened to unbalance him. He stood so close to the angel panel on the wall behind him that his head had become part of the painting.

"Stop this now. We don't have much time to deal with the situation. Your father's expecting me in his office and we can't let him think that we suspect anything."

"My brothers are going to kidnap Caterina. My father wants her to disappear. Mabruco's one of them." Lorenzo paced back and forth. "We have to do something." He lunged towards the priest. "Haven't you heard a word I've been saying?" He grabbed his arm and Padre Valentine feared he was going to tear it out of the socket.

Caterina had almost been lost. And what would have happened to Lorenzo if Santo's plans had been brought to fruition? The fourth angel seemed to be smiling at him; perhaps, there was a place for him in God's kingdom someday for afterall he'd been given a second chance.

"We'll still do everything that we planned but we'll do it tomorrow," Padre Valentine said. "I'll marry you and Caterina at sunrise, hide her in the church during your mother's funeral then afterwards, at night when everyone's sleeping, you'll leave for Diamante." There was no need for Caterina to know what he'd found out; once again, it made no sense to tell the truth.

Lorenzo was staring at the carpet as if the burden of his thoughts had made his head too heavy to lift. He looked up and for a moment, the priest saw Anna. "Everything will be fine." It was to her that he spoke.

"I was supposed to show my father some sketches I was doing for *Mamma's* tombstone."

"When?"

"A little while ago."

"Then you better go," Padre ordered. Lorenzo turned away from him.

"I don't know if I..."

"I'll go with you and tell your father that you're late because we were praying for your mother."

"Caesare had something to do with Clorinda's death. I think he may have killed her."

His words were muffled and Padre Valentine hoped that what he had heard was not what had been said.

"Do you know what happened?" Lorenzo asked.

"There was some kind of accident. I don't know what actually happened but Caesare didn't mean to harm the girl." Padre Valentine was thankful that he was an expert liar; there was a good side to everything.

"Why did you keep this from me?"

"I had to promise your father that I would say nothing."

"Why?"

"He didn't want your mother to find out and I would never do anything to hurt her." His love for Anna had given him words to soothe her son; God had shown him mercy again.

They left the sitting room and made their way down the corridor. "I don't want Francesca to know anything about this," Padre Valentine said.

"I agree. This will be our secret Padre."

The value of not telling the truth was a lesson Padre Valentine was not proud of teaching Lorenzo. They descended the stairs and approached Santo's sitting room.

"I must have dropped it," Lorenzo said as he picked up his notebook that was lying outside of the door. Padre Valentine followed him into the room; Santo and Benito were sitting in the chairs facing the fireplace.

"There you are," Santo said.

"We were praying," Padre Valentine said.

"I brought the sketches to show you." Lorenzo handed his father the notebook.

"Benito, pour us all some brandy," Santo said. "Let's have a drink."

Padre Valentine looked at the statue of *Gattamelata*; he hated it almost as much as he hated Santo Marino.

The sun had not yet risen as the team of horses pulling his mother's carriage sped across the fields taking Lorenzo, Francesca and Padre Valentine to the stream where Caterina and Shadow would be waiting. A short time later, Lorenzo tied the reins to a branch of an oak tree and flew down the trail. This day would change his life for within the twenty-four hours it had been allotted, Lorenzo would marry his wife and bury his mother; it would be impossible to erase anything that happened from his mind.

"Look at what I just found," Francesca said. She pulled her hand from underneath her cloak.

"Oleanders," Lorenzo said.

"*Mamma's* Gabriella flowers."

His mother was blessing their marriage, Lorenzo thought. She wanted this day to be a celebration of their new beginning and not a mourning of her passing; Lorenzo would honor her wishes. Dinner last night with his father and brothers had been beyond difficult and afterwards he'd barely slept, but when they met at the stables this morning, everyone else in the villa was still sleeping; so far, everything was going well.

"I'm glad we're leaving tonight," Francesca said. "I don't like the way Benito looks at me. Men like him think they can fool women with their smiles."

Lodovico and Matteo would love Francesca, Lorenzo thought.

"Caesare though, well, I feel sorry for him, Lorenzo, about his leg, but he frightens me."

"By tomorrow morning, you'll be hours away from here," Padre Valentine said.

"Why can't you come with us?" Francesca asked.

"My place is here."

When would they see Padre Valentine again? Lorenzo did not know and this was the first time he'd thought of this.

"There she is," Francesca yelled.

The trail had widened and Caterina was facing them from behind the fallen tree trunk. The sun was rising in a grey painted sky; the pine trees lining the opposite shore had lost their green and the blue had drained from the stream. This absence of color and brightness was of no concern to Lorenzo for he did not need them to see Caterina's beautiful face; he had memorized every detail of the woman who would soon be his wife. Lorenzo raced towards Caterina.

"I tried to clean up in the stream," Caterina said, "but..."

Worthless words, Lorenzo thought. He had not seen her since his mother had died and his father had banished her from the villa; he pulled her towards him. What did it matter that her dress was dirty and her hair unwashed? Did she think his love depended on such trivialities? Their bodies sank into each other and he craved to know her again.

"Are you all right?" Lorenzo traced the outline of her torso with his hands. "No one has harmed you?" He longed for their first night as husband and wife; the passion they had released at Dreamer's Rock would be pale compared to what their love would express the next time they were together. He held her closer; she was safe. A part of him now belonged to Caterina and if anything ever happened to her, that part of him would also die. Loving someone completely and unconditionally was sublime but it also had its price; Lorenzo would court death should his life ever not include Caterina.

Shadow jumped over the log and Francesca handed the flowers to the priest. She dropped to her knees and when the wolf's body came into contact with hers, she fell onto her side and they became entangled in her cloak; Padre Valentine felt as if he were watching two children play. He looked at Caterina and Lorenzo; they were locked in a passionate embrace. By tomorrow morning, he would be alone. Padre Valentine did not want to stay at San Michelle any longer but where else could he go? He had nowhere to belong.

"We must start." Padre Valentine helped Francesca to her feet. She took off her cloak and lay it on the ground; he gave her the flowers then patted the wolf's head. As they walked towards Caterina and Lorenzo, a band of gold stretched across the sky.

The women embraced; it was the first time they'd seen each other since the morning Anna had died and they'd found out that Bruno had also passed away.

"We have to get back to the villa as soon as possible," the priest said to Lorenzo.

"I know, Padre."

Caterina held the cedar box her *Pappa* had made her when she was a child. She was standing between Francesca and Lorenzo, Padre Valentine was facing the stream and Shadow was lapping water.

"It was Lorenzo's idea," Francesca said. "He knew that you'd want it in Florence and that was the only reason I wore that stupid cloak; it had an inside pocket."

"Open it," Lorenzo said.

There was a lavender stalk and crimson rose petals on top.

"The lavender's from your cottage and the flowers from the rose bed you were working in the day I returned to San Michelle," he said.

Life had changed so much for Caterina in the past three months; she hoped that the future would hold some quiet.

"Did you see what's underneath?" Francesca picked up two holy cards. "St. Catherine of Siena and St. Frances of Assisi."

"Did you ever find out if you have a name saint?" Caterina asked.

"*Si*. St. Lorenzo. He was a calligrapher who was born over three hundred years ago. I think he was Spanish but I'm not sure."

"We'll find out in Florence."

"I remember you telling me about St. Catherine waving to you."

When Caterina was an old woman and looked back at her life, she would have very few memories without Lorenzo; it would be almost as if they'd always been married.

"Francesca will take it back with her and give it to you tonight when it's time to leave," Padre Valentine said.

"You will come to Florence and see us, Padre?" Caterina asked. "Won't you?"

"Of course." He placed the cedar box on top of the tree trunk.

The emptiness inside Caterina for her *Mamma, Pappa, Mamma* Anna and Bruno would never go away; she was glad that there would be no emptiness for Padre Valentine for there was no more room in her body.

"Let's begin," he said.

Lorenzo held Caterina's hand; Francesca was beside her and the wolf close by. The jeweled cross hung around Caterina's neck, the cameo brooch was pinned on her shawl and the sketch tucked inside her blouse near her heart. The early morning breeze gained momentum; it stirred the fine sand at the edge of the priest's cassock and swirled it upwards, dusting the long black robe with golden flecks. A random beam of light flashed across the sky and passed through the priest's body and in that instant, Lorenzo sensed that Padre Valentine had undergone some kind of transformation. Francesca handed Caterina the oleanders and the priest began their marriage vows.

"O Lord by our humble prayers, and in your kindness assist this institution of marriage which You have ordained. Let the yoke of their marriage be one of love and peace. Let her be true to one wedlock and let her be fruitful in children. May they thus attain the old age, which they desire..."

Francesca took the flowers from Caterina and Lorenzo unwrapped a handkerchief that his mother had given him. "This will have to do until we get to Florence." He placed a ring woven from strands of his hair on her finger.

"It's perfect," she said.

"My woman in the wind." Lorenzo kissed Caterina.

"I'm sorry, but there's so little time," Padre Valentine said.

The kiss ended before it began and when it was over, Lorenzo felt that it had yet to start; this was not a propitious way to mark their new life. The first time a husband's lips touch those of his wife's, there should be lingering without hurry. When they were settled in Florence, he would kiss Caterina over and over again to make up for this one, in their new life, Lorenzo would never rush their love.

"Sign this now." The priest placed their marriage certificate on the tree trunk.

"Caterina Romano and Lorenzo Marino are married on this day, August 25, 1913," Lorenzo said aloud when they were finished. "I'll keep it." He folded the paper in half and placed it in his pocket.

"I'll go over everything once more, then we must leave," Padre Valentine said. "The sun's about to rise."

They huddled together.

"You and Francesca will take the carriage and return to the villa. If anyone asks where you've been, tell them you were praying with me. I'll take Caterina to the church now. Leave a horse tied up. We'll wait till you've been gone for a few minutes before we set off. Afterwards, I'll return to the villa. When *Mamma's* funeral is over and everyone's sleeping, you and Francesca will meet us at the church. I'll say I have to return my vestments and in this way, I can stay with Caterina until you get there. I've already made arrangements for horses. Then, the three of you are to leave for Diamante; the old priest will be expecting you in his church."

"You'll take care of Shadow until we can send for him?" Francesca asked.

"Of course." Padre Valentine wasn't sure what to do with the wolf after they'd gone but he'd think of something; he had to keep the animal safe from harm.

"And Shadow will be with Caterina until we arrive," Lorenzo said.

"Caterina will never be left alone."

"Can you do a favor for me before you go, Padre?" Caterina asked.

"Of course."

She turned around and when she faced the priest again, she placed the jeweled cross, the cameo brooch and the sketch in his hand. "These are from Lorenzo and I want you to bless them so that whenever I look at them, I'll always think of the day I became his wife."

Padre Valentine bowed his head, said a silent prayer and blessed the gifts. Caterina folded them in the handkerchief, turned around then tucked the bundle inside her blouse.

"We must go now," Padre Valentine said. He picked up the oleander flowers, Francesca's cloak and the cedar box.

"I can't say goodbye to you, Francesca," Caterina said.

"That's good because you're not." She kissed her on the cheek, spun around, did three cartwheels and disappeared down the trail.

"And I will never say goodbye to you." The eyes of the sea, Caterina thought. She snuggled close to Lorenzo; no matter how many years she looked at them, it would never be enough.

"Only a little while longer, then we'll never be apart again."

"I wouldn't know how to live without you, Lorenzo." He circled his arms around her but there was still too much distance between them. Could there ever be enough closeness? Caterina wanted to be more than one with Lorenzo but was this possible? If it was dangerous for a woman to give a man this much of herself, it was too late for her; she had gone past this point.

"And I wouldn't know how to live without you."

"*Mio amare*," she said.

"*Mia amare*," he said.

"*Sempre*," they said in unison.

"You must go now Lorenzo," Padre Valentine walked towards them. "I'm sorry but there simply is no more time for you and Caterina to be together."

His bride stood beside Padre Valentine and Shadow was close to her; at least, Lorenzo knew she was safe. He walked backwards for as long as he could, he kept his eyes on her and she kept her eyes on him. Time would have to be endured until he could see her again; Lorenzo was thankful that the hours were few compared to those in the lifetime they would share. Finally, he turned away; he had to leave her now if he ever wanted to come back. Lorenzo would always remember the way Caterina looked when Padre married them; as the years of their marriage passed and he saw her in other ways, it was this picture that would remain. As soon as they were settled in Florence, he would draw a sketch of Caterina; he hoped that he could capture the very moment that she became his wife.

Francesca had covered almost half the distance back to the carriage by the time Lorenzo caught up with her.

"Do you have the cedar box?" She took the oleanders from him.

"*Si.*"

They walked along in silence. In the past few days, Lorenzo had been to Dreamer's Rock with Caterina, his mother had died, Bruno had passed away, he'd discovered Caesare had killed Clorinda and his father and brothers had planned to kidnap the woman who was now his wife; he couldn't get away from San Michelle soon enough. There was no reason to return for he and Caterina would have their own villa in Tuscany, the region where Leonardo was born; that's where they belonged and where they would raise their children. Padre would send Shadow as soon as they were settled and Lorenzo would convince the priest to move to Florence and live with them. By this time tomorrow, they would be on their way.

His mother's carriage came into view. He and Francesca released one of the horses from the harness and saddled it for Padre Valentine and Caterina.

"Let's go," he said.

"Did you ever think that letter would lead to this?" Francesca asked.

"What letter?"

"The letter you got in Florence that told you to come home."

The only people who knew about the letter were Lodovico and Matteo; Lorenzo hadn't even told Padre Valentine.

"Give me my cloak." She put it on the back seat.

"How do you know about the letter?" Lorenzo asked.

"I was the one who wrote it and sent it to you," Francesca said.

They climbed into the carriage; Francesca grabbed the reins and tapped the horse's back. The carriage moved forward.

"I knew your *Mamma* wanted to see you and after she came back from Naples, I could tell she'd never get well again."

Don't ask any questions, Lorenzo thought. Just let her speak.

"Was there ever a time in her life that Caterina didn't love you? She read your letters even more than your *Mamma* did."

"I don't know when I would have come home if it weren't for your letter."

"Then, I'm glad I sent it."

It was mid-morning when Padre Valentine walked through the doors of St. Ursula's Church; Caterina and Shadow followed him. He dipped the tip of his index finger into the holy water in the basin of the stone pedestal font and blessed himself. Caterina did the same, then repeated the ritual for the wolf, dabbing the holy water between the animal's eyes. The priest bowed his head in front of the picture of St. Ursula. "*O, Dio who knowest us to be set in the midst of great perils, help us to overcome the evils which we suffer for through Thine assistance. Through Christ our Lord, Amen.*"

"Come," he said. They walked down the center aisle of the church's nave. The statue of St. Pammachius was perched on the ledge in the recess on the far wall. He had to say mass next week in his honor to celebrate the end of summer but there was no reason to be joyful.

"Padre." Caterina pointed to the stained glass window behind the altar. "Do you remember that this was where I saw my first rainbow?"

"*Si*. You asked me all the time where you could find painted glass."

"And you used to tell me it was buried in the sand on the beaches."

They reached the transept of the church.

"This is where I'll stay. In the chapel with the statue of St. Rose that *Mamma* Anna bought for you."

"Absolutely not. You'll stay in the sacristy. Mabruco put a lock on the door because of the new chalices."

"Why do I need to lock myself in a room?"

Padre Valentine should have had an answer but he didn't.

"I have Shadow and *mio Pappa's* lavender with me. I'm staying here."

Why did she have to argue with the priest now when his mind had no energy to dissuade her?

Caterina passed under the arch-shaped entrance of the small chapel; Shadow was at her heels.

The walls and floor were grey stone and except for a narrow wooden table along one side covered with irregular shaped candles, it was unfurnished. The statue of St Rose was set against the wall in front of them, positioned in the middle of a ledge, which also held a vase of Anna's favorite roses; a few of the red petals had turned pink. A waist high wooden railing with a kneeling board separated the room into two sections.

"You can't stay here. There's nowhere for you to sit; the floor's too cold to lie down on and even if I lit all the candles, the chill would stay. There's a chair in the sacristy and a rug on the floor."

"This is where I'll wait for you and Lorenzo and Francesca. My thoughts of our new life will keep me warm and I can cuddle up with Shadow." She patted the wolf's head. "Let's light a candle together before you leave."

She went over to the table and picked up a long matchstick. The priest straightened one of the slim cream colored candles and held it while she brought the wick to life.

"For *Mamma* Anna and *mio Pappa* and *mia Mamma,*" she said.

For you, Caterina, the priest said to himself.

A few minutes later, he exited the church, mounted the horse and raced back to the villa. There had been no need for Padre Valentine and Caterina to say goodbye for he would see her later that day; his thoughts turned to Anna's funeral.

Caterina spread her shawl on the floor and Shadow lay down on it, his front paws pointed towards the entrance. She reached inside her blouse, removed the bundle and unfolded the handkerchief.

"See how beautiful *Mamma* Anna was?" Caterina had put off thinking about *Mamma* Anna's death until she could be with Lorenzo; this was the second mother she'd lost but her love for him was so great that it would absorb this sadness. She'd wait to cry for Bruno too; her tears wouldn't hurt as much if she were in his arms. The love they shared would fill her and for the first time in Caterina's life; there would be no room for emptiness.

She brought the cameo brooch close to Shadow and traced the swirls engraved in the golden oval frame with her fingertip.

Caterina knew their first child would be a girl and Lorenzo had already decided to name her "Caterina Rosa." She'd name the next daughter "Anna Nella" after her mothers and when she spoke with her, she'd use both names. She put the brooch down and picked up the jeweled cross. There wasn't any light to make the aquamarine stone glow but the rays of the Tuscan sun would bring it back to life. Shadow's wet nose touched her hand.

"Do you remember how frightened Lorenzo was the first time he saw you?"

"Edoardo" would be the name of their first son and the first thing she'd teach him to grow would be lavender. Caterina would wait until she had a son with the eyes of the sea before she used the name Lorenzo. She put the cross beside the brooch. He'd want Lodovico and Matteo to be godfather to their sons; Francesca would be the only godmother for all of their children and she'd probably teach them to do cartwheels.

"You'll be giving rides to a lot of children you know and Padre Valentine will be kept busy baptizing all my babies." She patted the wolf's fur; Caterina hoped that someday Padre Valentine would live with them in Florence; perhaps she could care for him when he was old.

"I am the woman in the wind. Did you know that?" She unfolded the sketch in front of the wolf's face. "That's me. On the edge of the cliff. Aren't I brave?" She placed it next to the cross.

"Do you know what I'm going to do with these gifts my husband gave me?" She put her arm around Shadow's neck. "Isn't that a lovely word? Husband."

"They will be the inheritance I give to the first child Lorenzo and I have; the cameo brooch, the jeweled cross and the sketch will be for our Caterina Rosa. And I know that she will be born with the mark of the rose and the eyes of the sea."

Caterina folded everything up in the handkerchief and tucked the bundle inside her blouse. The wolf raised his head and shifted his body so that once again it was positioned forward. She rested against his shoulders. In a few hours, Padre Valentine would return and shortly afterwards, Lorenzo and Francesca; her new life as Lorenzo's wife was set to begin. The mystics were right; their love was blessed.

All she had to do now was summon up the pictures of their time at Dreamer's Rock and it would be as if she was with Lorenzo again; Caterina was thankful that she had the same mind as Leonardo. She closed her eyes. No matter how age changed Lorenzo's face, it was the young Lorenzo who had shown her love for the first time that she would always remember. There, she was looking at him now; she drifted away. When she awoke, it would be his face that she saw again; sleep came to her but not to Shadow. The wolf focused his eyes on the open space in front of them and kept every one of his muscles tensed and poised for action.

CHAPTER TWENTY-FOUR

Lorenzo was positioned at the rear of his mother's coffin, across from Caesare and behind Benito; his father was at the front. He grasped the brass handle by his side and planted his foot on the granite step. All of a sudden, the coffin dipped and propelled him forward.

"Ben...tho," Caesare yelled.

If his mother's coffin slid downwards, Lorenzo hoped it would crush his father and Benito.

"Pull the handle towards you," Benito ordered.

The coffin jerked and the four men regained their equilibrium. What had caused his father to lose his balance? Francesca was standing behind the workhorse hitched up to the wagon that would take his mother's coffin to the gravesite; Rinaldo sat in the driver's seat and Padre Valentine stood below him. There seemed to be others clustered around but Lorenzo had trouble focusing; the heat of the noonday sun combined with the exhaustion in his body was beginning to overtake him. He blinked several times, the scene took shape and within a few minutes, he understood what had happened. Lined up in the driveway were the servants and workers of San Michelle as well as villagers from Cetraro, an act of love for his mother that had taken his father by surprise.

They completed their descent and walked towards the wagon, passing by men and women with bowed heads who were mouthing silent prayers as their fingers slid soundlessly from one rosary bead to another. Their clothes, though worn and faded, were meticulously clean; rips and tears had been carefully stitched, boots and shoes polished. The women wore dark kerchiefs and the men black armbands. Faces already red from the sun had been reddened further from scrupulous scrubbing, hair had been trimmed and washed; their bodies smelled fresh.

As they approached the wagon, Lorenzo acknowledged Sisina and Armida. Blankets had been layered on top of the rough wood at the back so as to protect his mother's coffin from being scratched. Benito offered to help Francesca into the carriage so that she could sit next to Rinaldo; instead, she cut in front of him and approached a group of children holding bouquets of wildflowers.

"For *Mamma* Anna?" Francesca bent down so that she'd match their height.

"*Si,*" their voices chimed sweetly.

Fortunata tapped her on the shoulder.

"*Bella,*" Francesca said. She kissed the girl and took the bouquets from all the children.

After Francesca had gathered the flowers, Benito offered for a second time to help her into the carriage.

"I'll walk beside Lorenzo," she said.

Padre Valentine nodded at Rinaldo; he flicked the reins on the horse's back and the wagon moved forward. The priest followed with Santo beside him; Benito and Caesare were next, then Francesca and Lorenzo. The cortege passed the villa and traveled through the section of the estate housing the barns, stables and pens; it skirted the edge of the servant's enclave. Who would live in the cottage that Caterina and Edoardo had shared? Lorenzo did not care who occupied his villa. They crossed the open fields bordered by wooded areas cut by trails and through which streams flowed; even though Lorenzo no longer wanted to live at San Michelle, there were parts of it he planned never to forget. By the time they reached the perimeter of San Michelle, it was the middle of the afternoon.

The site that his father had approved for his mother's burial plot was a natural elevation that faced east; Benito had selected it because the sun would rise over her grave every morning. Would Lorenzo ever be able to reconcile Benito's dual nature? How could he be distraught one moment over his mother's death and the next, be merciless towards the woman who had given her the care and solace that had not come from her husband and sons? If Lorenzo were to choose a color from his palette to paint Benito, it would be grey.

Something in the periphery caught his father's attention and for the second time that day, he was surprised, for those who had lined the driveway had followed them to the gravesite. They removed the coffin and carried it up to the grave, which Caesare had excavated earlier. His oldest brother seemed calm with no trace of the seizure he'd suffered yesterday. Despite his abhorrence for Caesare, there was something tragic about what had happened to him; of his two brothers now, it was Benito whom Lorenzo feared the most. When they reached the top, they set the coffin on the ground.

"It's time to begin the prayers," his father said.

They stood in two straight lines parallel to the coffin; Santo, Caesare and Benito were on one side and Padre Valentine, Lorenzo and Francesca on the other. The open pit into which his mother's coffin would be lowered afterwards separated them.

"*Lord Jesus Christ, who willest that no man should perish...*"

Padre Valentine's words faded as Lorenzo was consumed by thoughts that weren't about his mother. He grieved her loss but his concern for Caterina had overpowered these feelings. She looked so tired and worn this morning; of course he never told her but the heaviness did not escape him. How much sleep would it before she was restored? The ride to Diamante tonight was long and he hoped that she found some respite in the church.

"*...Thou has redeemed me, O God of truth, who are blessed for ever and ever.*"

By late afternoon, the prayers had ended. When Padre Valentine turned around in a circle to bless the crowd below, he set his white alb into motion. The sun shone on the gold designs embroidered on the chasuble and rays of light beamed into the air. The priest was a celestial vision with the same ethereal quality that Lorenzo had seen in Francesca the day he'd been reunited with his mother. Padre Valentine was a holy man; Lorenzo had to find a way to convince him to be a part of their life in Florence.

"Now let us say together, one of Anna's most cherished prayers."

At the conclusion when Padre Valentine blessed himself, something a teacher had taught Lorenzo a long time ago surfaced in his mind. Emperor Claudius the Goth had imprisoned St. Valentine for defying his orders and secretly marrying young lovers. His fate, Lorenzo remembered, was execution; he was beheaded. A shiver ran up Lorenzo's spine and at the same time Vito Mabruco ascended the mound carrying three bouquets of his mother's vermilion red roses.

Mabruco handed the first bouquet to Lorenzo's father and the second to Benito; they placed them on top of the coffin. Lorenzo went over to Mabruco for the remaining bouquet.

"For Caesare," Mabruco said.

Benito took the roses and approached the coffin with his brother. He placed the bouquet in Caesare's arms and guided him with his hands so that they lay the flowers down together. They returned to his father and Padre Valentine moved beside Lorenzo.

The four men left the gravesite and made their way to the wagon. Mabruco was in between Lorenzo's father and Benito and he was the only one talking; Caesare followed behind.

Francesca was staring into the distance, oblivious to Mabruco's presence. The wildflowers she had gathered from the children were spread on the ground by her feet. He picked them up and they returned to the coffin and scattered them over the roses.

"From the *bambina's, Mamma,*" she said.

Lorenzo reached inside his shirt and pulled out the oleanders Caterina had held that morning; there was still life in them. "From Caterina, *Mamma*. My wife." He lay them down with the others.

Padre Valentine was staring at something; Lorenzo followed his line of vision and met his father's eyes. Without any words being exchanged, they both realized that somehow, Mabruco had found out that the priest had married Lorenzo and Caterina and now, his father knew as well.

Almost two hours had passed since his mother's funeral had ended; it was early evening and Padre Valentine would be in the church with Caterina and Shadow. Mabruco had brought his father and brothers back in his mother's carriage and they were waiting for Lorenzo and Francesca in the villa.

While Francesca talked to Rinaldo, Lorenzo walked down the pathway. Most of the roses had been clipped from the shrubs in his mother's flowerbed; the exact one Caterina had been working in the day he'd returned to San Michelle. Stems had been snapped in half and the roses hung limply, they had died a slow death in the day's heat. Bits of leaves and broken branches and loose petals were scattered on the ground. Clusters of unopened buds had been squished; the imprint of boots that had stepped on them marked the earth. Lorenzo felt as if someone had committed an act of defilement on the roses and concluded that it had been Mabruco. He had barely seen or exchanged a word with the man this summer. How was it possible to hate someone who was almost a complete stranger but then again, how was it possible to hate the men whose blood you shared?

How had Mabruco discovered the truth? He wished that he and Padre Valentine had time to discuss the situation after his mother's funeral but what difference would it have made? Sometimes talking was an absolute waste of time. Lorenzo reviewed what he and Francesca had done when they returned to the carriage house earlier that morning. They had wiped the exterior of the carriage and its seats with rags removing any trace of dust or grime. He'd pulled out the grass intertwined with the spokes in the wheels and Francesca had put the horse in its stall. Everything had been done in haste. What clue had he left behind?

Rinaldo climbed into the wagon and the horse made its way to the barn; Francesca walked towards him. There was no spring to the curls in her hair, no swing to the movements of her arms and no dance to the steps her boots took; Caterina's spirited friend had become a forlorn waif.

"We better go inside now," Lorenzo said.

"How much longer?" she asked.

"Only a few more hours." What his father knew was of no consequence; it could not alter their plans, therefore, there was no need to tell Francesca.

"We have to have dinner with them, don't we?"

"But then we can rest until it's time to leave for the church," Lorenzo reassured her.

"And I have to be nice to Benito. Padre Valentine says that we can't cause any trouble."

"He's right."

"I'm only doing this for Caterina."

"I know," Lorenzo replied.

"Caterina probably loves you more than me."

"No," Lorenzo said. "Just in a different way."

Francesca smiled and they walked towards the stairs.

The embers in the fireplace were cold, it had been a day with too much sun and there was no need for Rinaldo to build Santo a fire tonight. Santo slid his hand down the smooth white column in front of him; the statue of *Gattamelata* would remain in the center of the mantle. He would not give Fiorina permission to alter the fireplace in anyway. Sisina set the tray with the silver pitcher and two crystal glasses on the round table between the chairs. She was thirty years old and had been in his service for sixteen years. Sisina was attractive in an uncomplicated way; it didn't take as much effort or money to keep women like her happy and in some ways, Santo envied Vito Mabruco.

"I've prepared the water according to your instructions," Sisina said.

"*Bene*. Then, after only one glass, Lorenzo should sleep until tomorrow afternoon," Santo said.

"*Si*. And when he awakes, he'll only have a headache," Sisina added.

"How will I ever be able to repay you and Vito?"

Vito and Interzino were passing by Anna's carriage house early that morning to bring the wagon that would carry her coffin back to the villa. They saw Lorenzo and Francesca leave and Vito followed them. Interzino returned to the villa and told Santo. It had all been so simple; Santo couldn't wait to tell Buccella.

Was it Lorenzo's audacity or his stupidity that angered Santo the most? He wasn't sure. What Santo couldn't believe was that a Marino son was actually married to a servant girl. He shuddered. If they'd ever had a child, it would be as worthless as a bastard but the shame it could bring to his family would be incalculable; blood should never be mixed.

There was a period in his early life when Santo didn't adhere to this tenet, for it had been to his advantage when Anna married him but as time passed his need for this belief disappeared. Unfortunately, Anna's didn't and in the end, what had brought them together tore them apart. Love could be fickle but Fiorina was an excellent choice for his second wife; their marriage had brought the *Ndrangheta* and the *Camorra* together and Buccella was ecstatic with the endless possibilities. Now that Anna was dead, he'd get Padre Valentine to remarry them; Santo didn't want any complications to mar this union. Yes, he still needed the priest.

"Working for you has been an honor, *Signore*," Sisina said.

"Are you anxious to start your new life?"

"Very much, *Signore*. Armida is happy that you are letting her come with us."

"She belongs with you and her brother. Buccella tells me that he has a beautiful villa waiting for you."

"I am ready to be a *Signora*."

"Fiorina and I look forward to dancing at your wedding," Santo said.

"It will be my honor, *Signore*," Sisina said.

Santo smiled. "Have all the arrangements been made for Francesca?" he asked.

"*Si*. Armida's getting her bath ready and I've prepared her the same drink; Francesca will also sleep well into tomorrow."

"And when they both awake, the servant girl will have disappeared," Santo said.

Sisina nodded.

"I will be glad when this day's over. It's been very exhausting for me." When Santo woke up tomorrow, it would be a new life at San Michelle; his three sons would be with him and there'd be no more meddlesome women. It was too bad that Eugenio Mella didn't have another daughter for Lorenzo; Santo would ask Buccella to find someone appropriate.

"Is there anything I can do for Benito and Caesare?"

"*Non*. They're having a rest before dinner. If you see Lorenzo though, please remind him that I am waiting."

Sisina left the room.

As soon as darkness had fallen, Benito and Caesare would go to the church; Interzino had already taken Padre Valentine there. Santo did not want the priest harmed, he intended to deal with him later; nevertheless, he had made it clear to Benito that nothing was to stand in the way of getting rid of the girl. Suddenly, Santo felt chilled; he needed Rinaldo to build him a fire after all.

Lorenzo opened the door to his villa and Francesca went to the staircase and leaned against the wooden banister.

"The children were so sweet," Francesca said.

"Fortunata's going to miss Caterina," Lorenzo said. But Caterina had given the girl the gift of reading and writing and so, they would always be a part of each other.

"So are Elda and Ermenigildo," Francesca said.

What would Padre Valentine tell everyone tomorrow?

"I can't believe that *Mamma's* not upstairs," Francesca said.

Neither could Lorenzo. Even though his feelings for Caterina were beyond what he had ever dreamed possible, it was different than the love he had for his mother; it couldn't replace it and he didn't want it to. Lorenzo's life had been blessed; he'd known the love of a mother and now, the love of a wife.

Sisina approached them. "*Signore*. Your father's waiting for you in his sitting room."

"I must go," Lorenzo said to Francesca.

"Armida's preparing your bath, *Signorina*."

"That's wonderful," Francesca said.

"And I've prepared you a refreshing drink."

"Sisina," Lorenzo said. "Thank you for your kindness to *Mamma*." These were words that his mother would be proud that he spoke.

"*Sì*, Sisina. *Grazie*," Francesca said.

"I will miss the *Signora*," Sisina said.

"I'll see you at dinner," Lorenzo said to Francesca.

Francesca and Sisina walked up the stairs.

Lorenzo knocked on the door of his father's sitting room then entered. His father was pouring water into a glass; he hoped that he didn't have to talk much before he could have a drink. Actually, Lorenzo hoped that he didn't have to talk at all; there was nothing he ever wanted to say to him again.

"Have some," said his father. "It's been a long day for all of us." He handed the glass to Lorenzo.

The scent of flowery cologne floated across the table. When had his father started to wear perfume? Lorenzo drank the water in one gulp; the cool liquid rushed down his throat but did not quench his thirst. He licked his lips. How could they still be dry?

He set the glass on the tray. The features of his father's face started to loose their shape like melting wax on a candle. How could there be softness in a man of such hardness? Was anything possible? Could a man who sold his soul to the devil ever find redemption?

"Would you likesome more?" his father asked.

The parchness within Lorenzo was spreading as if he held a desert. His father was filling his glass. Why was his hair slicked back with oil? He never styled it like that when his mother was alive. And when had the jowls under his chin gotten so long? They were almost touching his shirt collar.

"Here. Drink this." His father walked around the table.

Why on earth was he wearing pink lipstick? Lorenzo collapsed. His father stood over him. The buckle on his belt widened until it was too big for his eyes to hold. What was in his father's hands? Why were there red petals floating down over him? That couldn't be a purple pencil he saw; his eyes were playing tricks. He squinted. Why was St. Catherine looking at him? Blackness swallowed Lorenzo.

CHAPTER TWENTY-FIVE

The light that passed through the stained glass window behind the altar barely illuminated the space in front of the chapel; it was early evening and Caterina had been asleep for a few hours. The cold from the stone floor had invaded her body and her limbs were stiff; Padre was right, the sacristy would have been more comfortable.

Caterina had prayed in this church with *Pappa* and sat beside Elda during mass; she would miss her godmother for if Elda hadn't nursed her, Caterina would have died. Before she left today, she would bless herself one last time with the holy water in the font where Padre had baptized her. Caterina wanted to begin her new life in Florence but a part of her was sad as it meant she had to leave this one behind; sometimes even good choices were laced with regret.

St. Ursula's Church was small and it was easy to feel God's presence here; Lorenzo had told her that the cathedrals in Florence were bigger than his villa and Caterina wondered if it would be difficult to find God in them. She buried her face in Shadow's fur and longed for the warmth of Lorenzo's body. The wolf tensed his muscles and she pulled back. He leapt forward and charged out of the chapel. An instant later, she heard the door of the church open; she scrambled to her feet.

"Caterina," Padre Valentine called out.

This was the first time she'd seen him wearing something other than his black cassock. He hurried down the center aisle towards her; Shadow yelped by his side. They sat in a pew facing the altar.

There would be no questions about *Mamma* Anna's funeral; Caterina had already decided. She and Lorenzo were married now and they would comfort each other in their suffering; this was something a husband and wife should do for it would bring them closer and Caterina wanted to be as close as possible to Lorenzo.

"Is everything alright?" Caterina asked.

"*Si.* Lorenzo and Francesca will be here in a few hours."

"Did Santo suspect anything?"

"*Non.*"

"Did you get the horses?"

"*Si.* Interzino left me the wagon. I told him that I wouldn't be finished for awhile and I'd be too tired to walk back to villa afterwards. He was going into the village to get one of his friends to take him back to San Michelle. Everything will be fine Caterina and soon you will be on your way to a new life."

"There's no need to stay at San Michelle anymore? *Mamma* Anna and Bruno and *Pappa* and *Mamma* are all gone." She touched his silver crucifix. Someday, she hoped to meet Fiore; he was probably as wonderful a friend to Padre Valentine as Francesca had been to her. "You trained my mind, Padre, and you know that I'm right. Why can't you come to Florence with us?"

"I can't leave."

"Why?" This would be one argument that Caterina was determined to win.

"Who will take care of our people?"

"Santo can find another priest for this church. He found you after our old one died. Didn't he?"

The priest patted the wolf's head.

"We were all together this morning, Padre, when you married Lorenzo and I. You and Francesca and Shadow. We belong to the same family now and we all have to start our new life together, at the same time, in Florence. It would be wrong for any of us to stay behind." There was no weakness in the reasoning on which her argument was based; the priest would have to concede defeat. "Interzino left us the wagon. There's room for everyone, even

249

Shadow. It's a sign, Padre. Don't you see? We can all leave for Diamante as soon as Francesca and Lorenzo get here."

Padre Valentine stood up and streams of muted colors flowed through the stain glass panel and washed over him; it was as if he was part of a rainbow. He did not want to stay at San Michelle anymore and his secret was safe so what reason was there for him to do so? He and Caterina had arrived at the same conclusion, albeit for different reasons. Caesare had suffered another seizure yesterday, thus securing Santo's dependency on Fiore. If Caterina knew the truth about the priest's life, which of course she never would, she'd say that this had been a sign from God that he could leave San Michelle.

The situation merited reflection; Padre Valentine could craft a new life in Florence by changing his name and altering his appearance. He could join a community of scholars and spend the rest of his life studying. How would Santo find him? The priest could finally reclaim his life. All this was possible. Even by his standards, the argument was irrefutable; as long as Caesare was alive; no harm would come to Ortenza and her mother. Padre Valentine suddenly knew that God had not forsaken him and that when it was his time, He would welcome him into the kingdom of Heaven.

As the priest turned around to tell Caterina what she longed to hear and what he longed to say, Shadow growled. Caterina popped up and her shawl slipped off her shoulders; Benito was walking down the aisle. The wolf lunged towards him. Benito fired one shot that hit the animal between his eyes; Shadow dropped to the floor and Caterina screamed. Caesare appeared in the doorway.

"Lock yourself in the sacristy." Caterina ran into the room and Padre Valentine moved towards Benito.

What was Caterina supposed to do? Hide? Yes, she told herself, hide. The storage cupboard was too narrow and its shelves were lined with gold chalices. That wouldn't work. She ran to the window but it wasn't wide enough for her body; the room held her prisoner. She dashed underneath the desk, crammed into the small space and pulled the chair towards her. What were the muffled voices saying? A horrible wail pierced the air. The cries of a wounded animal, she thought. She covered her head with her hands and her mind processed what her eyes had seen; Benito had shot Shadow.

Loud bangs crashed against the door. Caesare was in the church. What if he broke in? Maybe if she could shrink herself, he wouldn't see her. The banging stopped. Caesare and Benito had gone away; Padre Valentine was going to save her.

The door burst open, the chair flew out and a large hand grabbed her and yanked her forward. Caterina banged her head and a flash of blackness came and went. Caesare picked her up by the waist as if she were a rag doll and shoved her through the doorway. She fell on the stone floor; Shadow's body was beside her and the fur on his face was matted with blood.

Caesare was grunting and snorting like a wild boar. She pushed herself up and he grabbed her by the hair; she feared her neck would snap. She smashed her fist against his nose and blood spurted onto her face. He cried out and released her and she tore down the aisle. The door to the church was open. She ran past rows of pews then slipped and fell face down. She wiped her hand on her blouse and it was covered with blood. The base of the baptismal font was a few inches away; its stand was clotted with clumps of flesh and grey matter and thin ribbon like red rivulets ran to the floor. Who was the man lying next to the stone pedestal? Why was he wearing a red dress? She pulled herself up. Where was St. Ursula's picture? Who had poured paint into the holy water? A putrid stench filled the air and Caterina bent over. Why did the man have on Padre Valentine's silver crucifix? Caesare lumbered towards her. Blood was dripping from his chin. Caterina fled from the church.

Someone jumped on her back and the hard ground scraped her cheek. Her body flipped over; Benito had tackled her. He sat astride her body and Caterina thought his weight would crush her.

His knees squeezed against her ribcage and she feared the love in her heart for Lorenzo would explode on his chest and she'd lose it; she couldn't let this happen for Caterina would die without Lorenzo's love. She had to push Benito off her. She tried to squirm but her back was flush against the earth. A piece of rope was flying through the air towards her; it looked like a bird. Why was Caterina wasting her time thinking such ridiculous thoughts? Benito raised a hand and his weight shifted and Caterina caught her breath. She pummeled her fists on his chest. Benito's hand cracked against her face and the rope he held cut her cheek; the sting of his slap filled her eyes with tears and Caterina was blind. Benito tied her wrists together and she thought that her veins would burst open and she'd bleed to death. This wasn't her time to die; she and Lorenzo were going to Florence to start a new life. She could see again.

Why was Mabruco standing beside Caesare? What was the gardener doing here? She saw an image of Padre Valentine drowning in a sea of blood in her mind. Why was she having this nightmare? Reality could never be like this. Or could it? It was once before. She remembered running through the dark in the storm and hearing her *Pappa's* voice but not being able to find him. She was lying on her mother's grave and then Lorenzo found her. Caterina closed her eyes. She'd count to ten and when she opened them, she and Shadow would be back in the chapel waiting for Padre Valentine and Lorenzo would find her again and he'd hold her in his arms and she'd forget this horrible dream. There was never any blackness when Caterina was with Lorenzo. She opened her eyes.

Mabruco was kneeling at her feet and Benito was still on top of her.

"She broke Caesare's nose?" Mabruco said.

Her face was too numb for Benito's slap to hurt. Mabruco bound her ankles with another piece of rope and Benito sprung off her; she twisted and turned on the ground like a writhing snake.

"What are we going to do about Padre Valentine?" Mabruco asked.

"That wasn't supposed to have happened," Benito said. "I lost control of Caesare."

"Your father will understand."

"We'll have to get rid of his body," Benito spat.

The emptiness inside Caterina started to grow.

Interzino took his place beside the two men.

"Throw the priest into the sea," Benito ordered. "He'll keep Clorinda company."

Caterina's lungs refused to fill up with air.

Benito pulled a cloth out of his pocket and stuffed it into her mouth; Caterina gagged. How could *Mamma* Anna's handkerchief choke her? She forced the bitter substance that had crept up her throat back down. It was easier than Caterina had expected; *Mamma* Anna was helping her.

"Interzino," Benito yelled. "Help Vito clean up the church. There must be no traces left. It will be as if they both just vanished. No one will ever know what happened to them."

"Do you want me to tell your father what happened?" Mabruco asked.

"*Si*. I'll contact him after we meet Buccella in Naples."

What was Benito saying? Caterina was going to Florence, not Naples. She tried to spit the handkerchief out but couldn't. Why wasn't *Mamma* Anna helping her anymore? Where were Lorenzo and Francesca? Why was she alone?

Pain cut into the side of her body and her back arched above the ground; Caesare had struck her ribcage with his wooden peg. Benito laughed and Caterina released a silent scream.

"Throw her into the wagon," Benito said.

Her upper torso soared over Caesare's shoulders and her chin banged against the muscles of his back. If it weren't for the handkerchief, her teeth would have cut her tongue in half and she'd be rendered mute for the rest of her life and would never be able to tell Lorenzo how much she loved him. *Mamma* Anna had saved her words; she hadn't abandoned her after all. Caterina should have known better; this was a sign from *Mamma* Anna and she was

253

telling her that Lorenzo would be here any minute.

Caterina felt as if she were a sack of potatoes that someone was bringing to Bruno's kitchen. Her bound wrists dangled precariously close to the ground. If Caesare dropped her, she'd smash her face and Caterina would be as unrecognizable as Padre Valentine had become. She couldn't let this happen. How would Lorenzo find her if she didn't look the same?

"Caesare," Benito said.

He turned sideways and almost smashed her against the edge of the wagon.

"Put the blanket over her."

She landed on the hard wooden surface and her head struck a corner of the wagon.

Who were these people, Caterina wondered. She didn't know their faces. Their smiles were friendly, but why was she with them? And why were they speaking words that she couldn't understand? She stepped away and turned around in a circle; she was in the middle of a large crowd surrounded by a din of noise. Why was everyone hurrying and rushing about? Where was everyone going? Then it donned on her; Caterina knew where she was.

She was with Lorenzo in Florence and it was market day and they were in the Piazza San Lorenzo. Families were together and everyone was carrying bags, some were stuffed with clothes while others had loaves of bread. Men were even buying suitcases. Caterina looked around. There was a mountain in the distance and grey smoke spilled forth from the top and shaped itself into loose curls as it ascended into a gorgeous blue sky. The day was lovely and much too warm for this long coat. Why was she wearing it? A breeze passed by and Caterina could smell the salt of the sea. Men and women were crossing a wooden bridge and entering the largest structure she'd ever seen.

The building was one of the cathedrals in Florence that

Lorenzo had described to her; his villa was small compared to it. A man waved at her; he must have seen Lorenzo enter the cathedral. How did he know that she was looking for him? Were all the people in Florence this kind? Caterina got in line. Lorenzo must be trying to find God for her. She hoped that Francesca wasn't doing cartwheels; Padre Valentine was probably praying and he wouldn't think that this was appropriate behavior. Caterina was happy that they had begun their new life in Florence.

"Wake her," a gruff male voice said. "It's almost time to board."

A hand tapped her cheek then grabbed her arm and forced her to stand up. Caterina had been sitting on a pile of suitcases. Who was this face? His teeth were broken and his breath smelled of tobacco and old food. She pulled back and he tightened his grip.

Benito walked towards her. She rubbed her wrists; the blistered skin reminded her of the sores on *Mamma* Anna's body. She shuffled her feet and the side of her body throbbed. The coat she had on was unbuttoned; it was snug at the shoulders and the sleeves were too short. The front of her blouse was splattered with blood. Was it Padre's or Caesare's or Shadow's? Her rose birthmark was red. Was it hers, too? She slipped her hand inside; the bundle was still tucked between her breasts. She hadn't lost the cameo brooch and the jeweled cross and the sketch; Lorenzo was with her.

There was a ship in front of her that was bigger than Lorenzo's villa; people were standing in line and crossing a gangplank and boarding it. Where were they going? The ship was so long that she couldn't see where it ended. There was a smokestack in the middle. Where was she? Why had Benito brought her here?

There was a name printed in large block letters on the side. Caterina silently mouthed the word. Carpathia. She repeated it to herself. Carpathia. It was a word that she had never seen before. What did it mean? What was a "Carpathia?" Where was Padre Valentine? He'd be able to tell her what a "Carpathia" was.

A man wearing a black suit with a white shirt that reminded her of Lorenzo's father walked towards her.

"Did you get the ticket?" he asked Benito.

"*Si,* Arduino," Benito said. "I put it in her pocket when she was sleeping."

"*Bene,*" the man in the black suit said. "She'll fit in perfectly with the other 2,500 poor people in steerage who are leaving Naples today." He snickered. "Who wants them in Italy anyway?"

Naples, Caterina shuddered; where was Naples and why had they brought her here?

"Has everything been arranged?" Benito asked. "Did you get the papers?"

"*Si.*" He waved them at Benito then shoved them into the pocket of Caterina's coat. "I told you, there's nothing that Arduino Buccella's money can't buy."

Benito laughed and Caterina wondered what was so funny.

"They'll ask her for them at Ellis Island," Buccella said. "She needs them to get into New York. There's some *lire* too. You don't want the Americans to send her back to Italy do you?"

Italy was her home, Caterina told herself. She wasn't going to leave. What were they talking about?

Benito spat on the ground in front of her feet. "Does that answer your question?"

Buccella stared at Caterina. How could someone who didn't even know her have so much hatred in his eyes? "Don't worry," he said to Benito. "It's almost over."

Why was Buccella soothing Benito? Caterina was the one who'd been hurt.

"It only takes three weeks for the ship to cross the Atlantic Ocean and get to New York," Buccella said.

Was the Atlantic Ocean bigger than the Tyrrhenian Sea? Caterina didn't know. How far away was New York? Could Lorenzo get there?

"She'll disappear in the Americas and never bother your family again; especially your little brother," Buccella said.

Caterina couldn't disappear in the Americas. She couldn't live without Lorenzo. She was his wife. They were married. They belonged together. There was no way she'd let them use an ocean to separate her from her husband. Caterina knew that she had to escape. She brought her arm up to her side and angled her elbow. She massaged her forearm with her other hand as if it were sore. She could fool them. They weren't that smart. She waited for a few moments then jabbed the man holding her in the soft belly of his stomach. The pain she inflicted on him was as much as what she inflicted on herself. He buckled over and she lunged forward but Buccella moved in front of her and it was as if Caterina had struck a brick wall.

"Your father was right," Buccella said to Benito. He wrapped his arms around her as if they were a vise. "She is a bad one."

Caterina would pretend Buccella was Santo and ram his body with hers; she hated Santo so much that she was certain she could knock him over. She shoved against him but he knocked her back. He slapped her face and his ring ripped her cheek; warm blood ran down her face.

"Are you alright?" Benito asked.

"*Si,*" Buccella said. "Take her," he told the other man.

The man grabbed Caterina's arm.

Buccella took a handkerchief from his pocket and wiped his ring. It was black with an "N" insignia. Caterina prayed that the initial wouldn't be imprinted on her face; she didn't want to be branded like an animal.

"I want to see Lorenzo." Caterina planted her feet on the wooden deck and stared at Benito. "I'm his wife."

"You are nothing and you will never see my brother again."

What if Benito's words were true?

"Let's go," Benito said to Buccella. "I want to check on Caesare."

"Don't worry." Bucella patted Benito's back." I'm sure Fiore's taking good care of him."

Fiore, Caterina repeated to herself. Wasn't that the name of the man who gave Padre his silver crucifix? It couldn't be the same person, she reasoned. Why would Padre's best friend be taking care of Caesare?

"Let's have a brandy first?" Buccella said. "We could go to the bar that your father and Padre Valentine liked and have a drink in the priest's memory. And then we'll contact your father and tell him that she's gone."

Benito nodded then said," We'll have two brandies."

"And don't forget," Buccella said. "We have to buy Fiorina a new coat before we leave Naples."

"I remember," Benito chuckled. "My father's wife likes nice things."

"Women are such problems," Buccella said.

"Francesca won't be," Benito said. "I'll make sure she's a good wife." He and Buccella walked away.

Caterina had to save herself so that she could save Francesca. What could she do? The crowd swallowed Benito and Buccella. The man pulled her forward; she strained against him. Lorenzo's love would make her strong. Her feet slid towards the gangplank; she resisted. She wasn't going to let the ship take her to the America's, she belonged in Italy with Lorenzo. Someone bumped into them and the man loosened his hold. She had time to escape. Caterina wasn't going to New York; she was going to Florence. The man whacked her then dragged her across the gangplank; she was on the ship. The force of the crowds propelled them forward. Without warning, the man released her; he disappeared into the throngs and Caterina was alone.

The time to escape was now. All Caterina had to do was get back to the gangplank and get off the ship; it was so simple. Her body gave one last surge of energy; she turned around but everyone was going the opposite way. They pushed her farther and farther down the deck and Caterina feared that she would fall backwards and they'd trample her. She grabbed onto the railing, yanked herself forward and leaned over the side; the gangplank was gone.

Caterina watched as the harbour receded from view. It got smaller and smaller then disappeared completely. The ship was completely surrounded by water. Where was she? Was this the Atlantic Ocean? Caterina did not know.

She lifted her hand from the railing and pressed it against her chest. She still had the cameo brooch, the jeweled cross and the sketch; Lorenzo was with her. She would find a way to get back to Italy and be reunited with her husband. The mystics at Dreamer's Rock had blessed their love and there was nothing that anyone could do to keep them apart. The wind rushed against her face; Caterina would love Lorenzo Marino forever.

ABOUT THE AUTHOR

MARIANNE PERRY is a second-generation Canadian-Italian with Calabrian and Sicilian roots. She was born and raised in Sault Ste. Marie, Ontario, Canada. Except for the years she taught junior high school in Toronto, she has spent her adult life in this Northern Ontario city.

LEARNING is integral to Marianne. She holds a Bachelor of Arts Degree in English and Geography from Laurentian University, a Bachelor of Education Degree and a Specialist in Dramatic Arts from The University of Toronto, a Master of Education Degree from The University of Western Ontario and a Graduate Certificate in Creative Writing from Humber College. A past member of the Board of Trustees, the National Arts Centre Corporation and the Board of Directors, the Northern Ontario Diabetes Network, she received a recognition award from the Canadian Association of Colleges and Universities Student Services Association for her work in establishing the first campus safety for women program at Algoma University College in Sault Ste. Marie.

Marianne's life reflects her passion for TRAVELING. Her first trip was with her family to Expo '67, the World's Fair in Montreal, Quebec. Since then, her adventures have included: a hot-air balloon ride over Kenya's Masai Mara; a journey down Ecuador's Rio Agrico, a tributary of the Amazon River; paying homage to Leonardo da Vinci's grave in Amboise, France; a 2,500-mile road trip from Dallas, Texas through Mexico to Guatemala City; exploring Central America's Mayan Temples; boating at the base of Iguazu Falls in

Argentina; a helicopter viewing of Australia's Great Barrier Reef; first-time backpacking at the age of 52 in Italy and France; witnessing the sacred Hindu rite of passage on the west bank of the Ganges River in Varanasi, India plus several trips to her beloved Italy. For each of her adventures, she has compiled extensive photo albums and maintained detailed journals, which she refers to when researching material for her novels.

Marianne's first JOBS were working at a drive-in movie theatre, selling shoes and making television commercials. Her adult employment has included teaching English, Dramatic Arts and Career Planning at the elementary, secondary and post-secondary levels; university management positions in student services and communications; developing Life Skills lectures for women in transition; hosting a radio show; and managing an educational bookstore and a law firm.

The mother of two grown children, Marianne and her husband live on the shores of the St. Mary's River, which drains Lake Superior on the outskirts of Sault Ste. Marie, Ontario Canada. She is writing her second novel.

CONNECT WITH THE AUTHOR ONLINE:

www.marianneperry.ca

RESOURCES

Readers interested in genealogical research with family that have immigrated to North America and landed at Ellis Island, New York will find www.ellisislandrecords.org an excellent resource. I was able to obtain a copy of my grandmother's Passenger Record, which included her date of arrival plus her ship of travel from this site as well as a copy of the Ship Manifest that listed her name, age and place of residence in Italy. For those whose relatives landed at Pier 21 in Halifax, Nova Scotia, www.pier21.ca has extensive immigration records as well as ship arrival databases. I would also recommend readers consult ancestry.ca. I was able to find my grandparent's 1915 wedding certificate here plus begin the Perri family tree. The historical record collection at familysearch.org is also valuable.

A standard google search on the internet will provide information on Cetraro and Mottafollone. Both are located in the province of Cosenza in the region of Calabria in the county of Italy. Two sites on Cetraro are en.comuni-italiani.it and www.comune.cetraro.cs.it. Information on Mottafollone may be found at en.comuni-italiani.it and www.comune.mottafollone.cs.it.

A standard google search on the internet for Calabria will produce numerous websites.

The Villa San Michelle is fictional but The Grand Hotel San Michele does exist.It is a turn-of-the century villa situated on a 124-acre estate that overlooks the Tyrrhenian Sea. The resort has a private beach and is located in Cetraro and a short distance from Mottafollone. I stayed there while exploring this area and researching my grandmother's early life. Its website is www. sanmichele.it.

An earthquake struck southern Calabria and Sicily on December 28, 1908. It was centered on the city of Messina, Sicily and registered 7.2. Its effects were felt for a radius of 300 kilometres. The twelve metre tsunami that followed devastated the coast. Reggio Calabria in southern Italy was severly damaged and authorities have estimated that between 100,000 and 200,000 lives were lost. For readers interested in learning about this natural disaster, a standard google search on the internet will provide several links.

For readers interested in the 'Ndrangheta, a criminal organization based in Calabria, a standard google search on the internet will provide several links.

The following books were also valuable:

Blanchard, Paul. *Southern Italy South of Rome to Calabria.* A & C Black (Publishers) Limited. 1996.

Bolton, Roy. *A Brief History of Painting 2000BC to AD 2000.* Constable and Robinson Ltd. 2004.

Dunston, Lara and Carter, Terry. *Travellers Calabria.* Thomas Cook Publishing. 2009.

Gastaut, Michelle. *Hotels and Country Inns of Character and Charm in Italy.* Fodor's Travel Publications, Inc. 1998.

Laneyrie-Dagen, Nadeije. *How to Read Paintings.* Larousse/VUEF 2002.

Postorivo, Mario Editore and Guzzolino, Francesco. *Mottafollone e la sua Storia tra Nobilta e Clero nelle valli dell'Occido-Rosa-Esaro.* Roggiano Gravina (Cs).1994.

LeBlanc, J.P. and Mitic, Trudy Duivenvoorden. *Pier 21: The Gateway that Changed Canada.* Lancelot Press. 1988.

Nelson, Lynn. *A Genealogist's Guide to Discovering Your Italian Ancestors.* Betterway Books. 1997.

Ody, Penelope. *The Complete Medicinal Herbal.* Key Porter Books Limited. 1994.

Rigante, Elodia. *Italian Immigrant Cooking.* World Publications Group, Inc. 2003.

Szucs, Loretto Dennis. *Ellis Island: Tracing Your Family History Through America's Gateway.* Ancestry Publishing. 2000.

READING GROUP QUESTIONS

1. Do you agree that Caterina Romano was an atypical woman for her time? Cite an example to support your answer.

2. Why is lavender an important symbol in *The Inheritance*?

3. What was Padre Valentine's moral dilemma? Do you think he resolved it successfully at the end of the novel?

4. *The Inheritance* explores the impact of opposing dreams on family dynamics. How do Santo Marino's dreams clash with Caterina Romano's? How do they alter their family dynamics and what is the end result in both situations?

5. There are several different family models in *The Inheritance*. The Marino's represent a nuclear unit whereas Caterina Romano and her father, Edoardo are a single-parent family. How do their family dynamics differ and what represents the greatest vulnerability in each unit?

6. Every detail in *The Inheritance* was chosen to help create an authentic sense of time and place. How did character names contribute to making the setting believable?

7. Flashbacks are one of the tools utilized to tell the story. How did Anna Marino's memories deepen your understanding of the

situation and help advance the plot?

8. *The Inheritance* examines the different kinds of love underscoring relationships. Describe the relationship between the following characters and state why they are integral to the novel's story:

a.   Anna Marino and Bruno, the cook

b.   Caterina Romano and Shadow, the wolf

c.   Caesare and Benito Marino

9. What twist surprised you in the novel? What happened that you didn't expect or what truth was revealed that caught you off guard?

10. Did Santo Marino have any redeeming qualities? Explain your answer.

11. What did you like the least about Caterina Romano and Lorenzo Marino? Explain your answer.

12. A rigid class system ruled the people in *The Inheritance*. How does food help illustrate the differences between the Marino family and the peasants who worked for them?

13. Conflicting loyalties have the power to alter family dynamics. How do they affect the Marino family and the relationship between Santo and Anna as well as their sons, Caesare, Benito and Lorenzo?

14. Would you consider Caesare Marino a thug or a tragic figure? What role did he play in *The Inheritance*? Explain your answers.

15. Why is art important in Caterina and Lorenzo's relationship?

16. Calabria is a harsh region and it serves as a perfect backdrop for *The Inheritance*. Cite one example that proves this point.

17. We all have family mysteries. What are the family mysteries connected to Santo Marino? How do they develop his character and advance the story?

18. What is Francesca Mella's family mystery? How does it affect Caterina and Lorenzo's relationship?

19. Why was the novel entitled *The Inheritance*?

20. Did you anticipate the ending of the book? What do you imagine might have happened afterwards to Caterina and Lorenzo?

ANGELS & BACKPACKERS

by **Marianne Perry**

Haunting memories, superstitious beliefs, eerie coincidences and an unexpected inheritance from a holograph will compel a woman to go to Calabria, southern Italy and solve the mystery of a century old land deed.

Marianne Perry's next novel, *Angels and Backpackers*, will be published in the future. Details to be announced on her website **www.marianneperry.ca**

For further information, email the author at:
marianne@marianneperry.ca